CW00672254

LIKE WATER LIKE SEA

From the same author:

this is not about sadness

Also By Mail

breach

When We Speak of Nothing

LIKE WATER LIKE SEA

Olumide Popoola

FEEDING THE AFRICAN IMAGINATION

Abuja – London

First published in 2024 by Cassava Republic Press

Abuja – London

Copyright © Olumide Popoola 2024

All rights reserved. No part of this book may be reproduced, stored in a retrieval system, or transported in any form or by any means (electronic, mechanical, photocopying, recording or otherwise), without the prior written permission of the publisher of this book.

The moral right of Olumide Popoola to be identified as the Author of this work has been asserted by her in accordance with the Copyright, Designs and Patents Act 1988. This is a work of fiction. Names, characters, businesses, places and incidents are either the product of the author's imagination or are used fictitiously. Any resemblance to actual persons, living or dead, events or locales is entirely coincidental.

A CIP catalogue record for this book is available from the National Library of Nigeria and the British Library.

ISBN: 978-1-913175-62-7
eISBN: 978-1-913175-63-4

Cover design: Jamie Keenan
Book design: Abdulrahman Osamudiamen Suleiman

Printed and bound in Czech Republic by Akcent Media Limited
Distributed in Nigeria by Yellow Danfo
Worldwide distribution by Ingram Publisher Services International

Stay up to date with the latest books, special offers and exclusive content with our monthly newsletter.
Sign up on our website:
www.cassavarepublic.biz

Twitter: @cassavarepublic
Instagram: @cassavarepublicpress
Facebook: facebook.com/CassavaRepublic
Hashtag: #LikeWaterLikeSea #ReadCassava

For Gabrielle, for holding space so tenderly and fierce.

For Natalie, for showing what is possible.

Dive into Nia's world with
a playlist carefully curated by the author.

These songs of womanhood, self-discovery, resilience,
liberation, and the enduring power of love form the perfect
backdrop for Nia's journey through grief, love,
and life in London.

Scan and listen on Spotify now!

Sometimes we must hold tight to steady ourselves amid the violent tumult of this world—and sometimes we must let go to unmoor ourselves from the stifling order imposed on this world.

– La Marr Jurelle Bruce [1]

*Sometimes we swim, sometimes we float,
other times we are drowning.
It's not always easy to know which is which.*

---

[1] Bruce, La Marr Jurelle, *How to go mad without losing your mind,* Durham: Duke University Press 2020, p.11

All Water Goes Somewhere

1

The Swimmer

Looking up from underneath, it made the sun blurry. The water swishing against my face, a thin layer, not enough to enter my nostrils. I was looking for her. I wanted to know what it was like, to be drowning, losing your breathing to suffocation.

Of course, I didn't last. I didn't have enough drive to do it, didn't have enough reasons. You would have to be invested in the idea, digging deep for this to be your final answer. Nothing like that was on my mind. I wasn't feeling despair. Not in that way. It is hard to take your own life. I think it is against your own body. Such an effort, incredible. I knew that before I jumped into the River Lea with my clothes on. You had to orchestrate the whole thing and pay attention to the variables.

The only thing I had done was leave Mum's after the not-so-unusual but still weird morning. For some reason I went straight to Hackney thinking, let's see this thing, drowning.

Mum was stable as we both called it but on the unstable side of that. She had been rummaging through a big cardboard box packed tight with clothes. I thought she was looking for something that belonged to Johari. It was ten years this year. I thought she was reminiscing, going to tell me a story I did or did not know about my dead sister. Instead, she brought out a long cotton skirt. Its pattern pulled me in briefly, blue and pink and red and green. Vertical and horizontal stripes. Flowers and swirls. It looked like something my mother would love. Something she had worn on a trip to Palestine in a completely different lifetime when she really worked not just as a fundraiser but also as a witness, as she said. I would have loved to have known the story of the skirt. The story of the trip, the stuff Mum had been doing when she included *really* in the telling, but her voice already had that edge to it. I could sense that tone even in the tiniest whisper and knew exactly where she was on the spectrum of a manic episode. It was the same with hospital admissions. I would dream she would die and she would be admitted, without fail, soon after that. Sectioned mostly but sometimes she went of her own accord.

The person who had died was Johari. I hadn't dreamt about her.

A couple of morning joggers slowed down when they saw me. I looked up, ready to defend myself. They looked like one of those couples who shared their hobbies and found that it made their bond stronger.

It was still too early for most people; Mum and I had found ourselves in the kitchen at 4am. She had woken early and I had not yet slept after leaving Temi in the club. I left two hours later. It couldn't be late enough for morning activities, I thought. Not on a Sunday morning.

'Do you need some help?' The woman of the pair asked.

So much, I thought. *But nothing you can sort out for me.*

'I'm OK,' I replied instead. 'Just cooling off my high.'

It wasn't truthful but then I hadn't said drugs. My eyes hadn't felt strained or hot or inflamed but the cool water was certainly soothing my eyelids. I was telling some version of the truth. It was promising, nice, the way the early sun was filtered by moving water before it reached my eyes, tiny leaves covering the surface that would slap against the concrete when a barge laboured through the water in the daytime. My long sleeve got covered in moss green. So cooling, the green, the colour.

Temi had talked about someone we knew who had rearranged someone else's living room.

'You get it, the woman went out to get some beers and came back to all the lamps rearranged, cushions moved about, armchair in a different spot, papers and books on a shelf instead of the table. All in the space of fifteen minutes. It was a completely different room.'

I looked at her in an 'and what' way.

I said, 'And what?'

'My friend lost it. She didn't know how to handle it.'

I had gotten tired, very tired at that moment.

'Let's go to the other place,' Temi had said.

I followed because that's what I do. I follow Temi and let her let me touch her, only to not hear from her for the following two weeks. And then we find ourselves in an all-nighter that lasts from Thursday evening until Monday morning if I can handle it. Lately, I couldn't always make it through. Here I was on a Sunday morning, sober, alone, in the river without doing anything, just lying on my back, the water holding me.

The joggers were still looking at me.

'Really. All okay here. I know it looks weird.'

I lifted my head and showed them my perfectly sound-of-mind face. I had issues, like everyone, but nothing that required institutional enforcement. At least I didn't think so. I waved and laughed.

'You wouldn't believe my night or morning. Honestly, I'm just cooling off.'

'Oh, okay then.'

They had been spot-running through the whole exchange, one foot touching the ground, the other one lifted, arms moving along, held up close to the torso. I was relieved their outfits didn't match.

'We'll be back this side in half an hour. If...'

'I won't be here, don't worry.'

I hoped not.

That skirt. Mum had waved it around, then draped it over her head, the fabric falling over her shoulders.

'Remember you used to do that, pretend your hair was moving when it was short.'

It was 5.30am by then.

'Mum, I was probably three or four.'

'Yes,' she'd replied. 'My skirts were much too long.'

She was laughing in that over-the-top way that you only recognise when you have a parent with serious bipolar. The shrillness that caught people's attention but they couldn't quite place. The way it seemed to threaten an unspoken balance. The turned-up-too-high volume, the eyes with something in them that I could never explain.

She pulled the chair close to the table. Inside I went oh-oh.

Two years ago, she had climbed the chair, then the kitchen table, had reached for the plant pots she had on the sill under the kitchen window, had picked up the mint and had thrown it against the opposite wall. Then the basil and the thyme, the heaviest, and the rosemary. I had been at hers because of another club night close to her flat. Not yet with Temi, but with a bunch of friends. A vase with dead flowers had followed. When I'd shouted, 'Why?' from the kitchen door, Mum said she was repotting. It was spring.

She had gone on to throw many more things that were above hip level until the neighbours below called the police. It wasn't that bad, a little loud, but they were always looking for a reason since the day the husband had helped Mum out of the bathtub naked. She had left the flat door open and he had come back from the terrace above, where he had his secret smokes, and seen the light on at 2am. Mum had fallen asleep in the bathtub. They had it in for us since then. When the police came, we asked why she had to be sectioned for throwing a couple of things around in her own flat. But the officer hadn't engaged. Of course, she had the shrill laugh then but there was no way he could know exactly what that meant.

Here we were two years later, another spring and a serious anniversary. I was bracing myself. I needed cooling down, something to keep me mellow.

She didn't climb the table.

I climbed down the river bank.

Mum had taken the skirt down and sat at the table.

'We should talk.'

There wasn't anything I feared more than Mum's talks. They could be like the repotting. Anything could land on you; anything was up for being dismantled and thrown my way. Things I wasn't ready to hear, details I couldn't stomach. I left.

The long sleeves were pulling downward, so were my sweatpants, and the shoes. I had wanted to take them off, my trainers, to spare them from getting dirty. Then I had remembered that here too, anything could come your way; tampons and pads from the sewage that the local water plant released into the river, the regular plastic waste from people too lazy to look for a bin. Fully clothed seemed like the best option, sensible protection for this experiment. I moved my hands, back and forth, the fingers spread a little. The water was too cold to stay for much longer, my lips had started to shiver. I was worried about the joggers. What they would do if I was still here when they got back?

Temi had been rushing us, taking shortcuts I didn't know, through back streets that smelled.

'Maybe it was the light.' There was no telling if she was listening. 'It could have been the light affecting her, that's why she moved the lamps. It happens with mania, light sensitivity.'

I stumbled behind her. Her Doc Martens were echoing back from the arches we were under. Her long shirt was hanging over her ripped shorts, moving around her legs where I wanted my hands to be. She stopped suddenly and pulled me close.

'It's not that I don't like you. I like you a lot.'

Inside I was ducking. Were there pots coming my way?

She kissed me and I sucked on her lips until she pulled back.

'It's just, you don't talk. You're not really...here. You just disappear and hang on. Metaphorically.'

Her eyes fixed on me as she walked backwards, her hands waving me to follow her. I did.

We felt like grandparents once we were inside the club. Most people were ten years younger but the music was hot. We danced and kissed some more and she whispered something in my ear that I couldn't hear. When she went to the toilet I ran out and took the bus to Mum's. My head leaned against the window. I texted Temi, making up an emergency I had to attend to. I would catch her next time. It was the first time I had left before her. It was also the first time Temi had talked to me like that. I had complained about her non-committed ways. I had told my friends about her infrequent libido, if that was what it was, of her having a string of lovers, of her not knowing how to be close. She was stringing me along, she wasn't serious, she wasn't out. My friends and I had gone over it again and again, but to Temi I had only ever said, 'Sure, I'm free, let's go out.'

Before the skirt, Mum had asked what was wrong. How things were going with that woman. And that she hadn't expected me that night.

There was water everywhere. The river was full of it.

I climbed back onto the bank and sat on the bench with my knees close to my body, arms wrapped around my shins. It was dripping from everywhere, the water melting into the wood. I could see the joggers coming up. They were smiling when they saw me sit on solid ground.

'I should probably get home, inside.'

'Probably.'

They were no longer running but had come to a full stop. The guy took my hand and pulled me off the bench. The woman flanked me on the other side. She picked up my phone, my Oyster card and the keys I had left on the grass before I stepped into the water.

'It might even be a warm day today.'

'Yeah, looks like it,' I replied.

We walked and my trainers made a slurping sound.

'How was the water,' she asked. 'Cold?'

I nodded. We passed the stairs leading up to the bus stop. I didn't say anything. It felt right, the walking.

2

The Dancers

Everyone is fragile at thirteen. They were no exception. Two teenagers from different parts of Hackney, finding each other in the same neighbourhood. Their friendship had an abrupt start, sudden and weird. Melvin had just moved into a three-bedroom flat with his parents and brother Ben. Ben was ten years older and not interested in helping Melvin settle into a new area, school, or anything really. He had returned from university because he didn't feel like finishing the degree in computer science he had started. He was deferring for as long as he could. Most days Ben spent at his girlfriend's house. Melvin was lonely. The first days at the new school had turned out to be okay but he didn't have anyone to spend the afternoons with. He was waiting for an opportunity, something to pull him into this new place. He would grab the chance, any chance, as soon as it presented itself.

Only a couple of days into his second week at the new school it came, an opportunity. It came as Johari. Melvin was at the local park, which he had seen from the window of their new flat. There was a lot going on. A small workout area with green-painted outdoor gym equipment. Playgrounds for younger and older kids. The designated bench for those who wanted to enjoy cheap wine and cider at any time of the day. He didn't quite know where to walk to and stood on a patch of grass to orient himself.

'Are you new?'

The girl in front of him had long braids that fell out under a baseball cap. Her jeans were very low. Melvin nodded. He looked at her shoulder where her jumper had slid off.

'Are you doing anything right now?' she continued.

He shook his head.

Her eyes were hard to make out as the sun was shining on her face.

She said, 'Come,' and started to walk, not checking whether Melvin would follow. 'Johari, by the way,' she continued with the briefest nod backwards as if she was throwing her name over her exposed shoulder. He could catch it if he felt like it. Or leave it. His choice.

'Melvin,' he replied, skipping a couple of paces to catch up with her. They stopped when she had led them to a small area behind bushes and trees.

Melvin wondered what they would be doing but before he could speculate Johari kicked off her shoes, stood still on the grass and lifted her head. A melody carried across from nearby.

'Follow me,' she said. 'If you want to.'

She started to move her arms in the air, parallel to each other, fingers pointing upwards. Melvin stumbled behind her as she moved with the melody. There were so many steps he got dizzy. He stopped.

She said again, 'Follow me, just do what I do.'

Melvin replied, 'That's okay, you go ahead,' but she looked at him, paused for a moment, shook her head, and pulled him back behind her. He tried his best to mimic her movements. After the first song, there was a break. Johari pointed behind the small trees to the brick building.

'They're having dance classes there. I'm having them out here.'

'And you know the steps?' Melvin asked.

She laughed. It was the first time he heard Johari laugh. It started as a giggle, warm and low. Then she opened her mouth and the volume picked up until her head went back in sync with the sound and he could hear the laughter coming from her belly. It ended in a reversal, the giggle leaving with a loud exhale.

'I have no clue what they do there but I like the music,' she said, her belly still moving with amusement.

The steps were all hers.

It wasn't a thing, being dancers. They never talked about the dancing. It was stress release. It was dealing with life and its fluctuations. Melvin knew this, even at thirteen. It was something that was useful, perhaps needed even, and on that first day they became friends. No elaborate sensing each other out, no questions about shared tastes. A simple 'Come' thrown behind her, and it was sealed. The right invitation at the right time. The right person at the right spot to invite on a random day. That is how depth announced itself. In the moments one could easily miss.

They weren't the type of friends who talked about everything. They were the type where Melvin followed and Johari stumbled ahead of him, looking back once in a while with a question on her face. Where are we going?

That summer they met in that hidden part of the park and soaked up the music and fell into the dried-up grass laughing. There wasn't a lot of grace to their steps. Most of the time they were huffing and puffing, their thoughts locked away from each other. By the end of the summer, they knew details about each other's lives. Not many, but some. What they didn't know was how the other lived, who they lived with, what their lives were like, outside of their spot in the park. Sometimes Johari brought a couple of other kids from her school with her, usually boys that were interested in her. They would join in, jumping about when the music came on. These boys laughed louder and fell into the grass more than Melvin and Johari did. They didn't take it seriously. Melvin smiled because it was ridiculous. This weird putting their bodies together in different ways without knowing anything about it. And in the park, for everyone to see. It was so weird. But it was something Johari liked to do. And they liked her.

3

The Swimmer

We walked to the next bus stop, water dripping off my clothes. We hadn't said much and they hadn't asked what I was doing. Who knew? I didn't, not really. I hadn't made a plan when I left Mum's, it was all coming together at the very minute that I was doing it. Maybe that was obvious. Crystal and Rahul settled in on the orange bum holder, or whatever one called it, and Rahul asked whether he could put his number in my phone.

'Maybe we can meet up under other circumstances sometime,' he said.

Crystal waited. I could feel the tension as if she was having to work hard not to move her head towards me.

'Sure, why not,' I replied. 'I'm not usually this far down the drain.'

We all laughed. The bus came but we kept our backsides glued to the orange plastic. They were on either side of me. I felt like I was held; two support structures helping to keep my body upright. There was purpose here, it was simplicity, and it was all I could manage. Me sitting there, the two on either side of me.

Rahul handed me the phone. While I typed my name and number, he wrote his number on a piece of paper, just in case. What that was supposed to mean I didn't know. In case more water poured over me? Was ink on paper safer than a mobile phone? And who carried a pen when they went out jogging? Crystal wondered so too and Rahul answered, 'I'm not quite sure why it is in my pocket, if I'm honest.'

It all made sense. These nonsensical circumstances. The bizarre details.

'I put both of our numbers... I mean we're not like a package deal...' Rahul continued when he had finished the writing that was large and in all caps. I would not be in danger of misreading either his name or number.

'I have options. Basically,' I replied.

We laughed again. It was the best conversation I'd had in my entire life. Not one thing made sense but we leaned right in, into the awkwardness.

'But you are a thing, right?' I couldn't help myself. I needed a little bit of help understanding what was happening here.

Rahul took my hand and held it. Crystal took his.

'We are,' he said.

My mother had asked the same a few hours ago. Were Temi and I a thing? I had started crying.

The three of us held hands and I asked them how long they had been seeing each other.

'Six years,' Crystal said. 'But we don't live together.'

'Not found anywhere?' Or they were still working on that property ladder opportunity, I wanted to add but Rahul answered before I could come up with my assumptions.

'It's not something we needed for us. We see each other all the time. We don't have to decorate the same space.'

I nodded.

Crystal said, 'We like being close but we like visiting.'

I put my head on her shoulder and thought of who I wanted to visit, Melvin or Temi, or anyone else, or whether I wanted to see anyone at all. Crystal put her arm around me and rubbed her hands up and down my damp sleeve. The cotton was slowly drying now that the sun was gaining traction. I wanted to kiss her but for no other reason than the fact that she was sitting next to me, her partner on the other side of me. She was unavailable. It was attractive. I was available, technically. But it was complicated in my case. I had to address some things I wasn't ready to look at. This, the sitting here, the sharing a moment that was much too significant for strangers, felt like it wasn't about me. It was generic, something you responded to because you knew that was the right thing to do. It wasn't about me personally. It suited me. I could be anyone I wanted in this scenario. I wouldn't have to show up as myself.

Another bus came up and I raised my head but when Crystal didn't move, I put it back on her shoulder.

Rahul stretched out his legs and massaged his thigh.

'Do you think you'll tell someone about this, this morning?' Crystal asked.

'This is not even a thing,' I said, and she replied, 'Okay.'

Three people came up to the stop in one go. We had been here for a good half-hour without anyone showing up.

Rahul said 'Good morning,' and it felt like we were making a statement. My clothes were still wet but I hoped that it wasn't that obvious. If not for their running outfits, it would have looked like we had gotten confused in the club, and now couldn't decide who was

taking who home. I liked the idea of us, a picture that couldn't be
decoded in one go. Was it all of us, or a combination of two, at which
time? No one paid us any attention and my mind drifted. Crystal was
no longer rubbing my sleeve; her arm was flung around my shoulder
now. It was touching Rahul's on the other side.

The skirt, Mum had said, was just because of Palestine. She wanted to
connect to the place because things were bad again. They were bad,
if that was the right word, all the time, but at the moment they were
worse than normal. There was no reason to put it on her head. When
she saw my face she said she wanted to make me laugh. I had just
come back from leaving Temi and found her up in the early hours
of the morning. She said I looked like my breath was stuck inside of
me, she said I had panic in my eyes. All I had thought of was the tone
of her voice.

And Johari. As much as Mum's voice alerted me, annoyed me,
made me pay attention... I had heard nothing in Johari's.

Temi had texted back but I had swiped it away before I could
read the message. I wanted availability, with her at least, but I wasn't
sure I could handle someone who could be quiet for months, leaving
me hanging again and again and then talk like she did the previous
night. It was confusing, unsettling, her contradictions. It didn't help
with all the things that were splashing underneath, inside of me. One
summary of a sentence and my whole self was captured. Where was
she in this? Why not leave me alone? Or stay properly?

Rahul stood up, shaking his leg. 'Didn't realise I got a little cramp.'

'Should we go? I mean it's probably time for breakfast,' I asked.

I didn't get up but I lifted my head. Crystal searched in the little
pocket at the back, right above her bum for coins. The lycra stretched
perfectly around her legs. I had noticed. Rahul was wearing shorts
and the running jacket that had the stray pen in it.

'I have almost £7,' Crystal said, counting the small coins and the
fiver.

'I didn't bring any,' Rahul replied.

'I mean, should we call it a day?' I offered. There was no way to
have breakfast for three with £7, not in this part of town. I was also
thinking of Mum and Temi, of things I should say or do, but mostly
I needed sleep. I wasn't quite sure what this scenario was, beyond
getting me out of the water.

'I have your numbers,' I said.

'You do.' Crystal got up and opened her arms. I leaned in, it wasn't awkward, not even with Rahul standing there. We held each other and I could feel her ribs lifting against my body. She put her head on my shoulder and I was grateful. I didn't want to leave the needy one, the one they had rescued. I wanted this to be an encounter, a two-way one. I would have gotten out of the water without them. I wanted them to know that. I knew how you had to do it, if you really wanted to do it.

Rahul touched my arm and rubbed my cheek very gently with the other hand.

'I'm all the way back the way we came so this is it. For now, anyway.' He paused. 'You might call.'

'I might,' I replied.

The bus came and I got on and waved before I placed the Oyster card on the machine.

It felt like young parents were sending their child off to college. Proud, yet fearful of what was to come.

Mum was at the kitchen table when I returned.

'There are pancakes.' She pointed to the plate on the cold stove.

'I need the bathroom first.'

She nodded and looked back at her portion.

I left the wet clothes on the bathroom floor, ran the water and stepped into the bathtub. The warmth spread right into the inner layers of my skin, unfolding and relaxing them.

I would throw the clothes into the wash as soon as Mum left the kitchen. The trainers separately. They needed a wash too. She didn't need to know. Not all the details. My phone was on the floor, next to my clothes. I leaned out of the water and was careful not to drop it in the tub when I looked at Temi's message.

You just leave me like that?

I put the mobile back on the floor and slid into the water. It was better here, I was held in, there was nowhere to float away to.

I wanted to see Melvin. I knew that. Mostly because I couldn't deal with Temi, not today. I had nothing to tell her. I shouldn't have left without her, without saying something. But also, because Melvin was where everything flowed in the right direction. Everything could fall away and I was still sure of who I was. I grabbed the towel I had left on top of the toilet seat and stepped out. Mum was still sitting at the table with her empty plate in front of her.

'Do you want to talk about this?'

I did but not now. She was having her *I can see right through you* look. Maybe she was manic but she was still able to read me better than I could read myself.

'It's not easy being in love,' she said, and waited.

'You freaked me out with the skirt.'

I couldn't see it. She might have put it back again or hung it up in her wardrobe.

'I wanted to make you laugh,' Mum replied.

I knew that. What to say about her voice?

'Do you think about her? Johari?'

'All the time,' she replied.

'I'm not sure I'm ready to open up to someone,' I said.

'It takes time,' she said.

'I feel I owe Johari.' I didn't know I was going to say that. I didn't even know I felt it but I was glad it was out.

'What could you possibly owe her? Nia, she adored you.'

'Having a good life.' I said it and it made sense. I also knew that I was running from everything that might have contributed to a thoughtful version of that at this particular moment in time. I was fine with that. 'Can we talk another time?' I continued.

Mum had done her elongated in-breath, exaggerated and complete with worry in her eyes. I suspected most parents had a varied collection of non-verbal responses up their sleeves. 'Of course.' Mum got up. 'We'll talk when you're ready.'

There was an edge to her voice. I wasn't imagining it. But my cliff was steeper.

4

The Dancers

They were hiding from the rain in a little wooden house above the slide on the playground.

'Just like that?'

Melvin nodded and said, 'Not just like that but yes. Here I am, without my older twin.'

It was a year into their friendship.

They held each other for a moment. It wasn't weird, it wasn't anything because what else could you do when at birth one of you survives and the other one dies and fourteen years later you told your best friend? What else could you say? There were no words for that.

The music came on but neither Johari nor Melvin moved. Not because it was pelting down, they had splashed about in the rain before, but because of this other silence between them. The rain was loud, which made the music even fainter, it didn't pull them the way it normally did. Only scraps of melody made it their way, carried by gusts of wind. They mostly imagined it because they knew it was there.

Johari looked at Melvin, when she thought he wasn't paying attention. Her eyes had a new depth, as if she was trying to reach all the way inside of him. Melvin pretended he didn't see it.

5

The Swimmer

I held the front door open with my foot while I looked for any mail I had forgotten to check for the previous day. When I looked up there was Temi, right across the road. She was sitting at the bus stop directly opposite the entrance. It was as if they had made it for occasions like this. When someone wanted to wait for you, outside of your door and wanted to make sure they didn't miss you but they didn't feel like standing. Her braids were twisted into Bantu knots. It was hard not to look into her face, beautiful and accusing. If there had been traffic, I might have missed her. Some days I walked a few stops and caught the bus somewhere along the way. But at 7am on a Monday it was almost slow on the street, even in London. Temi was in full view.

'Good morning.' I could hear her voice clearly, from the distance.

I crossed the road.

I was on my way to work. I was in a hurry. I didn't have time to sit there with her and make sense of my movements over the weekend. Instead, I said nothing, lowered myself onto the seating and waited. Temi looked at me.

'So, no reply?'

I didn't react. My eyes trailed the dirty paving slabs.

'Do you even know what's going on?'

The confidence, I admired her so much. I had never even texted her without a prompt from her, let alone followed up when she didn't reply.

'Next time you abandon me in a club, at least leave me some cash for drinks. I think that's global etiquette, an upfront apology when you stand someone up mid-date.'

'We were on a date?'

She had caught me, again, without me seeing it coming.

'She talks.'

'I need to go to work.'

Temi nodded, took out an Oyster card from her back pocket and waved it. We walked up to where my bus stopped and when it came, she got on with me and we went upstairs. The front seats were empty and she leaned her head on the window.

'I don't usually stalk people. I'm okay with you not liking me that much. If you just want to keep it casual. If that's what it is.'

Of course, there was an aura that came with that. It didn't seem like attitude. It seemed like my last chance.

I shook my head. She crossed her legs and pulled her cardigan around her. I didn't know why I had run out of the club Friday night. It had to do with what she had said. About me not being quite available, not quite present, in the larger sense of things. I was bracing myself for the ten-year anniversary. All these things were converging. How could I keep them apart and hold them at the same time? Johari wasn't available, she wasn't present and unlike my own emotional state, hers was utterly permanent, and final. Death was complicated, even ten years in. And with Mum and the mania, what could I say? Sometimes I wanted to have fun without explaining what that fun meant. Temi who had never pushed us wanted to make this, make us, a thing, *now*?

'I have a lot going on.'

'We all do.' I could hear the sweetheart, it would have been the perfect addition to round up the comment. It didn't come; instead, Temi sat up and put her face close to mine.

'Do you want to talk about it?'

I stared ahead. On the road, the pace was picking up. A cyclist was in front of us, holding up the bus. I always admired the bus drivers who didn't show any impatience but took whatever came their way and went with it: the slowing down because of cyclists/pedestrians/ dodgy traffic light cycles, the repeated ringing of the bell, noisy after-school kids.

'It's early. I don't think I can talk about much right now.'

Temi leaned back, her head facing away from me. She closed her eyes and folded her arms. I could feel her breath getting deeper and longer. In Camden, I poked her in the side.

'I need to get off.'

She didn't move.

'You coming?'

Her arm was limp when I lifted it. I dragged her from the seat. She looked at me confused, her eyes trying to fixate on something, her brain trying to make sense of where she was.

'You came to my house.'

I pulled her all the way out of the bus onto the pavement. We stopped at the corner. I could see that she was waking up, her eyes getting brighter.

'I need to get to work. Do you want a coffee?'

Temi worked as a research scientist in a cancer research institute. I didn't know when she had to be there, or where that was. I usually did the early shift in the health food store on Mondays. On the weekends we spent together, I left her at 7am to make it to *We Are The Earth* on time. When she was at mine, she left with me but I didn't know whether she stopped by at her home quickly. She seemed like someone who would want to change their clothes from a long weekend before being all serious about new scientific findings.

I liked the Monday early shift. It was quiet and subdued. The people who did come in at opening time would buy a coffee from the food counter and leave as quietly as they had entered. There was miniMum exchange, we seemed to all acknowledge a Monday morning this early was best observed in silence. No one ever asked for anything, they all knew what they needed and which shelf to find it on. I would help out with the produce delivery until 10am and then move to the natural remedies counter where I worked the rest of the week. Monday mornings were like a collective meditation: three hours of checking off vegetables, unpacking boxes and making the produce look pretty on the shop floor. Even the breaking down of the cardboard boxes and taking them to the back where we kept the recycling felt like an exercise in mindfulness. It would clear my head and any hangover, if I had one.

Temi nodded and we walked on in silence. A few metres before the entrance to *We Are The Earth* she stopped.

'You haven't answered.'

'What was the question?'

I didn't know whether she had asked me anything in particular but I knew what we were supposed to talk about. I had less than ten minutes before my shift started. Enough to get her a coffee and hang up my jacket. Enough to have a couple of minutes to shake off this weekend. Enough to make it on time, the floor managers were big on that. There wasn't enough time to deconstruct a relationship that had not yet become one. Temi's grand gesture, turning up unannounced at my house on a Monday morning before rush hour was huge. It was confusing, to say the least.

'What are your hours like? I'm starting work in five minutes.'

'I can meet you tonight.'

I agreed.

6

The Dancers

Arms floated upwards in a wave-like curve. Held there, mid-air as if someone had installed an invisible armrest. Middle finger dropped, tension in the elbows, the shoulders, the neck.

Head moving, turning from left to right, gracefully, dipping midway, then returning the same way it had come. Feet stomping, then pausing. Arms dropping by the sides of the torso. Head balanced, in the middle, still. Breath shallower, calming, then nothing.

Stopping all movement, savouring the tremor inside of the body.

'I was thinking about your twin.' The question fell out of Johari's mouth as if it was part of the routine.

Melvin bowled over, hands on his knees, still catching his breath. 'Sister.'

There was nothing else.

7

The Swimmer

I went to Temi's around 9pm. She lived in South Tottenham in a one-bedroom flat by herself. The living room was decked out with books and pictures, almost none of the walls were visible. It was a light room, two large windows opening onto the quieter end of the street and the colours from all the things lining or on the walls made it friendlier even, lively. A mosaic of bright colours. The pictures, all neatly hung between small bookshelves, were of things, rather than people. Close-ups of rocks with shadows and rays of sunshine illuminating patterns. The back of a block of houses with a large abstract mural of a maze on it. A painting of a street in the rain in purple and blue tones. Everything was in its place. She had clever storage, furniture with drawers and hidden lids that looked good *and* held her stuff. Magazines were stacked neatly on the side tables. Ceramic vases with dried flowers and empty ones on top of a stack of papers. In the hallway, there was a space and a hook for everything, from coats to hats to shoes. On my first visit, I had whistled, which I couldn't do. It came out like a bad attempt at making fart noises and had made us both laugh.

'Did you do that for me, or is this how it always looks?'

We had bumped into each other, the first time, without any entourage on either side and had found a great party to dance away the night. She couldn't have tidied up for me, our meeting was accidental. The taking home part was the deliberate end, or beginning, to a night of fun and sexy banter.

'Chaos gives birth to creativity,' she had replied. 'I've found I just can't have it in my head and my space at the same time.'

That's how I had been introduced to the scientist Temi. I had a science degree too, technically, although many times it was the scientific quarter that disputed the value of herbal medicine as a legitimate field, and not a sideshow, home remedy, a mother's way of feeling better and more equipped for the kids' colds she couldn't do anything about. Temi had told me that when she was in full work mode her place was immaculate. She had obviously been deep in some research that was close to a breakthrough because her free and wild outfit did not match the orderliness of her flat. Although the colours, the objects, the stuff that made it a home gave me a good sense of her. It said she would go places, she wasn't for staying inside a box, even if her things were boxed up and organised. They were so because of fun, the fun of discovery, and what was more joyous than opening a lid to see inside neatly placed items that you cared for?

'How was your day?' Temi asked after we had hugged.

'I got some rest when I came home from the shop. It's been a long weekend.' I didn't want to get into the details of what I had done since the club on Friday but it was difficult to be evasive and nonchalant here, in her space. As soon as the door closed, it felt as if I was trapped in a single shot of a camera lens. Illuminated, magnified, no escape. We would have to talk, about us, about what we wanted. It was moving in on me and I had nowhere to hide, let alone make a sudden and inexplicable exit.

She made me tea and we ordered takeaway. There was a Japanese place we both loved for the tempura and salmon teriyaki. When we sat down, waiting for the food, she offered again. We didn't need to do this; it was fine if it was supposed to be casual between us. She would handle it. But could I say so, to make it clear?

I couldn't bring myself to tell her that I couldn't stay because she knew so little. If I did, I would have to start with Melvin and his sister. How she was dead, had always been dead. That he couldn't possibly be his whole self if someone so central to his existence was missing. And my sister, Melvin's best friend, who had been dead for a long time too. My mother who had called me sixteen times since I left her Sunday evening. I spoke to her when I first got home, back to my own flat, right after leaving her. The other fifteen times were at 10pm, 10.01, 10.02, 10.30, ten calls between 11pm and midnight, and the last two at 3am and 4am. I had let it go to voicemail. There were some messages, saying 'Hello it's Mum.' There were others that sounded like she was caught in the middle of doing something, as if I had called her and she had picked up accidentally, unaware. I didn't know what to tell a woman I didn't know well enough how things were filling up inside of me, taking over and I didn't know which parts were the real ones.

'What did you do after the club?'

She wanted to bring it into the here and now, I wanted to stay in the past but by myself. I liked Temi. A lot. She was the smartest and hottest woman I'd ever gone out with. Once she tried to explain the details of her work, telling me that she had planned the new experiments the lab would be working on in the following week. Experiments she would be overseeing and which findings she would eventually write up and try to publish in a scientific journal. They were investigating cancer stem cells in brain tumours. I had looked at her with glazed eyes. Impressed but unable to hold my attention. It had been an early morning, after a long night out. It wasn't the light after-sex chat I had aimed for. She had laughed, pointed at my face and said, 'Maybe not.' We had slept soon after.

This smart woman was not someone to leave with lukewarm explanations.

'It just seemed more than I could handle at that moment,' I said.

'Can you explain? Last thing I remember is us dancing. It wasn't even serious. Other than what I said on the way.'

The bell rang and the food came. We spread the dishes out on her coffee table and used the chopsticks. I wanted to feed her. First with the sticks, then my hands, then have my hands go different places.

'Why? I mean why now? I thought you wanted something casual, that's why I hardly text you anymore,' I said.

I was leaning against the couch with my legs outstretched. She laughed.

'Really?'

'Remember after we started and had spent a bank holiday weekend together? From Thursday afternoon until Tuesday morning. Non-stop dancing and talking and fucking. I texted you on Wednesday and you replied, "Slow down, tiger."'

The laughter kept going although it sounded more surprised, then sad.

'Did you forget the rest of the message?'

'What rest?'

'It said "Slow down tiger. If I keep going like that, I'll miss the deadline for my paper." I was in the middle of something.' I could see her searching for the moment she had written me. 'I probably added how much of an opportunity it was, and that I'll get back as soon as I can. I'm pretty sure I did.'

I jumped up and got my phone from my bag. After an eternity of scrolling, I showed it to her. All it said was 'Slow down tiger.' I sat back down.

She came and sat on me, phone in hand. While she was going through her messages she started moving her hips. I wanted to pull her in but we were not yet done. If we were talking it would be better to get it over with although my head was already starting to get light and her lips seemed to be the only thing I could focus on. I tried hard not to reach for them with mine. We should clear the matter of the text, at least.

Hers said slow down tiger, devil emoji, tongue stuck out emoji, hearts as eyes emoji. And the rest of what she had already told me. And that by Friday 5pm she was a free woman again because that was the cut-off for her deadline.

'Six months,' I said.

'Six months,' she replied.

Six months of a misunderstanding.

She lifted her arm and I held it up while moving my hips, my lips going for her neck. She responded and pressed back into me, her head tilting, her hand on my neck holding me close to her.

'I guess I shouldn't mess with your hair?'

'You better not,' and her lips found mine.

When we had lost all our clothes my fingers opened her lips and I entered. I had wanted to be there all weekend. She moved into my hand, riding me and I leaned my head back. She touched the side of my face. I opened my eyes. She was staring. We looked at each other, not moving, not doing anything.

'Do you want to date me, or not?'

I nodded. That was the question. It was easy. I smiled and pulled her close.

'Not touching your hair, not even a little bit.'

She didn't laugh.

'I'm not going to mess up the hair-do.' I wanted to kiss her. 'Although I think sleeping will do that for you. Or for me.'

'If we're dating you have to give me a little more than this.'

I woke up at 4am in her bed. I wanted to cry. Not because of what she had said.

8

The Swimmer

'And if we were to think of a country, rather than a nation?'

I was in my element. I needed this time, away from all that had been going on the last few days. Melvin's was the place where I could park, where I didn't need to pretend. I was okay but I didn't need to name it. Not straight away; it would come out eventually, either way. Sometimes I got carried away on a topic, and the thoughts would bounce off each other without prompting. Even I could get caught off-guard by my reasoning. It made sense, and I could tell where it came from, most of the time. It only happened with Melvin. Knowing each other for this long made for a lot of letting out the seemingly random correlations your brain produced. I had never been guarded with him but over the years we had developed a particular kind of understanding. He had direct insight into me, no translation, no bridging. We already knew all of that – and the worst.

'A country is closer to a geography when nation is abstraction.'

I needed to speak about different things, away from the emotional floods which threatened to carry me away. Politics was a safe distraction.

Melvin smiled. He could see the synapses firing away. He once told me that my face looked like ironed satin when surely inside the skull there was major construction work going on, all the drilling exposing and unearthing the deeper thoughts I had.

'And geography is closer to earth and we can talk about beings. Beings who walk a particular patch of earth and have to live under the particular circumstances of that patch of earth.'

We were in the kitchen that I had put together last year with some friends when Melvin was away on tour. He had returned to a few brightly painted palettes that had been transformed into kitchen counters, the top finished off with poured concrete. I owed my architect friend who had brought in a couple of his mates to do something on a budget that looked like it belonged in a TV show.

'For you,' I had said. 'The colour.' It was a deep orange, apart from the polished concrete on top. It was perfect. In that complicated way.

'And the beings, okay people, these people should have a say, absolute say, about the ways of that place. We don't define place much but it pertains to physicality, something you can touch, whereas, I say it again, nation is pure ideology – is organised but mostly a construct that doesn't hold because there is too little to fill it with. I use organised rather than governed because to organise invokes a collective whereas governing, government, implies a selected, isolated elite.'

'An elected one nonetheless.' Melvin took off his shoes and flexed his toes. It seemed like he wanted to challenge me. *Have you really thought all of this through?*

'And how does this make a difference?'

'Because I might decide I want someone to take care of the larger affairs...'

I was disappointed with him. Melvin knew he couldn't get me with a half-hearted attempt when I had already warmed up. He should have said he didn't want to talk about theoretical things. I wouldn't mind but I didn't like it when he tried to get me to shut up. I was at the front door, my jacket was still in my hand.

'Take care? How can someone else take care of the larger affairs of your life? What are the larger affairs?'

'I mean things like the paving. The sewage even. I don't know. Things that affect you but are not about your own personal life. I would want someone to take care of that. Ideally, it is because I trust them to do a good job. I might think that they know enough. Maybe even more than me.'

'If you don't know enough to take care of your own life, you find people who do and speak with them.'

'Isn't it the same? Some people know some things I don't know at all. Think about farming, agriculture. I know nothing about that. All I know about is the body in space, the body in movement. That's what I'm good at. I don't want to think about farming, let alone make decisions about it.'

'You wouldn't have to, the farmers would do it. But you could have a say in how it affects other areas.'

I hung the jacket on the hook at the back of the door. Melvin was by the window that overlooked the backyard. You could see the apartments on the other side from there; some evenings we had sat in the dark watching the neighbours opposite. It was never interesting but we liked the clandestineness of it all. Melvin was good at filling in the gaps, making up a whole lot of stories for the young couple that never seemed to show any affection. Not as far as we could see.

I walked towards him.

'What other areas? I want to dance. I'm a dancer.'

'Precisely. If you were affected, in some way, let's say because it overlapped with something you were working on, you could be part of the committee that made certain decisions around farming. Not the major decisions, the farmers would make those. But those that addressed necessary compromises, if any were to be had. It wouldn't be closed off to you.'

'I don't want to—'

'Melvin. You think people just like the idea of leadership. But what does that mean? What does it actually mean? Leaders should inspire independent thinking, not following. People should know what impact certain things have in order to make informed decisions. But usually, leadership means that you believe some people cannot do it for themselves.'

'Yes, but you are forgetting that most people don't want to "do it for themselves". That's why they like leaders. They want to give away that responsibility. You can't forget that.'

'And a lot of that is because that is all we know. How can you be sure that it is what you want? If we all knew otherwise maybe it would be different. That's my point. Choice, free will, how are we sure we are applying that? How could we even?'

Someone was throwing their rubbish into the large containers in the yard. The metal made a dull sound when the lid fell back.

'I don't know for sure. None of us can be sure.'

We looked at each other. I knew he liked my honesty and the way my brain could work when it was in the mood. It was what had moved him, got his attention, in the first place all those years ago, when I was merely Johari's younger sister. I smiled. He smiled back. I had moved in front of the counter. The beautiful orange was broken up by my body. Melvin came over and placed his foot on the counter, stretching forward.

'You should come to the Monday class sometime. Be in your body more. You've already channelled all the abstraction in the world. Earth or not.'

I placed my foot on the palette that was Melvin's favourite colour, not reaching high enough for it to be on top of the counter. I bent over.

'It's not abstract Melvin. And you know it. Its simplicity bothers you, doesn't it? It can't just be it. Making decisions all the time.

Making decisions about life. And Mondays, I work early. I will never last until your 8pm class. You know that.'

There was nothing to say. This was both politics and the simplest way of ending back where we didn't want to be. You could swim away with almost any topic. Melvin took his foot down. I was still bent forward, foot almost flat on the front of the counter, knee pointing upwards. Melvin stepped behind me and placed his hands on my lower back, in the dip next to my spine.

'Now breathe.'

He moved one hand up.

'Let go.'

I folded, my forehead touching my knee.

'Straighten your leg.'

His right hand moved to reach for my calf, pressing. His left hand on my hips, pulling backwards. I stumbled.

'Straighten up. You can place that foot on the counter. I'll clean up after.'

I laughed. 'It's not the cleaning.'

'I know.' Melvin didn't miss a beat. 'Do you miss her?'

'It hurts. All of it.' I kept my eyes closed. 'Even after ten years, I can be flooded, out of nowhere.'

'You need to let go, that is the only way.'

My leg was angled but my foot slid along until it was on the counter. Melvin with his hand on my hip, the other one on my ankle, doubled over me, our bodies close now, his flaccid penis pressed on my back. I could feel his breath from a long way down.

'You are graceful with it all,' I said. My head almost touched my calf.

'It only looks that way. There is pain. You get supple with time.'

His face rested on my shoulder blade. I reached back, feeling for his ass, pulling him in.

'I know, but the grace… you are born with it. I'm just a farmer.' I laughed again.

'Who propagates the impossible,' he said.

'Not the impossible. I just believe in hope as a principle. It's a utopic possibility. Aspiring towards something, even if it cannot be achieved in its entirety, doesn't mean it isn't the right thing. It also doesn't lessen what happens on the way.'

My voice was slowing down and becoming heavy. Heavy because it was coming from deeper places in my body.

'If you say so.'

He was holding me tight, arms wrapped around my waist. I pushed with my ass and straightened my torso.

'Ugh. Painful. But good.'

'I told you.'

'What about the other leg? The balance?'

I turned around, the upper half of my cheeks on the counter, the other pressing into the wooden cabinet. Melvin knelt on the floor, lifted the other leg and placed it on his shoulder. My skirt slid back, the tension made the cotton from my underwear move and expose my lips. I could feel his lips on mine. Kissing, sucking. He looked at me.

'I didn't know political talk got you so fired up.'

'You get me so fired up.' I pulled his head back. 'The cause always burns, always.'

His tongue was playing with me but he stopped. 'Oh, now we call it the cause?'

'It always was, baby.'

I could feel his laugh more than I could hear it.

'So I read this today.' It was hard but I wanted to get it out. I pulled the paper out of the back pocket of my denim skirt.

'You copied? From the internet?' Melvin tilted his head back and his eyes were all mockery.

'Indeed. I will read it to you.'

He bit gently and all I could do was push out air, moaning. But I was determined. I was going to make my case. Right there, right then. Melvin had started to go in, everything was melting in my crotch. I raised my arm, finger pointing.

'"You have to act as if it were possible to radically transform the world. And you have to do it all the time." Angela Davis.'

'Mmh.' It was hard to tell if Melvin was responding or enjoying himself. He was transforming something in me, right there, right then.

I moved my hips, clenched the muscles deep inside. The ones that were like an elevator. The ones I had learned to lift and hold in Pilates class. The few times I had gone. This was the best use for that exercise.

9

The Dancers

Melvin had asked Johari if he could kiss her. They were both fourteen, it was a while after they had met. He knew he loved her; the awkward silences, the determination, the unusual decisions she made about being a dancer. He didn't tell her that. That he saw her that way, as a dancer. Johari would have laughed and pulled him to or away from their spot in the park. She was about the moment, the moment in the body. Not the label. He loved her, he knew that. There was something deep and pure and all-encompassing with her.

On a Thursday afternoon, they went to the movies. It was a romantic comedy. Melvin had suggested it; he wanted to set the tone, do it right, impress his best friend who he thought might be his girlfriend too. They sat in the last row. The cinema was almost empty. Johari turned to him and whispered, 'We can try. But I doubt it's going to be our thing.'

Melvin had shared kisses with a few girls, usually on late afternoons in a hidden corner in the park. But that was different. It was trying out, the excitement came from not knowing kissing, not from the other person. The film had a long night scene and the light in the theatre dropped. On-screen, the heroine was walking along a field at dusk, regretful of all the things she had not done to keep her lover. Melvin's hand reached to Johari, he turned her face toward him and kissed her. His tongue was searching into her mouth.

They tried. For the whole of the evening scene. They tried when the film cut to the night scene in the cottage where the character was staying and going over and over the actions that had pushed away their love interest. They tried during the morning scene, when the character decided, finally, after a sleepless night to make that courageous phone call. They kept trying during the scene after, which was two weeks later, where the heroine was forgiven, love was restored, and her friends advised her to remember not to do it again because you could only get so many chances.

She had been right. Johari. It was boring and colourless. Nothing like their crazy dancing. Nothing like their talking that was like dancing, only a very different type of dance. Melvin had felt her belly first, jiggling, and her mouth moved away. The laughter had been a relief, a way to stop the wet sloshing they were doing in each other's mouths.

'Man, this is like flossing with a slab of meat in your mouth.'

He had to agree. Their bodies didn't fit, it happened sometimes. Melvin realised he didn't want her, not like that. He wanted her time, time together. Not her body, not her sweet talk, not her exclusiveness.

Eight years later, Nia, her sister, and Melvin started dating. With permission.

Johari had laughed. 'Mate, you don't need my permission, you need hers.'

All Melvin needed to do was to remain her friend.

10

The Swimmer

Rahul wanted to meet the same evening I called. I wasn't sure what this meeting was about. Did he think along romantic lines? It was Crystal who had put her head on my shoulder. I already had one man in my life. I also had a woman. I needed to talk to Temi. Find out what the terms of our dating were. Did it mean exclusivity? I had slept with Melvin the day after I had gone to hers for our talk. We were showing real interest, Temi and I, but I didn't think that we were in a relationship yet.

I agreed to go for a run. Crystal was with her parents in Manchester and Rahul was feeling the lone runner blues. It was his thing, only being by himself while treading the ground when it was a choice. He didn't want to choose that way on this particular day and decided to ask me to come along. Healthier than the water, I assumed was his thinking. We did fifteen minutes and I was ready to swear off anything and anyone as long as we could continue the rest of the way walking.

'I shouldn't have gone that fast, perhaps.'

I wanted to reply but I was still panting.

'Not bad though, I take it you don't normally do this,' he continued.

It was funny. I laughed. He laughed. We went to the pub and gulped down some water. We ordered chips and washed them down with a couple of pints. He told me of his job as a supervisor for the residents at the periodontology department at Eastman Dental Hospital. I learned all about cleaning deep pockets, which wasn't an euphemism for pickpocketing.

'It's mostly just bad luck. Genetic disposition. Some people have a lot of debris and perfect gums. Others do everything right, floss and brush and still get it.'

My phone was on my lap, I had gotten it out when he started, so I could glimpse at it, secretly under the table. I was sure I would need a distraction from what was surely going to be the most mind-numbing conversation on a Wednesday evening. Strangely, I was absorbed by the details.

'You cut it back?'

'If it's bad we have to.'

'This sounds like torture.'

'It does hurt a little afterwards but the results are good. The gum flattens, the pockets close and you have a better chance of keeping the teeth.'

'Fascinating.' I meant it. If I had periodontitis in my future, at least I knew my way around now. 'It's a cliché to be a dentist though, for an Asian guy, isn't it?'

'It would be. Periodontology is a specialty.'

'You're more of an artist, is that what you're saying?'

He laughed. 'I'm more of a *If I have to stare into smelly mouths for the rest of my life I want to be paid accordingly*. And why is it a cliché anyway?'

I held up my empty glass and Rahul nodded. I went to the bar to fill them up with the free tap water they left out. Rahul was staring out of the window biting his lip. It was time to go back but it was so awkward. What was I doing? Did I want to do anything? Why were we even here? I had texted him, I had no excuse. I had started this whole evening. I could have taken some time off, stayed home, got some rest from the long weekend and the long week so far. It was only Wednesday. I filled my glass again and took both of our glasses back to the table.

'Anything exciting over there?' Rahul asked.

He was cute. I hadn't paid much attention because – well, because. Because this was all too many things in too few days. His hair fell slightly sideways over the upper part of his forehead. And it wasn't styled, we had just run our lungs out. Well, I had, but nevertheless we had been in motion. It was dishevelled but looked perfect and invited you to run your hands through it. Where the last part came from, I didn't know. I could have texted Crystal by herself. I didn't need to apologise. They were weird. The encounter was weird. Floating on a river was alarming, I got that. Hanging out with a person who looked like they were trying to drown themself, to give the person your number in case you ever wanted to hang out, was something else. I wouldn't have believed me. Not on that morning. I had a feeling about Crystal, a good one. I wanted to know her. I didn't want to sleep with her. And Rahul. He was funny. He was easy to get on with.

'I am rehydrating to make up for me stinking up the place with the aftermath of my amateur running efforts.'

'You're not smelly.'

'I was sweating like crazy. You were all *I stepped out of the bath* clean and perfume,' I said.

'We were practically standing still. I thought you went out dancing all the time.' Rahul wasn't trying to challenge me. It was genuine surprise.

'Who said that?'

'You. At the bus stop. You talked about the club. Yet again the club you said.'

The noise had started to die down. The pub was getting emptier. I heard him loud and clear.

'What?'

He got up and took the waters out of my hands and placed them on the table.

'Okay.' He sat back down. 'I'll be off soon. Early morning.'

'Flapping gums.'

'And other things.'

Later, I texted him that it had been fun. I wanted to do it again. Was there a reason he had steered us back to the River Lea on our run?

11

The Dancers

After the kissing that wasn't for them, they were even more inseparable. It was even easier now that they knew it wasn't their thing. They felt special with this bond that was not going to be eaten up by desire and the inevitable getting bored then annoyed then utterly pissed off with the person. No one lasted more than two months, not in their circles. At fourteen, two months was like a lifetime. After that, it often felt like a punishment.

When Jadyn turned up they were not worried. Their bond was strong. It was time to start having sexual relations. They talked about it. Then they laughed and tried to fill in the gaps that sex ed had left. How were you supposed to do it in a way that was pleasing to both parties? Johari doubted that boys her age had much of a clue. Melvin prided himself on having paid attention when they discussed sexuality in school, and after school with some of the older kids hanging around. You had to look for other ways to get details on the subject, like from his older cousin Eve who had just turned seventeen and was determined to teach him good manners. That's what she said.

'Melv, it's just a matter of being polite. You understand? It's respectful. You please the girl, the person, the boy, whoever it is for you Melv. You listen to them. Their body... You'll know.'

Melvin was eager for her opinion. Eve had a new boyfriend, Samuel who she said 'got *it*, all of it'. She was eager to share her newfound experience because she was happy and she wanted every girl to be as happy as she was.

Jadyn joined them on Mondays when he was with his Dad. His Dad lived on Melvin's street and Jadyn stayed over from Sunday morning to Monday evening. He slowed down one day when they were trying out a new choreography. With inspiration from the internet Johari and Melvin wanted to be more daring and included jumps and lifts but they had no idea where to put the focus on their bodies to keep them from falling over. There was a lot of trial and error. Then came Jadyn. He said he was good at gymnastics. He said they were doing it wrong. They had to be more deliberate with the gravity centre and how they steadied themselves. Jadyn didn't care for gymnastics. He

was just good at it. It happens sometimes. That desire and talent did
not converge. He was bored, he didn't have any friends close to his
father's house because his school was two bus rides away. It was
unnecessary to come to his father's after school only to go back to
his mother's in the evening. It messed up his day and the start of
the whole week. But his parents had agreed on this and they weren't
budging, much as he tried to change their mind. Their dancing gave
him a purpose. Mondays made sense again. Although he wasn't keen
on doing it so much, the dancing, he liked the idea of passing on the
knowledge. He didn't say it like that but it would have fitted. Jadyn
spoke in loaded half sentences, much more serious in his expressions
than he probably intended.

Johari and Melvin noticed the slight lisp and agreed that it suited
him. Jadyn had a strong walk. It was confident but there was a little
drag on the left leg. Melvin hadn't noticed it and disputed whether it
really was pulling slightly or whether Johari was slowing him down,
in her mind, to savour all the details. The way his legs lifted, the way
his bum got pulled apart for a brief moment when the legs were in
full stride, the way he pushed away air when moving as if he was
called to do it. Johari mused whether it inhibited his steadiness, the
almost imperceptible imbalance. Melvin threw a handful of leaves
her way.

'Stop! Ask him out already. His walk is fine.'

There were other things she had noticed. The way his T-shirt rode
up when he took off his jumper, exposing his midriff and the bits of
hair that travelled down into his trousers. But they never spoke alone
and she couldn't find the courage to ask him directly, whether he too
had noticed things about her.

Sometimes they left their respective schools earlier than they were
allowed to and snuck into the cinema in the early afternoon. Melvin
let Johari and Jadyn sit together. One time he left in the middle of the
movie to get more popcorn and paced around in the lobby until ten
minutes had passed. When he came back Johari avoided his eyes.

Jadyn always had to be at his father's house at 6pm, in time for
his mother's pick up. Sometimes, when Melvin and Johari were deep
into their practice, he forgot the time and had to run back to catch
his mother before she had to wait inside. It wasn't a good evening if
father and mother had to spend time together, waiting for their son.
The one they shared but who was the only thing they shared and
even that sharing was a division. One time, Johari ran all the way

home with him, leaving Melvin by his building. She lived the other direction but on that day Jadyn had smiled at her in a way that made her think it was time to approach this boy differently, to show she was interested in more than advice on their postures and shapes. She touched his arm while running, holding on until they arrived by the door to his father's house.

'Just in time, I think,' Jadyn said, laughing because they had sped the whole way as if someone was chasing them. Something was chasing them, or more precisely him. He didn't want another parent encounter. They didn't work, everyone knew it. Johari let go of his arm, raising hers while catching her breath. Jadyn put his hand on her shoulder and Johari turned to him. The door opened, first his mother then the father appeared. Jadyn let go of her shoulder and greeted his mother. He looked at Johari but she didn't know what his eyes were saying. It was clear that this tension had nothing to do with her, or her coming with their son. This was between the parents but Jadyn would have to carry it. Johari said hello and excused herself. She sprinted back the way she had come. At the end of the street, she turned around. The mother was waiting outside of the house by a parked car. Jadyn and the father were gone, probably to get his bag.

Johari didn't allow herself to bring him home again.

Their dancing started to look like they knew what they were doing. Jadyn didn't join in much; he mostly sat on the grass watching and commentating. Sometimes he stood up to correct them, to say 'No, here, like this.'

On those occasions, he showed them what he meant, where he generated the movement. Then he leaned back on the grass, his head on his backpack nodding appreciatively. 'Yeah, that's the one.'

It was a great summer, Melvin and Johari agreed.

12

The Swimmer

The letter was there. With a personal note. Hanna was like that, friendly and considerate.

'Owning property does not make me insensitive to the tenants' lives,' she said to me soon after I moved in. We had started chatting in the hallway after she had repaired things in the building. The chats became longer and she would stay for a tea, offered by me. Later she would bring biscuits, or cake, always self-made of course because she was German like that and believed the pastry from here had a lot of questions to answer for. The last two years, I had been to the pub with her at the beginning of December for Christmas drinks. She was the stereotype of a power lesbian, which I liked almost more than the flat. In charge, sporty and energetic. Hair kept short enough to not move much in the wind. That is where the stereotype ended because – although she assured me she was open to exploring if it ever came to it – she had been married to Stefan for years. Monogamously, not overly normative but very hetero.

The house was bought with her grandmother's inheritance and came with three units. Hanna lived a few streets away because 'it is not necessary to feel the person you're renting from is watching over everything you do.'

Hanna. You had to like her. She didn't have to try; she had a set of values that was sometimes at odds with what she was doing. She should have worked in a housing project that was more communal, but I had to admit she steered her retirement-plan-flats-for-rent ship well. None of us in the house had been unhappy.

But Brexit, oh Brexit. All that nonsense of an endless disaster, when she could go back to Berlin, her hometown, and be done with it. There was no telling where it would end, in the UK. It had taken forever but someone had bought the building at asking price. The buyer was not interested in keeping the tenants, except for the one in the basement flat, because they were converting the rest of the house into a family home.

Hanna left two cards, which I found on the windowsill by the front door. One had a flower decoration around a large *Thank You*. It read: *I never expected I would have to leave a friend behind, in what feels like my grandmother's house. I am grateful for the many conversations we have had, for the tips on herbal remedies (Astragalus works a treat!). Better things are still to come. You are a gifted person. Thank you for your friendship (if I may call it that).*

The other card said, *I'm sorry for any stress this is causing you. Let me know what I can do.* The picture on the front was a large smiley face with the arms outstretched.

The letter included my official two months' notice period, the details of the buyer, contact details of a friend of Hanna's who owned a house on the other side of the world (Shepherds Bush) and had a studio available (Hanna did try), and the waiving of the servicing fee that was normally included in our rent for the remainder of the tenancy.

Two months was tough. Not enough time to build up a deposit. My bed was empty and cold, or more specifically I felt alone and cold and there was no reason for the latter and I needed the former.

Mum was calling and calling; I had stopped looking at the phone when it buzzed. Temi sent a message about when to continue talking and was I free on the weekend, there was an art show she wanted to go to and she thought maybe we could actually start doing things together. Something other than clubbing and sex because she was starting to feel too old for the former and wanted more intellectual foreplay for the latter. I pulled the blanket over my head. Melvin was in his Thursday class, bending and stretching and making other people sniff the grace he had deeply embedded in his whole being. Except for his grief. I knew nothing of his sister, and that was enough reason for me to want to know. Now of all times. After knowing him forever and having shared almost all with him. I needed to dig at something.

I knew about his dead twin because his mother had told me once, slightly tipsy, when I stayed over on a bank holiday and Melvin had gone to sleep and I had stayed up. Our conversation had gotten carried away from Johari to siblings. Johari. Melvin's mother Olive adored her, much more than she liked me. I was the newcomer. Although I could see her approving when I had got a first in both the BSc and the post-grad diploma, it was a new-found respect, something that grew between adults but not because there was a natural spark between us. Johari had been in her life since she was a teenager, she was inventory. Fragile and quirky and full of beans, as Olive liked to say. She had something in common with my Mum, Olive: they were desperate for a cool edge that kept them in the younger half of life.

The letter. I had been dreading it. Somehow over the last six months, I had hoped the Brexit frenzy would put an even bigger damper on the property market. But it was still there, the notice, on my bedroom floor, demanding something from me that did not fit in this part of the year, where all I could muster was to lie back and look at the sky and wonder how to fly.

13

The Dancers

The Monday after Johari had run home with Jadyn, and Jadyn's parents had repelled Johari back down the street with their intense energies, Jadyn didn't turn up. Or more precisely he turned up but didn't join them on their patch. Instead, he went to the outdoor gym area and pretended he was working out. Melvin looked at Johari who shrugged her shoulders. They were in the middle of a choreography and although Johari was pulled away, always moving her head to see what Jadyn was doing, they continued. When the music stopped, they stopped. Johari turned to walk over to him but Jadyn was gone.

'You could just text him,' Melvin said.

'I know what I can and cannot do,' Johari replied. Her voice was sharp. As if Melvin had poured bicarbonate into some soapy water in a bottle and it fizzed out, bubbling over the rim like it didn't belong inside. Melvin's mouth opened and got stuck in shock. What had he done? He waited for Johari to catch herself, to recognise what she was doing, to say something. Johari pulled on her shoelaces, tightened them until it looked like her feet were squeezed into shoes two sizes smaller. She avoided Melvin as if she couldn't even fathom that someone else was here, in this moment, with her. Even if they had just spent forty minutes jumping and turning and extending their bodies together.

Melvin stared at her, his mouth still open. 'I get that you like him, but I haven't done anything.'

She looked up, finally finished with her laces. 'He's going through some stuff. Family,' Johari said.

'I haven't even said anything about him. I'm talking about you. Why're you rude to me? I haven't done anything.'

She didn't answer. She got up and picked up her backpack. Looking the other way she said, 'You coming?' She was about to move, leave for the day, expecting Melvin to follow like usual. He didn't move. He liked Johari. He liked their time together. He liked the weirdness between them, the way that words didn't always fill in what needed to be said. He understood that she liked Jadyn, that she would find a boyfriend at some point, that she would be awkward about that. He had expected that, the awkwardness. The way Johari was oblivious to the fact that not everyone would follow her when she said *go*. People would be left standing. wondering what she was implying, what she expected, what they were meant to do. Melvin picked up his bag and stood in front of her.

'You can just text him. You don't have to take it out on me. I'm your friend.'

He walked off. He liked to think that Johari was surprised; that she was the one with her mouth open now, standing with her face frozen in surprise, looking after him as he walked onto the sidewalk and then out of her view.

The next day she waited for him at the entrance to the park.

'Sorry. Not sure why I was a dickhead.'

'Okay,' he said. He wasn't sure if Johari knew that only changed behaviour made for an acceptable effort, not apologies by themselves. It was a small moment, her moodiness the previous day. He wanted to know that it was a one-off.

14

The Swimmer

Melvin hadn't been to mine for months. We hadn't seen each other
except for the few times I had stopped by his flat just after calling,
'Are you in, like right now?' It was like picking up an unfinished
conversation mid-air between us. Catching a thread and weaving it
back into the fabric that was our bond. We never needed a warm-up
period. I didn't ask him what else he did, romantically. He didn't ask
me. It wasn't about that. We were together for life, even if we were
not an item.

He put the shopping on the kitchen counter and searched for
onions. I hadn't been home much in the last week.

'There's an old one in the fridge.'

I brought it out and added it to the stuff he had taken out of the bag.
Melvin pulled me in and laid his head on my shoulder. I could feel
his breath, warm, pushing against my neck, my ear, my collarbone.
His arm wrapped around me and I stood in the embrace. Being held
by Melvin was a metaphor; life could never be flushed down the sink
completely when there was this.

'Twice in a week, treat.'

It made me happy to hear his voice, close to my ears, as if it had a
body, as if it had a shape. I could feel and hear it. My fingers pressed
around his forearms, then up to his upper arms, the muscles flexed
when I squeezed, which is what I was going for.

'Standing?'

The chairs were under the window, next to a small piece of wood
that I had drilled into the wall as a table.

'Holding.'

The letter and the cards from Hanna were on the kitchen table
now. After last night's broken sleep, I had put them there to have
coffee with. To give me inspiration. How could I find my new Hanna,
my new haven, my new place of dwelling without too much upheaval?
The logical thing would have been to go to Mum's, she had a second
bedroom that had been my bedroom at one point. It had been eight
years since I moved out but it was comfortable, with a sofa bed and
a small table. I stayed over often, both to keep Mum company and
when it was closer to get home to from wherever I was going that

night. The wardrobe was built-in, which was so rare, and would hold enough of my stuff. I would have my own space and the imposing on someone would be at a miniMum because Mum was happy to see me more anyway.

But there was the voice.

'The Germans are leaving us already, leaving the UK to rot in its own dystopian creation.'

Melvin was no longer melting into me. I could feel his thoughts rushing about. He was wired from a rehearsal with a musician who wanted him to respond to her set, without devising a choreography. A call and response, or more accurately a play and react.

'So you do have to leave? That's bad. Sorry!'

He squeezed me tight again, returning to me and my body.

'You know you always have a place with me, no question.'

I thought there were so many questions to clear up but I let go of Melvin and walked around the flat, the one bed I had lived in for almost five years. My living room with the large space in the middle, the place I retreated to when I needed to order my thoughts. The alcove was painted coral, the rest white and the large rug that covered the wood floor was green. It was warm and safe and it was not at all the right time to move, to leave anything behind, let alone a home that felt like one.

'I'll empty space for you.' Melvin had followed and positioned himself by the door opposite the windows. 'Just in case.'

I had nothing to answer. I had not listened to Mum's messages, I had not checked in. I lay down on the green rug, my legs on the armchair, my arms outstretched. I was welcoming the universe to lift me up into understanding and reveal what my next step should be.

Melvin started talking about the songs and the music, how it had swept him away when he first heard it but then what did sweeping mean, and how he had located the feeling in his tummy, connected it to his feet and the rest of his body had lifted and fallen. Not in line with the melody he found, but with the almost imperceptible shuffling of her feet that she was doing while singing the song to him. It was her breath and her nerves that carried him. I shuffled on the rug. It had creased and was poking my back.

I wanted to tell him about Temi and ask how I could see her without it being awkward, or perhaps it wasn't awkward and I was just having thoughts. Thoughts that needed this place, with the high ceilings, so that I could breathe out and let them float, not on water but right up to the ceiling, and there like a long, stretched-out whiteboard, my thoughts could attach and I could use my imaginary duster and erasable pen to make columns and charts and mind maps to organise it into manageable chunks, order it into colourful lists and flow charts. Except I never had that much need for detailed visuals. But I wanted the ceiling, and the space below it, and the floor to lie on. I moved my head to the right and smiled. Melvin was looking at me. He seemed happy, full with shuffling feet noise and the feelings that had stirred up in him. I was thinking of Temi. Would we ever have anything neutral; something that started on the right foot, where I could fuck her across my spacious room and tell her how her ears were sometimes on my mind, when we ended up on the other end, by the floor lamp. I would dash up to get a blanket and some cushions and we would stay lying on the floor because there, at the far end, we were hidden from the outside world. The windows couldn't reach it. It was a dead spot, a cosy corner to disappear in and make that beautiful love we made when we allowed ourselves to. I would bite her ears and she would moan and I could explain that it was the shivering that made me think of her ears. The way she trembled, the way her breath travelled from stomach to chest in little bursts, rhythmic, expectant.

I could feel my own breath stuck. I didn't even know where, it was so faint behind the pounding of my heart.

'One day we have to talk about your sister.'

Melvin's head jerked around and his face morphed from content with the world to alarm, major alarm stage.

'The one that died. The one you never talk about.'

'What are you talking about, Nia?'

'Your twin, your survivor's guilt.'

I knew I was wrong. The bile was pressing against the back of my throat. My own judgement, the very low blow I was trying to swing, hit me from the inside. I turned the other way, Melvin's eyes had lost their brightness. He was looking at me as if he was going to tear my skin off to see what the hell was inside. My little bookshelf was dusty. The shelf that held all my practitioner's books, the one behind the floor lamp. All the herbal knowledge I was still ingesting, in small portions, so that it could become part of me, that I would remember things, that they would feel organic to me. Not something automatic but something deliberate. This was organic too, this shooting straight out of my mouth without taking the route through the brain to slow it down and view the contents. What was I doing, what was I saying? And most importantly, why? My chest was clamped shut, it didn't conspire with me. Forcing Melvin to talk about his sister would not heal his or my wounds. My body was not compliant, yet it was deliberate. I turned around and Melvin was still staring at me. He went to the kitchen and I followed. My legs heavy, my head light – so light I had trouble seeing the short way down the hallway. Stars were blinking all over and I had to squeeze my eyes.

'How is your mother?' His voice had changed but he was still trying.

'She's manic.'

'She left a few messages but I was in class. I haven't been able to reach her. We should go by.'

'You should. I can't,' I replied.

I wanted him to do the work he was so good at. He could pull me out of any mood in the blink of an eye, but he did nothing to lift me out of the deep water.

'That voice. They probably need to put her medication up,' he said.

I looked at him. We had talked about this before, her voice. This part, when Mum was on the spiral, was always the hardest part to witness. When the doctor couldn't get the mania under control and she would be admitted so they could. When she was fresh on a high dose of medication that was trying to pummel her into an acceptable shape. Her face puffed up, swollen, her eyes glazed over, milky, and far away. And her speech. The words stretched until they were incomprehensible, the intonation flattened until it became monotone and scary, the slow-mo setting of a horror voice. The horror being the amount of medication that wiped out the person inside. It was a struggle for her words to make it into the world when she was like this. Being silenced wasn't a metaphor. There was too much of her spilling out at times and the pills were a violent way of stuffing it back, all down her throat again. Even I thought they were necessary, at times. When her mind was an open tap gushing. Running and running and not stopping, thinking that she alone could save the world and would do so with actions we had to try and undo in the weeks that followed. When there were hardly any facts in her stories and I had to make sense of the outrageous compositions of coincidences she presented that all conspired on the same person, her, at the same time. I had never had a psychotic episode. I did not know how it felt from the inside.

I started to cry. Melvin came to stand next to me. I wanted him to say everything was going to be okay. I wanted him to hold me. But he just stood where he stood.

'Your sister,' I started again.

'What do you mean?' His voice was calm, willing to let this go, to give me this one because of the stress but I couldn't help myself, I couldn't stop my mouth from pushing against him.

'The one that died. Your twin.'

Melvin fell away from me until we stood on opposite sides of the small kitchen and he seemed to have disappeared into space. So far that there would be no reaching. And still, I didn't stop. He looked at me and I continued.

'We will have to talk about her.'

'You're not right, you know that. Not like this.'

He picked up his keys and before I could answer, he had left.

15

The Dancers

'Do you want to go or not?' Johari looked at Melvin.

Melvin was thinking of Farah who had laughed and said, 'Maybe you can dance but she definitely can't. Why make such a fool of yourself? The whole school knows.'

It didn't matter to him. They needed to move, it didn't need to be pretty. And he disagreed. Johari was strong and with Jadyn and his gymnastics lessons, she had added acrobatic elements that had Melvin open-mouthed. He knew Farah was being mean. Johari did things other girls couldn't do, for lack of practice and for lack of talent. But Melvin liked Farah.

Johari's boldness was one of the things he loved most about her. In her mind, she was simply direct and honest. In fact, she was shy, that is why it came out so clear and unfiltered. She didn't have a game face. It hadn't taken Melvin a long time to catch her enthusiasm. There were music videos to copy, things to try that they had seen on TV. There were moves that seemed to burst out of their bodies. These sensations needed to be explored. The best work happened when their bodies disagreed on how they should translate a beat or an idea. Or the music. Sometimes they fell into the grass laughing, accusing each other of hearing another piece of music on invisible earphones. That they practised so many afternoons, sometimes even in the rain, and jumped to their own rhythm, twisted to the faint melody from the studio, invented ways of moving body parts back and forth, up and down: it was the most satisfying thing either of them had done. Melvin knew it was weird only because they could have gone to a centre and found classes they could afford, or were free. Melvin understood it, the weirdness. They were teenagers, not kids. There were places they could have gone. By then they could have joined the studio itself. They had been invited for a free trial period but Johari had said no, and Melvin had agreed.

Who in their right mind would spend all of their free time outside in London? Where the cold felt wet not only in winter.

Melvin knew everybody had an opinion about it. He had thought about how it looked, especially in the beginning. There were always kids and teenagers looking and saying something, adults smiling, sometimes laughing at them. Having this open secret, an intimate connection that was visible to everyone but which they couldn't understand the importance of was worth more to him than aesthetics. It was a secret because people didn't get it. This was about something between Johari and himself, and the world they lived in. About touching the world they lived in, and it touching them in return. All playing out in the sensations inside. It was precious. He could take a laugh or two because it felt good either way.

Once Farah said it, his legs stumbled over invisible roots and got caught in the grass. He could feel his skin making a dent in the air, his body shifting whole clouds of oxygen, disturbing the equilibrium of the park with ethereal waves that made it all the way to wherever Farah hung out after school and alerted her. He could hear her laughing in another part of the borough. It was mockery and it kept his body stiff and unmoving.

'Why don't we do something different today,' he said.

'What do you want to do?' Johari's face was open and inquisitive. How could he tell her that he wanted to spend the afternoon running after Farah, who hadn't even said she would hang out with him? He wanted to find her and ask her what he should do instead, what would be the thing that brought her attention to him, what could he do to stand out.

He hadn't told Johari about her. He decided that dancing wasn't for that day and they ended up at Johari's. Nia, her sister, was there and wanted to be part of their afternoon and they had no choice. They all sat in the small living room while their mother was cooking a meal she had heard about from a stranger she had talked to a few years earlier. It didn't come out well. SuSu, their mother couldn't remember how to make the dish and it ended up as half-cooked aubergines with chickpeas, the tomato sauce forgotten. Johari had eaten it without saying a word; she didn't look at Melvin and he knew he had to go along.

16

The Swimmer

Melvin didn't pick up the next morning but Crystal called. It was serendipitous. She had been on my mind, especially since I met with Rahul. The timing couldn't have been better. I didn't want the space to reflect on my behaviour with Melvin.

'I heard you've been by the River Lea again,' she said and I loved her voice for its sincerity. There were openings there, for jokes to be made rather than to engage with the facts she was alluding to. I appreciated the light toughness of her delivery.

It had been a week. I felt I had known her for years. Of course, this was the first time we spoke to each other after the Saturday morning, after the swimming while clothed in a bit of water that was not meant for it.

'Rahul was doing an experiment with me, I think,' I replied.

She didn't laugh. I wanted to but it was only funny if she went along. The pause was loud.

'I'm throwing a lot of things out with the bathwater, it seems.' I was trying and still, she didn't give me any way out. I had mistaken her honesty for an invitation to banter.

'Did you call anyone about this?'

'About what?' I asked.

I wanted to meet her in a cafe and get to know her. Not be in this non-starter of a phone conversation with the quiet in the background. There was space to imagine her flat, and I wondered whether Rahul was there. Maybe he was standing next to her, eyebrows raised, waiting for clues, his dishevelled hair sexy and ready for her hands.

'About being in the water. Did you call anyone?' Crystal repeated.

'Rahul wanted to go back down there,' I offered instead of an answer.

'He told me. It was his weird way of trying to find out what that was all about.'

There was no rush in her voice. There was no story in mine. I couldn't tell her what I was doing a week before, not yet, maybe not for a long time. It had been a moment, an urge, nothing planned. She was determined to find out how I could be saved and I wanted to sit across from her and look at her, taking in her essence. I knew that wasn't possible, what was a person's essence anyway, but I wanted to feel her.

'What are you doing today?' I asked.

It was a Saturday but she had called early. Either Rahul was still there or not yet. Perhaps there was a window of opportunity for me and I was up for taking my chances.

Two hours later we were at a small gluten-free bakery for breakfast. Crystal looked different. I hadn't had a clear picture of her in mind, more a sense of her than an image. An emotional cue.

'Haircut,' she said and rubbed her head. 'I am still faithful to my barber in Manchester, after all these years.'

I nodded my approval, although I had only ever been to the barbers to tidy up the edges of whatever hairstyles could be improved with a sharp hairline. Lately, I had got stuck on box braids.

Crystal worked for Project Guardian, a joint venture of the British transport police, the City of London, and the London transport services. Their job was to encourage the reporting of sexual offences on the Tube and investigate those instances. Her zealousness made sense now, she was trained in investigation.

'It can't be easy work,' I said and meant it. She was impressive but I knew that from last Saturday. She had a light-touch approach to things but she seemed to not shy away from going in deep.

At work, she was looking at patterns of reported incidents, working out if there were repeat offenders and passing on relevant findings to other teams who would go on and prosecute. All to make our journeys safer and to prevent future harassment.

'Like the Everyday Sexism Project.'

'Yes, something like it.'

I ran out of things to say as way of a reply, how important that work was, although I had never thought too highly about the police itself. I always wondered how one was drawn to a notoriously racist institution and hoped that the work one did would outshine the structure it was being done in. I knew the answer already. She was not the first person I had met, and liked, who believed that good people could make a difference, any and everywhere. I didn't want to argue about her own emotional health during our first meeting. And then how much healthier were my work environments? Did I know that? And health was my field of expertise.

We ate without talking for a while. The croissant was fresh. I hadn't slept well, and I decided I needed to force myself off caffeine for a while so I could get my circadian rhythm back in order. I sipped on the tap water I had asked the waitress to bring me.

Crystal was having toast with jam and a large flat white.

'I have a lot going on at the moment,' I explained.

'I thought so,' she replied. 'It's just better to get some help, professional, you know. It's so easy to fall through the cracks. I don't know you but I wanted to say it.'

'It might be hard to believe but I'm not falling through the cracks, I'm not sure I'm even falling, if that makes sense.' I ordered a lemon and ginger tea. 'I have people, I do. People who are holding me, or trying to.'

'It's not really about the people though, is it? It's about you.' Crystal ordered more toast.

I was meeting Temi at the Tate in an hour but I wanted to keep sitting in the tiny cafe and watch Crystal. She had ordered more bread. Her eating was not self-conscious. She was completely lost in the action and her enjoyment was spilling over to me. Butter and jam heaped onto the slice, then she cut it into small strips and licked the side of her hand when some of the jam dropped onto it. Eventually, she leaned back. She had eaten four pieces of toasted bread.

'I'm really full now,' she said.

We both laughed.

She drank some water. 'So much better.'

'Thank you for meeting me. I don't know what it is with you, with the both of you,' I said and wondered if I knew how to finish this sentence.

Her hands were folded on the table, calm and content.

'You paid attention,' I continued.

She was tracing a line in the wood on the table with her index finger while looking at me.

'I didn't think I wanted any. Really, I did want the cooling down. I wanted to hang in time, in space. The water was the only way I knew how to. I wasn't looking for help, I know how to do that. But there you were. Not shouting loudly, "What a weirdo," not reporting me to the police – and how strange that you actually work for the police.'

I had more to say but my skin got prickly; someone had opened the door and the draft was sudden. When I turned back, I spoke without meeting her eyes.

'You cared. It's rare these days.'

It was the ability to be moved by someone else, enough to stop you in your tracks.

She nodded. 'Perhaps it is, perhaps we're simply too scared to show it.'

She signalled for the bill.

'I do have to go. I'm glad you explained how you felt that morning. It makes sense, in some ways. I still think you should consider professional help.'

After the sensuous eating, this part of the breakfast was fast and clinical. She paid for the both of us, thanked the waiter in a friendly manner, got up, moved to the door and ushered me to the pavement where we parted minutes later. I saw her walk off in the other direction and felt dizzy. I had Temi to meet either way but the brash goodbye had left no real opening for a follow-up.

Temi was waiting on a bench canal side with three sunflowers tied together. She kissed me on the mouth when I leaned down to hug her, pulling herself up in the process.

'Is this our first date? As in not taking each other home after a party?' I asked.

'Who said this isn't a party?'

Her hand pulled mine as she laughed. Inside the turbine hall, we kissed and I held back from biting her ear.

'Why were you delayed?' she asked.

'Oh, something came up.' I didn't know what to offer as an excuse.

'I know, you texted. What was it?'

Here we were. Dating, officially, and since we knew each other for more than a year I had to say more to make this first date count. How to start? With Crystal, and Rahul, and the Saturday after I left her? Tell her that I had abandoned her while dancing, things sexy and smooth between us, no reason other than my own weirdness and I was now obsessing about a couple I had met when they thought I was going to drown myself? There was so much undoing in these seven days and here I was with Temi and her full attention on a sunny Saturday right at the Thames.

'It's someone I've just met but we had something to talk about. One of those chance encounters. I think I'm making friends with them, they're a couple. She wanted to catch up. We met in a gluten-free bakery in north London. She suggested it. I didn't want to cut her short.'

It was true. Somewhat. It was also my first lie. I could have looked for other places to meet but I wanted it far away from Temi and far away from anything that had to do with my other life. My real life. The one that I couldn't quite put into words at this moment. I hadn't explained anything and didn't want to add to the pile of unexplainable behaviour that needed unravelling in front of Temi. If we were calling it a relationship this wasn't a great start for open communication. But then we had not had our dating period yet, where we presented ourselves in the most favourable light and pretended to be entirely wholesome. I was doing that. I was showing her how much loving me would be a mature endeavour, healthy and accountable. I couldn't lead with awkward and questionable emotional states. Or the question of exclusivity, which I shoved away as quickly as it nagged my conscience. I could invoke the technicality of our surprise start and the lack of the relevant conversation to defend my sexual actions from the previous week, should they ever come up.

'Okay,' she replied.

There was no telling if she believed me.

The Tate was full and the tourists were walking around in groups, impressed and searching. We got our tickets and took the escalator up to the *Soul of a Nation: Art in the Age of Black Power* exhibition, holding hands and smiling. I stole glances while people pushed past us. Her hair was down now, the after Bantu knot effect, bouncy curls that framed her face. I liked it. Even more, I liked how we walked through the rooms, independently, sometimes lifting our heads to look for the other, pointing to a piece, smiling and nodding knowingly if we had already seen it. She waited for me when I trailed behind. Once we walked back together because she wanted to show me something. It was easy. So much easier than I had imagined. My theories on her had been informed by that misfired text, the one that had got lost in the cyber ether. It had seemed I was on her call list for lonely days, not that she was someone I could spend time with. Perhaps she had felt the same. We had not yet talked about what this might have prevented between us. I had answered her request for a date and here we were.

We ended up in a cafe across from the back entrance of the Tate.

'It was good,' she said, her voice flat.

'Oh,' I answered.

'Nothing oh.' She laughed.

'Then what?'

'It's important but all this emphasis on the US... Sometimes it seems we forget that there was and is a movement here too. I'd like more on here. Black British movement. You know? Why not have a major exhibition on that? When they show local artists, it's always just a room or two.'

Her head was turned away, towards the window and she waved.

'A colleague of mine.'

She mouthed 'Check your inbox,' and the woman nodded, smiled and waved back as she turned the corner.

'Tell me about your work,' I said when she turned back to me.

'Now I want to say "Oh".'

I laughed. 'Why?'

'Too dry. The day-to-day of it isn't all that glamorous.'

'What else do you want me to ask?'

Instead of answering, she switched gears. 'What do you want to do? I mean for the rest of the afternoon? Are you free this evening?'

'I am. I want to spend time with you,' I answered. Crystal was no longer on my mind. The two situations were unrelated. I didn't pay attention to the fact that the meeting with Crystal held more depth for me, although it was the first time we had met.

'Good,' Temi replied.

We decided to go to mine. On the way, I told her about the sold house and my impending homelessness. I had considered Melvin. It was where I wanted to be. I needed him. I didn't tell her about pushing him away, about being mean. I didn't tell her that Melvin and I had slept together again, just a few days ago. It wasn't going to continue, I suspected. I had some repairing to do. He was not the type to go for casual sex when things were on a barely speaking basis. I didn't tell Temi that he had been my longest relationship. And that I had been happy, entirely happy. Until it felt like I knew him too well. Until it felt like I could not get over my sister if I was too close to him. Yet each time I was looking for her I went back to rekindle the physical side between us. Sometimes it took me weeks to figure out that I was grieving again. Melvin and I were always organic, it was hard to see the loss that prompted me to reach for him. Perhaps he needed it too. I never asked. Sometimes he asked whether it was a good idea, or why we were back on. I usually laughed, then replied, 'Because you're my prince'. He rarely laughed in response. Prince was not one of the things he dreamt of being. Not in or out of bed. It would have amused him, this strange confession, if he didn't have a question mark about my motives.

'I'll probably stay at my Mum's for a while to figure out what to do. This flat was such a good deal, I have to consider my options,' I said to Temi.

Living in London was like trying to gain entry to an exclusive club, especially when it came to housing. I couldn't do the sharing any longer. I had left Mum's after uni and moved in with five others in Vauxhall. It was great. Social, formative, cheap. It helped get me through post-graduate studies. After that, I wanted alone time. I wanted the possibility of someone I was in a relationship with to come and live with me. I had had a couple of longer ones, relationships, other than the one with Melvin. One still at the shared house that broke off six months after I moved into my flat. Then Lena, who I was with for three and a half years. Before Temi. In between Melvin, always Melvin. Next to Melvin, Lena was my longest relationship but she never came up when I gave anyone a rundown of my significant relationships. I had to dig through my entire romantic history before my memories delivered her to the forefront. It had been safe and lovely. I had learned how to be there, be intimate with someone who did not know Johari, have someone know me who had met me once I was without a sibling. But it had not translated into deep love. We had similar interests but they manifested in different ways. That's how we met. At a seminar on digestive health. Only she saw it as something that went along with allopathic treatment, that helped alongside it. She suffered from chronic constipation, that's how she came to herbal medicine. For the rest she was sceptical. We both loved travelling but she needed to make itineraries before we even got there. Long detailed handwritten lists in her notebook. Sometimes with different colours. I believed in psychogeography. I wanted to get lost in the moment. That's how I learned about a place, the way it felt when you experienced it while walking. It was also how I let go of the stressful weeks, not knowing what would happen at any particular time. Our opposite approaches didn't complement each other. We weren't a good match.

'I have two months,' I said to Temi. 'I might get lucky.'

We stopped by a small greengrocer and bought tinned black beans, spinach, rice and salad. At mine we stood in each other's way, chopping and deciding what spices should go into the bean stew. She looked through my cupboards for a pot to boil the rice in. I bumped into her. We laughed. The way her body moved through my kitchen, the way her head lifted and tipped back briefly when she laughed, the way our hands grazed the other. Her mouth was moving and speaking about her work at the cancer research institute.

'I like that I am a scientist and look younger and different to people's expectations about scientists. They always think I am on a tour from a university, or of course that I work at reception.'

'Does it not make you mad?'

'It does and it doesn't. To be honest I don't care enough about the people thinking like that for it to reach me. I am too focused on important things. Looking at tissue samples. Evaluating whether new treatment ideas work. Studying the people for whom we are trying to make a difference. I know my worth. They are the ones with a need for learning and I leave them to it.'

She laughed again and I could tell she wasn't talking about an ideal scenario. She didn't care. I wanted this ability to shift the focus onto myself, not for my problems but away from other's perceptions. It seemed self-reliant.

We sat down to eat at my little kitchen table. The food was spicier than I would have made it and with more flavour than I could normally get out of a tin of beans. We decided we were good at being sous-chefs to each other. Her foot crept up my leg and stretched into my crotch.

'Will I be able to visit you at your mother's?'

'Yes.' There was a mushiness in my tummy. She was planning ahead. She thought we would still be dating two months from now. 'Of course, it wouldn't be like this, I mean the affection.'

'Of course not.'

We ate in silence and did a lot of smiling. Her eating was precise. She put small portions onto her fork and chewed properly. In-between she looked at me, smiling, her eyes communicating. She didn't rush but there wasn't much pleasure in her eating. It wasn't lavish, it didn't spill over. Her food went onto her fork and then into her mouth, just as it was supposed to.

'I have an important anniversary coming up. I can't tell you the details today. I'm not... ready, it's all a bit much right now. I just wanted you to know, a sort of explanation. There are days when I am not sure what is going on. I need some time to figure that out.'

Her knife and fork were on her plate and she had stopped chewing. I had all of her attention.

I bit my lip. 'You always think it is done, that you have figured it out, the sadness. You know that it comes in waves, you know what the grieving means, that it goes and comes at its own pace. You know all of that. Also that the days do get easier and they have been for many years. It's not a recent death. It's not on my mind often, really. But once in a while, it creeps up. With no warning you find yourself swimming again, and then it seems like you're being pulled away, and you have no control over it, you can do nothing but float on your back, slowly. There isn't anywhere to go, and there is no reason to steer yourself into another direction, and how would you do that anyway, and before you know it you are at the dam that has been holding everything back. The next thing, out of nowhere: there is that deep drop. No direction, no knowing where it will propel you to. You don't know where you will get caught, where you will end up. It's not up to you.'

Temi sat absolutely still. Maybe that is why I had said much more than I had intended to. Her eyes were clear and had not moved from mine. I didn't know where to look, so much had come out. My exhale was loud and I pushed consciously, trying to relieve the tension in my body.

'That's what happened,' I said.

When I raised my head again Temi was still looking at me.

'Are you in the drop, or past it?'

I raised my shoulders and let them fall again.

She nodded.

Later we took a bath together. Temi leaned back and complimented my bath oil. The tangerine smell was uplifting. I had changed to it a few years ago, leaving the usual suspects of rose, lavender and similar florals behind. I wanted to be covered in sensual sun, my nose telling my brain that we would get lifted. All of us. Brain, senses, feelings and body. Temi's breasts stuck out of the water, the nipples half in, half out. There was a quick pull inside me.

My hands played with the water as if I could catch it, if only I found the right angle.

17

The Dancers

Melvin had stayed at Johari's. It was a Saturday morning and because he was coughing he didn't go along when Nia and Johari went to the shops. Johari told him to relax and recover. To stay in her room and get better. This cold that was taking hold of him had had him gasping all night. In the morning it had turned chesty and he was miserable. Johari was going to walk him home in the afternoon, after making him a delicious soup.

'Better than Mum's cooking, I promise,' she had said before leaving.

She knew a thing or two about food. At least about the three dishes she had perfected: chicken soup, vegetable lasagne and fried rice. 'Staples', she called them. For the off times, when SuSu, her mother, would forget to cook. Or when she decided she would only eat something in blue and yellow, and their dinner ended up a selection of blueberries with yellow squash, yellow peppers and sweetcorn. All uncooked because her energy was rising and it made it difficult to focus on one task, impossible to find the patience for preparing food properly.

Johari and Nia would be back shortly. Melvin had slept the night in Nia's room while she had shared Johari's. Now he was lying on Johari's bed looking at the sky that was visible through the window. His chest rattled and wheezed. His mother was starting to think he was developing allergies because he sneezed frequently. Melvin was sure it was because of being outside all of the time, dancing through all weather. He didn't tell her that. Olive was unaware of what they did most of the time. Letting her know that he got rained on and stayed in wet clothes because he didn't want to rush home seemed a sure way of jeopardising his freedom. He didn't mind the damp, he always thought he would dance it off. They only left when it was pouring. He needed to lift his legs and arms and feel the air's resistance. Of course, most of the time there was none. It would seem like they floated neatly through it. Still, he could feel the weight, he could hold the air with an upturned palm, he could push it away too. Windy days were not his favourites. It was as if someone was being too obvious. He enjoyed the way his body needed to push against the force and that sometimes he could throw himself against it and be held. He was not holding air, it was holding him. More than once he had let himself fall; had given in completely after a turn or a twist, leaned or jumped into the gust and let go. A couple of times Johari stood aside and only when he returned from the sensation did he notice her staring at him. He liked the wind because it cleared his mind. There was no attaching to his thoughts, there was only sensation. He liked that, the letting go. Decisions on where to place a foot, how to fold or bend no longer needed to be made because if the wind was strong those would be made for him. Still, he preferred when the difference between outside and him was more porous. As if it was one state, different matter, his body and the world around him, but in a seamless conjunction.

Melvin opened the door to go to the toilet. He stopped. SuSu was standing in the hallway naked. A bundle of lavender was tied around her waist, hanging on her left hip, hitting her leg when her body swayed from one to the other side. Her arms reached upwards, her eyes open. Melvin wanted to sneak back into the room but she had seen him.

'Hello,' she said.

What was he to do here? What was the decorum for meeting a friend's mother naked on a Saturday morning? What type of chitchat was appropriate? Where could one find speech when his brain was repeating *don't look, where to look, don't look, don't look, don't look...*

Her voice was warm, her eyes distant.

'Melvin. Your cough!'

'It's not that bad.' Melvin kept his eyes on the carpet in front of her feet.

'Can you get my coat for me, please? It is chilly after all,' she continued.

Blood was rushing to his cheeks as Melvin lifted his head to follow her arm. She was pointing to the coat stand by the entrance door. He stepped so quickly that moving his legs to get there, lifting the coat off the hook, returning and stretching his arm out to hand it over was one singular event. His armpits were getting hot and sweaty.

She took the coat and draped it over her shoulders. 'Better. The draught, it always slows me down.'

'Okay,' Melvin said and escaped into the toilet. It was the most excruciating journey that he had made for a long time. There wasn't a noise from the hallway and he couldn't be sure whether SuSu was still there or not. He wouldn't leave the bathroom then. Not until Johari returned. After he flushed, he closed the toilet seat again, washed his hands and sat down. His throat felt dry, the cough pushing against his airway. He swallowed again and again, determined not to make a sound. He didn't want to draw attention to himself. He also didn't want to miss anything, he needed to know what was going on. SuSu had started humming. He needed to think of something else. Not the naked mother on the other side of the door. He made himself think of a poem they were discussing at school that week, Imtiaz Dharker's *Tissue*. He couldn't recall all the words but he remembered the video recording of the poet introducing and reading the poem they had watched. The sentiments had stood out. Tissue. So fragile and transparent. It could fall apart at any minute. Like SuSu seemed to be doing in the hallway.

Movement resumed. A stomping, then a dull noise of something hitting the floor. He cracked the bathroom door just as Johari and Nia unlocked the door to the flat. SuSu had thrown the coat stand to the floor, it was heavy with thick jackets and coats. She was squatting at the end that was meant for hats.

'Mum!'

Both sisters rushed in. Johari caught Melvin's eye and turned back to her mother quickly. Melvin opened the door enough for his body to be visible. There was a smell of pee. It wasn't coming from the toilet. He knew he had flushed.

'Come on, get up. You need to wear some clothes.'

Melvin could see Nia's face as they pulled her up and into her bedroom. Johari seemed to have made sure she never had to look at Melvin, or that he could not see her properly. He had no idea what her expression was like but he knew she didn't want him to see this, not quite that much. Her back was warding him off, daring him to peep. Not a playful challenge, the seriousness was ingrained in her body now, the muscles were tenser than her posture, or her movements, required. Her breathing was quick. He got a sense of a hissing, putting him in his place.

'We have a guest,' Johari said while she closed the bedroom door.

Melvin moved fast to get back into Johari's room, where he had left his bag. His throat was still tickling. He still hadn't got a glass of water but the kitchen was now hostile, somewhere he couldn't fathom making it to because it was not on the way to the front door. He wanted to get out of the flat as quickly as possible. It wasn't even

SuSu. It was Johari. He didn't understand her reaction, why she wanted to hide this from him. At other times she had invited him over, knowing her mother was in a manic phase. He had seen things, he had seen SuSu.

One time they had come into the flat on a day when it rained heavily and SuSu had sat in the living room, her hands and feet shaking to a rapid rhythm. She had talked in so fast a manner that all Melvin managed to say was 'Pardon me?' She didn't stop to repeat herself or slow down. Johari had started cooking and left him to sit in the living room with SuSu until Ben, her father, came home half an hour later. Ben had said it was okay to go home if he wanted to. And SuSu had echoed that everyone was free or should be free, including Melvin and that she was going to see to it that everyone did know they had rights. She would organise a campaign that educated everyone in every detail of what it meant to exercise these rights. That was all that Melvin had understood because right after that exclamation her speech sped away again and he could not catch it even if he wanted to. He had excused himself and eaten with his own mother, Olive, instead. That time SuSu had emerged a week later, after a lot of sleeping pills-induced long nights and adjusted medication, with a subdued manner. Melvin had seen her briefly when he dropped Johari's jumper off, the one she had forgotten a couple of days previously at their usual spot in the park when she had suddenly run back home without walking with him to the corner like they usually did.

Johari had always acted like he was supposed to see it, he was supposed to get used to it and know that it was normal. What wasn't normal was to shut it away. That only the not-knowing, never having seen someone with any real symptoms of a mental illness was weird. Some people had bipolar and sometimes you would notice. Melvin had taken it as it came. Interested, open, sometimes lost. He had never made fun of it, he didn't gossip about it, it didn't really register most of the time. There were strange encounters and questions that were inappropriate, there were actions that were unusual for a mother her age, actions that were unusual altogether. But it hadn't bothered him beyond the discomfort of the moment. Like the naked encounter in the hallway. He would remember that. It was embarrassing. Mostly for him because he didn't know where to look. What would stand out more was Johari's back. The way it squared off against him, as if they had passed a threshold and somehow he should have known not to pass it. He had done absolutely nothing but follow her instructions.

'Wait for me. I'm making you soup,' she had said before leaving for the shops. 'It'll help.'

Before Melvin could get out of the room to leave the flat Johari stood in the door.

'Sorry about that,' she said.

'Is she okay?' Melvin didn't look at her.

'I'm sure she is. She hasn't slept in a few days. She needs to sleep,' she replied.

'What normally happens, I mean...' For a moment it seemed like they were back to normal. Not talking about everything but giving pointers to stake out a frame.

The door shut much louder than she had planned to. He was sure of that. That she didn't want to slam it, only close it so they could talk. But it was pointed, the sharpness of the noise. What was normal? And where were they, as friends, at this particular moment, in relation to it?

'You have your stuff? I'll make you soup another time. Sorry, I know, your cold.'

'Hey,' Melvin replied. They were standing in front of each other. 'Don't worry about me. I'll get some Lemsip on my way home.'

They hugged briefly and he was out of the flat half a minute later.

18

The Swimmer

Being with Temi was one of the things I dreamed about when I was away from her. More than her touching me, I loved how she pulled me in, how she offered herself. I longed for her when she disappeared, which I now knew was not disappearing after all. My body would protest her absence.

I found the space behind her ear and kissed her but the sex that followed felt stilted. Something we should do. The day had had more than enough intimacy. I wanted to return to our light-hearted connection, full of banter and not a lot of knowing each other.

'Do you need some space?' she asked.

'Why?' I rolled to the side.

'You've been lying there, lost in thoughts,' she said.

I smiled. 'You. I mean that was...'

'You're not exactly glowing,' she replied and got up. 'More of a frown.' She grabbed a T-shirt of mine that was hanging on the doorknob. 'Is this clean?'

She turned around again. Smiling, but to herself.

'Yes. Only tried it on, never actually wore it,' I said.

'Okay.' She slipped on the T-shirt I had got for free at a natural health fair a while back. The dark green made her brown even more earthy. If the light hit her from the right angle there would be a bronze glow, I thought. My thoughts were running away again. I almost expected her to get her things, which were half in the living room, half in the bathroom, pack up and leave but I could hear her walk to the kitchen and minutes later she was back with two cups of herbal tea.

'You have a selection,' she said.

'Occupational hazard,' I replied.

'Danger: might keep you healthy and alert?' She was teasing.

My laughter came with the feeling of excitement. This was a 360-degree woman. Someone who could and did capture me in more ways than I was used to. With whom my mind could run away in playful banter and stay present in a conversation about research methodologies. What was wrong with me?

'Which one did you use?' I asked.

'The flu mix. You look like you have a sore throat.'

She was turning me on again, and all the thoughts I had about other people dissolved into a small ache in the depths of my stomach. Her hand trailed the outside of my leg, kissing it once in a while. Each time it startled me. She didn't allow me to touch her. She didn't allow me to do anything. I was on my back with my legs spread and each time I wanted to roll onto her, or change position, or have my way she said, 'Did I say you could move?'

It was hard to stop thinking like that. The letting go was too open. I was exposed and I was too naked.

'I can't do this,' I said.

'What? Showing me yourself? You can say stop. It's up to you.'

She was down again. I wanted to come so bad and behind my closed eyelids, images were racing. Johari running. Johari crying. Johari laughing and laughing and then shouting. Mum shouting and laughing. Johari turning towards me, pointing at me, smiling, then tapping her index finger on her temple. I pressed my eyelids together and stroked Temi's head, careful not to mess with her hair too much.

'I don't care about the hair, you know. Not when it's down,' she said.

And she disappeared between my legs again. I leaned into her.

I asked her to stay. Her surprise was genuine and I could see she was unsure. Was this a start of hot and somewhat cold on-and-offness of my own, similar to what I had complained to my friends about Temi? Or would I know what I wanted from her when we spent more time with each other?

Snuggling up in the bed, we were silent for a long time. She drifted off to sleep and hours later I did too.

19

The Climber

Nia came home a couple of hours later. SuSu was waiting to hear her enter the flat. She was lying on the bed, the skirt next to her. She could feel it. The way the mania was spreading. It made her body lighter, it pumped it full of energy. It was good, at this point, but she couldn't tell whether it would build. When it tipped over she couldn't stop it, even if she had wanted to. It became scary then, uncontrollable. Nia was looking at her the way she did when she was worrying. She could see it and feel it and then went past the question in her daughter's eyes and lifted herself out of the constraints until all faded into the background: her appetite, her sleep, the pauses between thoughts and words, restriction.

She could hear Nia closing the door carefully and slipping out of her shoes, which made a dull sound on the carpeted hallway floor. A few moments later her daughter closed the door to the bathroom. She imagined her stepping into the water. Walls between them. Her thoughts slower; perhaps Nia was ready for bed. It was morning now, time for breakfast and to wash away the sleep from the eyes. SuSu had planned to meet a few friends for brunch in a cafe with a colourful garden area. Flowers and plants dominated the space, interspersed with industrial lighting, shelves and furnishings that belonged inside and transformed the space into a living room without a roof. When it rained, they pulled out a canopy over the metal frame that blended into the background. Drinks and food, everything was overpriced there but they had got a reservation for the table at the far end, which had the best view and the most privacy.

She and Nia needed to talk about the anniversary. It was too late for a formal event now. Nia had been adamant that she wouldn't participate if they organised something without her consent. Nia wanted it to be small, only Melvin, herself, her Dad Ben. SuSu wanted to celebrate Johari. She would have been thirty this year. Ben had made a passionate plea to his daughter. He was the dreamer of their circle. The one who would dig for meaning and ask for it to have its space. He too thought their daughter was wrong. Ben felt it was important to mark this because ten years was yet another departure. Things pushed themselves deeper into memory, recollection became harder, the details faded. What was left was the fabric, the things that had grown into the flesh, that had become organic, not specific. You could not separate entirely what was based on fact, what was based on nostalgia. Like a palimpsest, there was writing but you couldn't make out exactly what it said, and who had written it. History or imagination?

It required an organised ceremony, in Ben's opinion. Bringing the bones back, he wanted to say but Nia would have been alarmed if he had talked like that. It would have reminded her of her mother.

Ten years meant that Nia's circle of friends had changed almost entirely. Hardly any of them were aware of the dead sister.

Nia had said, who cares, other than us? Why drag everyone into this? And what about Mum?

They no longer did family dinners but Ben had invited them to his flat. He still lived alone, although he and Aisha had been together for six years. She lived a few streets away, her kids called him Ben, and loved him, and were of course no longer living at home. They had never done so during their relationship. It made it easier. No interference. Not for them, not for Ben, or for Aisha. Aisha sent her regards and that was it. Nia would see her another time, either for dinner or an evening out.

When they had sat at Ben's, a couple of months ago, SuSu had looked at Nia. Nia had looked at Melvin who was quiet in the corner of the sitting room, waiting for Ben to call them to the kitchen in which the table barely fitted when it was folded out to its maxiMum capacity. Once they sat down it was cosy and lively. But before that, upon entering, it felt like it was impossible to make everyone fit. Ben was in the kitchen finishing something while they were waiting for his cue in the living room. Nia didn't want to be here; she had voiced her opinion many times on this. *Not another memorial. Not with me. I will refuse.* And here they were.

Melvin's breathing was as perfect and steady, deep and deliberate as an advert for a mindfulness course. The way his chest rose in his perfect posture meant he was too alert for this conversation. If he had time to straighten his spine and keep it there when they were about to talk about the memory of his best friend he was using his body as a distraction.

SuSu said, 'Just remember her, Nia. It doesn't have to be about the tears. I want people to know that I had two daughters. Beautiful ones at that. And they still are. Both of them.'

She didn't understand why her daughter found it so hard to imagine other people loving Johari. That it was important to them, even if it held a different weight than it did for them.

After the dinner, Melvin and SuSu were by the front door, getting ready to leave. Nia was still in the kitchen with Ben. Melvin said that there was shame. That he thought Nia wanted to avoid it.

"How do you let your own daughter die," someone had asked SuSu.

It was in the psychiatric hospital after the first anniversary.

SuSu had made it and held on to the flowers at the grave, at Johari's funeral, grateful for everyone and their kind words. For the arms that offered to hold her, if briefly.

A mother should not bury her child, this is not how it is supposed to be, children should outlive their parents, that is nature's way. It echoed everywhere.

She had been grateful for the food friends had brought. The months after Johari's death, and then to the memorial a year later.

The funeral had been a lavish affair. A celebration of life. Although it was too unreal, too real, too soon, too unbelievable they had gathered themselves and everyone who had known Johari. A hundred guests had met at the community centre near the cemetery. About a third of those had been at the grave a couple of hours earlier. Guests had prepared messages to read out about the wonderful person, the older sister, the exuberant woman they remembered. Flowers were abundant. Melvin had prepared a dance. A solo he performed alone on the grass patch next to the grave. It was short, only a few minutes long and without music. Just his body and a memory that pressed from the inside, that tried to come out of his skin and find its own form again. He was dancing to get rid of the muscle memory. The memory of Johari that would not leave his body. It was sad and joyous because sometimes the beauty was in the saddest places. The very saddest ones. The places you could not look at and could not look away from. It was beautiful because you met it. You walked towards the sadness and said, 'Here you are. I am here too.' You touched it and found solace that in the end, you were one with it. It was like a separate person that you had to hold close to let it enter you. Otherwise, it could never leave.

Melvin's dance carried with it the shape of Johari's sadness. The one she had not been able to shake. And his own. And both were entirely different.

It was beautiful because the most beautiful thing is when you let someone see it, the you that is so hard to fathom for anyone including yourself. The you that shies away, always retreating, always fleeting. When you grasp it and put it into form and say to someone 'Here it is.' This is how I fall apart.

The guests looked at him with clasped hands, solemn, endeared. Some were crying. Some uplifted when he jumped and turned at the same time landing with his toes on the grass, gracefully, arms outstretched, eyes closed. There was nowhere to look. He couldn't see anything because the point was to be present, not to look for a way out. It was easy to remember her, the dead friend, in his movements.

SuSu's heart had jumped out of her chest as family and friends watched Melvin. Her legs wanted to move too. Kick her feet up high, jump over low stones laid out along the paths. Pick up flowers and toss them everywhere. She managed to stand still with everyone else except for the shaking of hands, the embraces, the gestures of comfort and shared grief.

During the celebration at the community centre, she had laughed and sometimes cried. She had remembered her daughter in the endless stories that people offered. The puzzled anecdotes. The wisdom that came in retrospect.

Her daughter. A twenty-year-old woman who had jumped into a river one night. Unexpected. And never surfaced again until they fished her out of that river the morning after. Someone had seen her jump and had seen her swim. They had called the police and the fire brigade. They had said in an exasperated voice, 'Someone is swimming in the river, you have to come, please come quickly, I don't think this is going to end well.'

They couldn't find her. Not until the morning.

The memorial a year later was similar. Not as many people came but it was moving. Melvin didn't dance, he read *A Litany for Survival*, a poem by Audre Lorde that talked about those who were always afraid, mostly for good reasons but also no matter what happened. That they had to remember they weren't meant to survive and could choose to do so. They should speak in defiance. The memorial was in the back room of the pub where the caterers had already set up the food and the guests were standing in a half circle, watching him standing in front of a little fireplace. He didn't say anything else, and the poem weighed heavier this way, without explanation, without 'it wasn't quite like this for Johari but...', without giving context to why he had chosen this particular piece of writing. Maybe he was speaking about himself, choosing to speak to survive this, the absence of his best friend.

There were tributes again. Hugs and the shaking of hands. A togetherness that was still carried by the disbelief. She was not coming back. Johari.

The evening after the one-year memorial, Ben, who was still her husband then, held SuSu as she released her legs, kicking the blanket that was crunched up. He held her from behind, arms tight against hers only leaving her lower limbs free. Her movements were violent, strong. They echoed her voice that hit the ceiling and escaped through the cracks in the walls until it found its way outside the building.

She had cried at the funeral a year earlier. And she had managed. She had sat with the sadness and accepted that every day was there for her to make something of it. Without her daughter in it. She had cried with friends who had looked at her searching her eyes. The pain was there, day after day, knocking on her temples as if to say, the time is not good right now, but I'll come anyway. She had buried herself in Ben's arms, and he in hers. She had held her other daughter, the one that was still alive.

Eventually, their house had become quiet. Dampened. A place where the insides got mouldy.

She had moved. Every day a little. At first only to the kitchen sink to dispose of a cup or a used plate. Then to the cooker, and to do that she had to touch the fridge, open it, take things out. Slowly each day she had widened her circles until there was food to be eaten, until she had made it out of the house again. She had enjoyed working again as a fundraiser for an umbrella organisation that supported a number of small charities that worked in Palestine. Small projects that did targeted work. One was providing water purification units in schools and nurseries in Gaza. Another one helped Palestinian children deal with the trauma they had experienced. She made it into the office for a few hours at a time, attended short meetings or sat behind her computer for short spells of writing on a funding bid. Her work was meaningful to her, it made a difference. That was all she could manage, lend a hand in affecting something good somewhere else, however small it was. Her own house was quiet and subdued and she couldn't change that.

Then after the memorial, one year after Johari's death, her screaming stopped in the early morning hours. The neighbours had knocked on the door and Ben had apologised. SuSu stuffed it back in her throat, sealed it with all the best intentions.

She had agreed with Ben. It was heart-breaking, soul-destroying, unbearable. And yes, they had to find a way to heal without shattering neighbour's windows with high-octave exclamations or sounds. In the morning she was exhausted, but the energy wouldn't leave her.

Ben was putting on his suede jacket that was rough on one side. She had not seen him wear it all year. The rough patch caught her attention and held her eyes. It had dragged on the ground once when it got caught in his daughter's bicycle when he was teaching Johari, Nia running next to her sister. It had been an unusually warm March day and they had all gone to a playground that had a fenced-in basketball court. At mid-week morning, it was empty and Ben had shown Johari how to cycle while SuSu sat with her back against the fencing eating grapes and watching both of her daughters. Johari with a deep frown, concentrating. Nia, not yet three, running around with her arms high up, shouting, 'You can do it, Hari, you can do it, you can do it.' Nia had been more eager for this to work than Johari, and Ben had wiped his brow, sweaty from holding on low to the learner's bike while running after her, bent over. He took his jacket off and held onto it with his free hand, smiling at Nia. 'You are next, then I will say you can do it, do it, do it.'

'Yes,' Nia had said, skipping along as the jacket rolled up in between the spikes. Johari had pedalled and pedalled, her face scrunched up, her hands gripping the handles. She found her balance and Ben let go, his jacket dragging on the asphalt.

SuSu had laughed and clapped her hands because Johari had looked up briefly to find her eyes. *Do you see me, Mum, do you see this? I can ride it, I can do it, I can really do it.* Ben had caught up with her before the bike could topple over. The jacket had survived, minus one side that now looked like a lawnmower had taken to it. He held it up with one arm and boomed into the empty court,

'This is the trophy, the proof that my daughter, Johari Zahara Lewis, has mastered the art of transportation with her own two precious feet. She is a skilful peddler, an artful rider, an inimitable sportsperson and shall be celebrated from now until forever.'

Johari had buried her head in his legs as he embraced her. Then she ran to SuSu who was clapping and singing again and laughing.

Nia was jumping up and down clapping with her mother. 'You did it, did it, did it.'

They had spent the rest of the afternoon practising. At night both of the daughters had slept well. One tired from concentrating and peddling. The other from cheering on and running alongside.

Why Ben was wearing this jacket to go out a day after the first anniversary she didn't know. But she couldn't shake the memory of her dead daughter's face from that day. The fearful, concentrated one, then the relieved and proud one. And Nia alongside, with steady pride, the faithful younger sister for whom Johari was everything the world had to offer and thus the only reference she needed.

A month after the one-year anniversary SuSu had turned up at Ben's workplace, a national newspaper he had worked at for more than twenty years. She knew his colleagues; she knew the offices. She had hardly slept the previous week; she had hardly slept that month.

She found herself stepping up onto the editor-at-large's desk, shouting again until all eyes were on her.

'Why do this, write things, if you're not making things, if you're not making someone's pain better?' She wasn't talking about hers. 'Why not say the things that need to be said and instead hide behind objective reporting? We are guilty this way. Implicitly, implicated. Unless you say how it is, you are guilty.'

It went on until Ben, who had been out on assignment and who arrived after she had made clear what she thought of the cowardly reporting, begged her first with his eyes, then with his arms, in which he tried to wrap her.

SuSu stepped down, her voice shrill, carrying with it not only accusations but also names and dates of people who had been killed in Gaza. Some of these names she had carried for years. The suffering had built up inside of her until she could no longer make herself believe that there were ways in which she could be helpful, ways in which she could make a difference if she kept the things she had seen inside of her.

She had been sectioned a few days later.

Ben had left her six months later.

Nia had lost respect for her father. 'Of course, she is out of control. You act like you didn't lose a child.'

Ben had replied, 'Nia, I'm trying to be there for the child I have left by keeping my job.'

In the hospital, that second year after losing Johari, SuSu had talked about her daughter, who was so good with her legs. First riding a bike, then dancing.

A plump woman with dark hair, the one she had spent most of her time with, had said it. 'How do you let your own daughter die? You must be ashamed.'

20

The Swimmer

I called Mum back, she answered after the first ring.

'Hello Nia, darling. So good to hear your voice. I am out at the moment but the timing is great, come along.'

My mouth opened to ask how she was doing. Before the *H* was formed, Mum jumped in.

'I'm looking to sweep the pavement and have bought the best flowers for the job. They are not lilies as they would be useless but they are not roses either because those were the ones that Ben used to buy me when we were first dating...'

'Okay,' I replied, worried now.

'...I don't need to be thinking of Ben, not today, or this month, anyway. You know what your father said to me the other day? It was related to Johari and also you. That you were your own person and I should stop with making comparisons, which I don't do at all. I thought it was odd to say that, and he went on to explain, you know how your father is, he is always a bit dramatic. Never mind, of course you are like her, in some ways, she was your role model, it's only natural. Who wouldn't look up to their older sister? Ben said it was a long time ago and you were a woman now, an adult and you know how adamant he gets with his voice, don't you, when he wants to make a point. He was really going for it, only because I said my two babies were still my two babies and you were the younger one.'

I felt cold and got up to put on a long-sleeved shirt. Mum didn't leave any space between sentences, I wondered how she was able to breathe.

'The flowers I have are the kind whose name I have forgotten but they move their heads well when I shake them and they will help dust the pavement. I will have a small shop outside with treasures from all over the world, all the things you said I should tidy, you are harsh sometimes, aren't you, when all these things have meaning and mean something. They will come into the shop and people will understand how we are related, all of us, as people, so that is why they are related to Johari too, and you to her and them to you. I've already taken the old suitcase, you know the one I mean, the large one from grandma, old-fashioned but perfect for the job and it stands up on one side if you lean it against something. My friend Lav will make shelves that fit in perfectly, I've already booked him for the job and asked him for a purchase order, he said he is busy this afternoon but I can probably get him first thing tomorrow if I go through his office, isn't that great, I wonder if he has an assistant or is he the assistant. It's so good that you are calling now, I need you to help me put together the shed that I bought at Homebase. I brought it here with a taxi, did you know that the minicab office by the park has a new person taking bookings now, I could hear it straight away but then I walked there and didn't recognise the face either. The shed is standing here and needs protection. I've asked the kids from around the corner but they didn't want to do it, not even for twenty pounds, maybe I should have said forty? What would they do with forty pounds? Do you think they would help their parents, maybe a nice dinner? The shed needs to be assembled ASAP, just outside the building, where there is a bit of grass, you know where I mean, next to the bins. It will be going from high to higher then lower again, the suitcase. I think you should be able to do it, call Melvin, I talked to him yesterday, he is around and can help, he'll do it if you ask him, or I can...'

'Why did you buy a shed, Mum?' I asked. My question went into the wall, headfirst, diving. It was almost impossible to separate the mass of words and make myself heard.

'You can't have a shop without a shop. How is that possible? It needs a building...'

'And the suitcase?'

'That is the teaser, the announcement, the advertising...'

'So why the shelves?'

I was tired and knew this wasn't going to go my way of logic but the tiredness made it hard to decide what to do. Let her rain over me and then hang up? Call Dad and ask him to call the psychiatrist to adjust her medicine?

She had blamed me. That I had made her go to the hospital once. I put her there, she had said. It was my fault because I had called the doctor, the number she had given me the previous time she had a manic episode. In case we didn't know what to do. In case Dad wasn't around. I was thirteen. The doctor admitted her because she had locked herself in the neighbour's kitchen. The Celals, the neighbours who lived across the road, were family friends. She wouldn't come out for the whole night although the adult sons pleaded and pleaded with her and indulged her requests of a sing-along to invoke the peace energies. Which oppressive energies she wanted to counteract, she hadn't said. Just that it was essential, needed, the world was falling apart. The suffering.

I had returned home to sleep so that I could go to school the next day. Johari and I shared the bed that night because I was afraid. Afraid that Mum would be gone for a while. Dad stayed at the Celals' flat, holding the fort outside of the kitchen, speaking to her in his soothing voice, pleading too.

'Let these people sleep. Come home. What's going on? What are you thinking about?' In the morning he came to wake us to get ready for school. He boiled eggs and put old bread on the table. He sliced apples and I thought I hadn't eaten sliced apples since I was a preschooler. He had arranged them in a spiral on the plate and set them in the middle of the table. His eyes looked tired and his voice had a different tone. Heavy and raspy, on the way to a cold brought on from lack of sleep. The phone rang. The Celals' mother said they heard a crash in the kitchen.

'Call the doctor. Ask her to call me at the Celals' house. You have the number?'

He was speaking to Johari. Fifteen-year-old Johari who wanted nothing more than to storm out of the house and move her limbs in the dusty morning weather in the green part behind the school. She would call Melvin as soon as it turned eight. Olive didn't like night-time calls, she had said. 'Not when you see each other every day anyway. Unless it's an emergency it's not necessary.'

Of course, so many things were an emergency when you were in the throes of puberty. Especially for us, for Johari, with Mum not being too well.

Johari had nodded to Dad's question and I had recited the number. Mainly to show Dad that he could go. He didn't have to worry about anything here, we knew how to do this. Johari and I had left the Celals' flat after midnight, and finally slept after 2am, once Johari had nestled into me and started breathing heavier. I felt full of tired calm. Not as stressed as I was other times when Mum was being sleepless at our own house. I felt guilty. Ashamed. Because Safet, the oldest of the Celals' kids, owned a small optician's shop on the high street. He would have to open after a sleepless night. He couldn't keep it shut; his schedule was always full.

I knew how it was when Mum was up all night, unable to leave us out of the equation. My own system flooded with chemicals then, which would help me make it through the following day something pumping independently, me watching myself perform the rituals of my life: washing, dressing, school, learning, speaking, eating. But unlike Sefat I would sit at the back of the class, keeping my mouth shut, speaking to the friends I had, the ones who didn't know what was going on at home. I had overheard them discuss Mum and what could be wrong with her. One time I was coming around the corner, they could not yet see me, I had not expected them to be on the other side. Four classmates were talking about her. My mother. That it must be a psychosomatic disorder. I didn't know what that meant. I did know it was not bipolar.

I didn't need much to function in my day. Sefat did. I only needed to drag myself into position. Something inside would keep my body upright and going. One step of the ritual to the next. You just had to let it happen. When I saw Dad rushing back to the Celals' I thought of those rituals. Why Mum just couldn't do it, one little illusion at a time.

Mum was still talking. I didn't know what to do. To go over and try to get her to sleep was of no use. At this point, it was hard to stop her.

'The shelves are for the drinks.'

I was back in bed. I had returned here after Temi left to meet a friend for breakfast. She had kissed me on the lips. Looked into my eyes and said, 'Stay in bed, babe, it's been a long week.'

When the door closed behind her I wanted to cry instead of laugh. It had been a long week and I had made it longer. More confusing. It was Sunday. I was alone. I would not go swimming or lie on a river. I wouldn't call Rahul or Crystal, people I didn't know to distract me from the things I had to face with the people I already knew and loved.

I should have called my father. That was the sensible option. To say, 'We're still meeting at yours on Monday, aren't we? Can we go and sit by the river, leave some flowers, light a candle?'

I wanted to do that. I wanted to talk about my dead sister, right by the water. Not where I had got in, not where she had. I wanted to walk along the sloping River Lea until we found a patch of grass wide enough for all of us to sit on. Melvin, Dad, Mum, me. But Mum would be there. And the words that kept coming and coming. I couldn't keep them away from me and I couldn't save her from the torrent that made her run down the track that would inevitably lead her down the same road she had been on many times in the past. The finish line, the hospital door. Instead of cheering, her marathon would be met with the opposite: a quiet so loud it could extinguish the past and the future.

Mum kept talking. I put the phone on the duvet and got up to move the cups Temi and I had used half an hour ago into the kitchen. When I came back her words were still flowing evenly through the phone. As much as she was in what the doctor called a heightened state, that elevation in her voice was steady. There wasn't a lot of variation in her pitch. The excitement remained as if it was raised brows, fixed mid-movement.

'I need to go,' I said and hung up.

My mind went back again to that time fifteen years ago. The doctor had called at the Celals' flat. Had talked to Dad, had heard Mum in the kitchen who was now making fresh yoghurt, 'like you always offer me,' she had said. 'I want to thank you for all that you do for us, you wonderful friends, wonderful neighbours. Let me make your food for you.' She didn't know how to make the Turkish dishes she mentioned in her sing-song voice. She didn't know how to make yoghurt either but she would start on that. Although it would take at least a couple of hours. She intended to stay the course.

Dad had pleaded again. Later in the evening, he told Johari and me the details because Johari had asked over and over again.

'What did Mum say, what did she do? Can you tell me?'

Dad had pleaded with Mum because by now she surely needed the toilet. Surely. What about a refreshing shower? Or a bit of sleep?

Apparently, his words would have been drowned by the noise of pots being taken out of cupboards. Mother Celal had stayed in the living room after the initial commotion. She had simply sat there all night, eventually leaning her elbow on her knee and her head in her palm, pulling her legs up onto the couch. She didn't comment on Mum's activities, not like the men of the family. It was life, simple and complicated. Sometimes things went on with people and you simply had to sit it out. Maybe it was normal to her and not just because she had seen Mum manic before. It *was* normal. This losing your mind, something leaving and it coming back differently and with more pressure. Sefat had gone to open up the shop. Mesut had stayed with Dad.

And their Dad, who was signed off sick from his job as human resources manager for a large gym because he had hurt his back badly and couldn't sit all day without lying on the floor, stretching.

The doctor had said Mum needed to be admitted.

It became my fault. I had called. She would have not needed it. That's what she said.

I took my backpack and filled it with my water bottle, a banana, an orange, some crisps that were left from earlier in the week. I walked until I was outside of Melvin's place.

Melvin came to the window. He looked at me. I was waving. This was the scariest it had ever been between us. He just stared. It hit me. That he could not let me in. That he could look at me for a while longer still and then disappear inside the flat, where I could not see him. I was lucky I had caught him here, by the window that looked onto the street.

My hand went up in a greeting. I waved again. I could see his thoughts behind the skin, inside his forehead, deep inside his brain. I didn't know what thoughts they were, whether they included me. He walked away and I couldn't see him any longer. I crossed the road to the front door that led into the building and reached as the buzzer came on. I pushed it open.

21

The Dancers

Monday after school Johari waited for Melvin at their usual spot. It was mild, and the younger schoolkids were on the playground running off the hours their brains had spent in concentration.

'Did it go all right, yesterday?' Melvin started. He was standing by the wall that divided this section of the park from a formal garden with circular beds that had seen better days. In another era, most likely. Ivy was spreading on one end of the wall, and creeping over the edge. The other end of the wall was completely bare as if the different sides belonged to different tenants who had decorated it in their individual styles.

'All good,' Johari answered. She was stretching already and was leaning into her lower leg. The weather had turned that week, a sudden heatwave. The music from the studio started. The windows must have been open as the music was louder and clearer than usual. Johari moved her head. Melvin still had his bag in his hand. He was searching for her eyes but Johari wasn't looking at him. He went to put the backpack down by the wall, together with his jacket. He had seen SuSu naked, which by itself seemed the least embarrassing fact about the previous day's morning. They needed to talk about it. The flowers tied around her waist. The way Johari had pushed him out of the flat.

'Is your father back?' Melvin asked.

Ben had been on an assignment in another city.

'He is coming today,' Johari replied. 'I called him yesterday.'

Melvin wanted to know about Johari. About the pushing. Why they were here in their usual spot pretending that dancing was the only thing on their minds. Melvin's PE teacher, a gymnastics enthusiast, as he liked to call himself, had said, 'Dancing is a great way to allow the body to take care of your emotions.' Melvin believed that. They had done it for the past two years. Allowed their bodies to shape the conversations they were not having.

Conversations about themselves. The things they left unsaid. The things they didn't know needed words and which they did not know the words to. This was different. This was an *I was thinking about your twin* moment. You would want to bend over, hold onto your knees and spit it all out while catching your breath. Perhaps nothing would come after releasing saliva from your mouth. Maybe that was all there was to it, to put it out in the world, the words giving it shape, rather than the body.

Johari did not let anything leave anywhere. Not from her mouth or the rest of her body. She moved along to the music while Melvin watched her, sitting on the grass with his legs outstretched. Her body didn't open to the outside. It reminded him of closing. Arms folding inwards, eyes without focus, the gaze turned off as if it could soft focus inwardly until there was only one small dot of darkness. The nothingness that encompassed all of life. Behind it, she would hide. In plain sight.

Jadyn arrived and threw his backpack next to Melvin's. He hadn't been around for a couple of weeks. Melvin laughed. Of course. No conversation and then the one who doesn't care about dancing but has all the moves comes swooping in. He stretched his arms up. 'I like that beat,' he said. The music was as clear as if they were playing it from a speaker next to them. Jadyn bent into a backflip, landing with soft feet in time with the rhythm. Johari clapped. She reached backwards until her hands met the grass. Jadyn put one hand under her back and one hand under her leg lifting it for her to flip.

'You're getting there,' he said.

No one paid Melvin any attention. He would have said, yes she is but not any time soon. Jadyn had used all his strength to move her leg and drag her body with it. It had looked good only because their bodies wanted to be close to each other, there was a synergy, attraction.

Then Jadyn showed her one of his jumps.

'You stretch your leg forward as if you're aiming an arrow.'

Johari laughed. Melvin looked at her. How was that funny?
He wouldn't get up again. Johari was ignoring him and Jadyn was doing his thing. He hadn't been around that much lately only stopping by once in a while. He showed her a few more things and Johari tried her best to imitate his effortlessness. Then he had to leave as suddenly as he had arrived.

'Can't be late. It doesn't work out well if I'm not there on time.'

'I understand,' Johari replied and gave him a hug.

'It'll work out, you know,' Jadyn said to her.

Melvin was surprised. What was working out? Their dancing?

'See you next week, Melvin.' Jadyn raised his hand and ran off.

Melvin took his time to start. He knew exactly what he wanted to say but he was hoping something else would come out of his mouth. His mother had said that things changed. Nothing in life stayed the same, not even for a minute. That maybe they needed to find different activities as they were getting older, that other things were becoming more important, relationships, dating. That maybe at this point in time, they weren't at their most intimate. That talking hadn't been their thing. They either had to find that, the words, or give each other space to let things work out without explanation.

'I don't need to be part of this, you know,' Melvin said.

Johari sat with her bag in between her legs, searching for something inside.

'I mean,' he continued, ' if you want to have your time with him and I'm in the way...'

He wanted her to say anything but she looked ahead onto the grass, still rummaging in her bag until she fished out the smallest bottle he had ever seen.

He started laughing. 'Why bother, does that even have any water inside?'

She smiled. 'I saw it in the shop. It was cute, I couldn't resist.'

She unscrewed it and within a second the bottle was empty but she held onto it shaking it as if to coax out any hidden liquid. 'Please,' she said, 'I need more... please.'

Melvin took his own water bottle and poured some into her open mouth. She sputtered and laughed.

'You don't have to exclude me, you know,' he said, smiling too but not ready to let the moment pass. 'You don't like talking, I know that. But I need you to say something about this. Otherwise, I won't keep coming. You never wanted an audience and I'm not going to start being yours.'

Her head jerked around. He had surprised her. Things were shifting and instead of expecting people to follow her, she had followed Jadyn, expecting Melvin to provide the backdrop.

'What is this thing with Jadyn? You couldn't look at me today but you can hug it out with him?

Johari took her time to close her bag. To crunch up the tiny water bottle, to lift herself up and get ready to leave. She waited, not looking directly at Melvin but waiting. He grabbed his bag and stood close to her.

'Some things I think Jadyn gets because he has chaos at home too. It's different but he knows what it means. When your family is not the safest place.' Her hand was squeezing the water bottle, the noise was annoying, the plastic contracting and releasing.

'Maybe you...' Melvin started. He wanted to say that she could share more. Explain it, let him in. He had seen things but she was pushing him away. She looked in his direction but avoided his eyes.

'You ready,' she asked.

They walked out of the park together and parted ways when they had to turn into their respective streets.

The next day he joined her dancing again.

A week later it seemed like all was indeed working out good, like Johari had told Melvin. There was no trip to the hospital. Ben had talked to her doctor who had prescribed strong sleeping medication. After a few good nights things went back to their regular rhythm. The sisters at school. Ben and SuSu working. Melvin still waiting for a conversation that Johari didn't seem to want to have.

22

The Swimmer

Melvin and I stood in the kitchen. His hands were on the kitchen counter, my thumbs were hooked into the straps of the backpack. My eyes were looking at the floor searching for clues to put together a word, then one more until I arrived at a whole sentence. I didn't know what the word would be, let alone a whole sequence of it. I needed to explain myself. To ask Melvin to suspend judgement for a couple of weeks until I could find myself enough to speak to him like his friend. Not this version of a person who was spilling out of her boundaries, like my Mum, but quietly, differently. As fast and loud as my mother could be, I could get quiet and lingering. I looked like I always did. I performed all the steps daily life required of me. And I had said 'We need to talk about your twin.'

'What's going on with you? Is it because of Johari?'

'I think so.' I was relieved Melvin had some understanding about me, of course he did. He was the one who knew me. That is why I wanted to hurt him.

'Have you decided what you want to do, I mean tomorrow?' he asked.

Melvin spoke factually. He too knew how to keep rituals going.

'I texted Dad on my way here. It would be good to meet by the water. What do you think?' I said.

It was getting louder outside. The street was waking up from the Sunday lunch lull and as the weather was good everyone was on their way out. I looked at my phone. Just then it rang, Dad's name flashing up on the screen.

'I'll call you right back Dad, okay? I just arrived at Melvin's. Is tomorrow still good? Can we meet at the river? Just us?'

I looked at Melvin. 'Dad is fine with it and said he'd get some snacks from the Lebanese place we all like.'

'Sounds good.' Melvin's voice was warmer. 'What time? I'll bring Lucozade.'

Johari had downed that drink with conviction as if it was raw vegetable juice. 'So good for you.' I could hear it. Her voice. Praising the most famous of drinks in our circles, at least in our age group then.

We decided to meet at 4.30pm and I typed a message to Dad. That he should call Mum too. And pick her up. I was on the early shift and would be off by then. We could walk together, find a place, and still enjoy the light and warmth of the day.

'Sometimes I wonder why you never speak about it.' I couldn't stop myself. My fingers were still on the phone while I spoke.

'We talk about Johari.' Melvin wasn't looking at me. He didn't seem like he needed to face me, he was sure of his words.

I was preparing to load my sharp tongue again, there were other things I wanted to say, to ask angrily. I wanted this day to be something else. Not a reminder. Instead a distraction.

Melvin continued. His whole body stayed turned away from me. '*You* don't really speak about her. Or you in relation to her.' He stopped. I was about to answer but he continued. 'Funny that word, relation. You don't *relate*. Not to her. Not anymore. If not for this date you could think she died when you were a baby.'

The ammunition went the opposite direction. I had wanted to fire away at him because anger was easier to bear than grief. Jealousy was delicious compared to it. Jealousy kept you alive, gave you energy. Grief stopped you, the fire in you, buried you. It had suddenly dawned on me that he had told Johari about his twin. Johari, who never talked about anything, who had said to me that I was so typical, meaning a stereotype, because with every little thing I ran to my friends and later to Melvin when we had started dating. Johari knew and they had done their weird outside dancing that all my classmates laughed about together and he still found time to share it with her. Here I was. Twelve years after we first got together. Our romantic relationship lasted six years. Two of them with Johari still alive. And after we split up we remained close friends. We were family. There wasn't a question about that. All of this time, not one word. The years of our relationship were filled with Johari. The dance practice that Melvin put over anything else, including me. Then her death. After her death we did nothing other than try to get our bodies to stop shaking from the impact. By the time we broke up, we were relieved to be sleeping with other people, holding their bodies close. Bodies that were quieter, that did not have an echo.

'That's not true.' I touched Melvin's arms, willing him to turn towards me. His face was calm. I had expected it to be closed off, defiant against me, but he was simply there. Factual, still.

When my mother had brought the box out of the closet I had gone 'oh-oh' on the inside. I was ready. Knowing we were going to be upended because that is the thing with anniversaries. It tugs on that old scab. I was not the one who we would focus on. Mum was.

Melvin was my 'I counted.' I was part of the exchange.

We looked at each other, Melvin and me. I wanted to show him how hurt I was. Missing my sister. Missing having a Mum in front of whom I could unravel. Lying on a river floating until I hit the ground again. Not having to find that ground. It being there. I wanted to show Melvin that I was ready to attack because behind that was the heartbreak. If he was my person, the one where I counted, who was I to him?

'I need to pee.' He didn't say anything. His eyes were still, giving no sign of what he was thinking. I went to the bathroom. I could feel my period coming. The box on top of the cistern had a selection of organic tampons in them. Once in a while Melvin came to *We Are The Earth* to restock, stopping at the natural remedies counter for a chat with me. There was nothing in my underwear yet but the cramps were a sure sign. I put a couple of mediums in my pocket.

Melvin was in the living room by the window. The one he had stood at when I looked in from the other side of the road, and when for a long moment I thought he would not open the door, he would not speak to me. It had never happened. There had never been a silent treatment between us. Periods of absence, as we both called them, yes. Little reaching out, yes. Especially when there were new lovers, or relationships. Not once had Melvin refused to speak to me. Or I to him. I walked over to him and traced his bicep, then my hand went inside his shirt sleeve. I put my head on his chest. He folded his arms around me.

'The shadow.'

'The shadow?' Melvin asked.

'I almost feel like everyone needs me to need more. More remembering her, more memorials with more people, more pain than I'm showing. Or that I have.'

He was warm, and a little bony.

'I'm not avoiding it. Really not,' I said.

'It's hard to talk with you about her,' he replied.

'Maybe that has to do with you rather than me.'

Melvin smelled of garlic. I shuffled my face to another spot where I no longer caught his breath directly. It was good here. Melvin and I.

'Maybe. So many things I haven't said to anyone really. How our friendship was. What it was to me,' he said.

He released me from his arms. 'I'm still mad at you.'

I knew he was. I had tried this before, the sneaking back in, hoping a conversation could be avoided or at least delayed when I had acted badly and did not yet know why or how to apologise. He was the last person to hold a grudge against me but he was also the last to forget an unusual or nasty detail. I couldn't deal with anything else today. Johari's thirtieth. She hadn't died on her actual birthday but the anniversary felt like we were marking this entry into a particular kind of adulthood. That she hadn't made. And I soon would. Without her example. I had been without my sister my whole adult life.

'Can we talk on the weekend?' I asked.

'Sure.'

We stood and looked out of the window. There was the day to get over, the anniversary day, all that came with it. There were things to give space. Melvin was one of those.

A seagull swooped across, dropping fancifully into the space above the road before flying on.

'They must be nesting somewhere. I see them a lot this year,' Melvin said.

'But there is no sea nearby.'

'No there isn't.'

I was struck by the crack in Melvin's voice. Liquid poured out of it, coating his tongue and leaving with his voice. I took his face in my hands and turned it toward me and saw the tears.

'I think sometimes I'm mad with you because you don't need her anymore,' he said.

I put my face back on his chest. I could feel the contraction in his stomach, his muscles trying to quell the urge to cry.

'You're right. I don't think I even miss her as much as you do. I *am* sad. I am. *And* I've lived my whole adult life without her. I've moved on. For the most part.'

I pulled him to the couch. Things had slipped out through our protective shells that didn't normally find light.

'It isn't a competition, either way,' Melvin said. He had stopped crying.

'It's not. Still. We should have asked what you needed.'

Melvin looked like I had kicked him in the same stomach that he had been holding in to make his crying softer. It made it so much more obvious. How discarded he was. By Johari. By me.

'Do you think you would have gotten back together? I mean at some point?' I asked. 'If she had lived.' I took a moment before I continued. 'We would have not lasted,' I said. 'Probably,' slipped out to give this context.

'It wasn't that between us –' Melvin said.

'Those thighs have a habit of changing their opinions,' I said.

'It was never that. You know that.' Melvin looked at me. 'I think we would have started something, an organisation or social enterprise. Something where we could have worked with each other and seen each other a lot. I think we needed each other. Being in each other's lives and doing something together.'

'Maybe at some point you would have talked more than danced,' I said. I was trying to be funny.

'Dancing is not less,' Melvin replied.

I had hurt him.

'We talked much more than you realised,' he continued.

If it had been breezy before, like air was flowing through the cracks in our shields, I now felt I was bouncing off duct tape that had been placed over the gaps, the openings. The conversation was sticky and I wasn't taking enough care to avoid being trapped.

'I know your time together was meaningful,' I offered.

'We talked, Nia! Is that so hard to acknowledge? It wasn't just the weird dancing that you all thought it was. Everything we needed we did in those hours after school. You just didn't take it seriously.'

I was stuck. Not understanding Melvin, not understanding Johari. Maybe I never would. But he had also kicked me. Not in the stomach but in the chest.

'I took it very seriously. There was no opportunity to not,' I said.

I got up and looked for my backpack. Melvin was sitting on the couch, his eyes searching for something beyond the window. He pulled up his legs, wrapped his arms around his shins and laid his head on his knees. He was crying again. The tears were falling onto his left foot. Barefoot whenever he could. I loved Melvin's feet. They were defined and un-calloused. There was a tenderness in them that held all that I saw in him. Maybe because I had seen what he could do with them, how he could carry himself on his toes, sometimes only on one or two, holding a beautiful shape, grounded while extending upwards. That is how I saw him. Slightly suspended, expanding. A concentrated stillness. I had come to expect that from him. This levitation. If you could be that still while bearing so much tension in your body... I had never said that to him. How much I admired his lightness, the way he gave himself to strain and ease, effortlessly.

We've had plenty of tension in our romantic relationship. It usually came with the promise of a defining lift at the end. I seldom felt like the more we walked closer to each other the harder it became to walk in sync. Today we seemed to not find the same route. No patterns that attracted our feet, metaphorically, to make sure we ended up facing the same direction.

Both my hands were on my chest. It felt tight like a construction truck had emptied its cement on it.

'I'll see you tomorrow. Let's all meet at the station. That's easier,' I said.

Melvin didn't lift his head. He wiped his face with the back of his hand and nodded.

My legs were heavy on the way to the door but as soon as I stepped onto the pavement, I felt release.

23

The Dancers

Nia waved when she arrived. Melvin was sitting on the grass, his trainers unlaced.

'It's me today.'

'Hi,' Melvin replied. He was in the middle of loosening the tongue of his shoe. All movement stopped. Except his eyes. His eyes gulped in the young woman in front of him, who had shot up beyond Johari's height the previous year.

Nia shook her long braids.

'Johari is at the physio today. She wanted me to tell you.'

'Okay. Thanks for coming all the way,' Melvin replied.

'Didn't want you to sit here and think she's let you down,' Nia said.

'You could have texted.' Melvin didn't mean it. It was nice to see Nia. They never got a chance to chat.

'Where is the fun in that?' Nia laughed and sat down next to him, taking off her sandals. 'I could jump in for her, if you like.'

Melvin smiled. 'Er… you don't have to.'

'Okay, then not.' Nia laid on the grass looking up. 'The sky is weird today.'

Melvin twisted his neck upwards. 'No rain though.'

'No rain,' Nia replied.

They remained in silence, following birds in their explorations. Laughing at a dog that ran to Nia, sniffing her feet and wouldn't leave her. It had to be carried away by the apologetic owner.

Johari had an appointment with a physiotherapist for a sprained wrist. The previous week she had tripped into the living room and her jumper had got stuck on the edge of the bookshelf. She had broken her fall well with both hands flat on the floor, levering herself into a perfect plank but then the shelf followed and caught her awkwardly on her arm. It wasn't serious, the doctor had said. Most likely not. But it needed some attention. The physio had called that morning out of the blue, he had space because of a last-minute cancellation. Nia had offered to tell Melvin. Johari had looked at her but then been too distracted to ask why she wanted to go to meet him, when she could just text her best friend. It had got lost in the morning commotion. SuSu picked her up from school and they went straight to the clinic.

Since the lavender tied around SuSu's waist two years ago, Johari didn't invite him to her place any longer. She was almost eighteen and they spent their time out doing their own things. When Nia turned sixteen, SuSu asked Johari to take her with her when she went out in the evenings. When they were going to see a movie, when they went skating. A few months earlier, the local community centre had started early end discos on Thursday evenings. They called it The Choice. Your choice to turn up on time or miss your mates making a fool of themselves. Everyone had laughed about it. Nia's friends, Johari, everyone they spoke to. Dancing right in their neighbourhood at a reasonable time so their parents were still up when they got home? What was the point of that? But it grew and people from other boroughs started coming. Melvin thought it was cool. Johari agreed it was worth a try. On their first evening they discovered the biggest investment the centre had made were blackout blinds and club lighting. The music system they hired. Local DJs offered reduced rates to get their name out. It was pumping. People laughed as they walked in in full daylight. As soon as they were inside they got serious with their club attitude. Cross-borough affairs were started. Relationships catapulted from one dance to 'Every Thursday yeah?'.

Nia watched Melvin when she and her friends stood in the corner until their exact right song came on. Sometimes Melvin came over to chat if they were still leaning on the walls and some of the best tunes, in his opinion, had already come and gone.

Johari had a string of boyfriends who liked to go there with her. They didn't want to stand at the side of the park, or wait for her to come out of another dance class, said with a drawn-out version of a n o t h e r as if it was the biggest nuisance they could think of. Most were intimidated by Melvin.

'What's up with this guy and you? You tell me you're not doing it? You're like twins and not in a siblings way.'

At The Choice Melvin was not a threat. Everyone danced. Some of them were much cooler in their moves than Melvin could dream of.

Since the dance studio offered them both free memberships they were now regulars there. Only Melvin had made it into their youth dance troupe. Melvin had also started coaching younger kids at their spot in the park when the weather allowed it. This day would have been a rare dancing like old days, just him and Johari. They hadn't found the time recently. Johari was annoyed when the physio called just before she was leaving for school. If she had been on time she would have missed the phone call altogether.

But her mother would have still appeared at the school gate.

Two years no episode.

Nia rolled onto her side to face Melvin. 'Do you miss it?'

'What?' he asked.

'Dancing with Johari, just the two of you. She says you haven't done it for a while.'

Melvin turned toward her. 'It's…' He took his time to complete the sentence, his thoughts visible behind his forehead. 'I do. I love the classes and being part of a dance troupe. I never imagined I could be a real dancer.'

'What's a real dancer?' Nia asked.

'Someone who dances all the time. Maybe someone who dances for a living. I don't know,' Melvin said.

Nia nodded.

'But dancing with Johari is different,' he continued.

'Not like real dancers?'

'It is. But more than that. It's about the dancing and not about the dancing. Does that make sense? It's our way of speaking to each other, being in the world, understanding what's going on. You know Johari is not the most elaborate of talkers.'

'She is pissed off that she is not part of *Intricate*,' Nia said.

'I was wondering about that.' Melvin scratched his head. 'How do I get her to talk about it?'

'You tell me. You're her best friend.'

Nia jumped onto her feet. 'Fancy some chips? Mum left some money, she and Johari are treating themselves after, she said.'

'Sure,' Melvin replied.

They walked to the chippy across the road. When they returned there was still an outline in the grass from where their bodies had been a few minutes earlier.

They chatted for a while. About GCSEs and A-levels. About The Choice and how crowded it had got. Melvin's family and what they thought about him wanting to pursue a dance career.

'Not so fond of the idea,' Melvin laughed. 'They'll come around. I'm eighteen in a couple of months. I make my own decisions now.'

'Have they seen you?' Nia asked.

'What do you mean?'

'I mean what you can do with your body... What else could you possibly do, other than dance,' she continued. 'That's yours!'

Nia had caught Melvin by surprise.

'What do you mean?' he asked.

'I can't explain. It's just you, it belongs to you. It's special,' Nia replied.

She smiled again. Melvin fumbled with his hands and looked at her.

'Thanks.'

He looked away.

'I like dancing with you at The Choice,' he said.

'Me too,' Nia replied. 'It's easy with you. Not like the other boys. They're always taking the piss.'

'You put your arms around me real close last time.'

'What?' Nia laughed. 'Did you notice that? My friend gave me a drink before. I was feeling adventurous.'

'Adventurous eh?' Melvin said.

'I have a sister who does everything differently. It was my turn to do something...' She was looking for the word. 'Bold.'

'It was bold?' Melvin asked.

'I wanted to kiss you but Araba pulled me away.'

The quiet between them was so loud they would have both put their hands over the ears. If not for their bodies moving closer, until their mouths were only millimetres away from the other's. Nia nodded and pulled Melvin's head to her. Melvin's lips tasted like watermelon from his Orbit chewing gum. Nia searched for his tongue. He put his arms around her pulling her closer. For a moment they were nowhere. Or more precisely nothing was there. Just the two kissing at the bottom of their street. Right in the park, in broad daylight. Then Melvin pushed himself away, looking at the ground.

'Nia...'

'My sister?'

'She's my best friend.'

24

The Swimmer

When I came up from the Tube Dad and Melvin were already standing by a lamp post that was covered with local ads and small notices. One was red writing on black background. I couldn't make out what it said but it pulled my eyes to it. As I walked closer it became clearer. *Black Minds Matter* and the web link for a Black therapists' network. Dad raised his hand, his head turning the other way. Mum was coming from the opposite direction to me, waving, with a large hat on that hid most of her face. She was carrying a big woven bag. We arrived where Melvin and Dad stood at the same time. She hugged Melvin first, then Dad and me. I followed in reverse order, staying for a moment in Dad's arms, his backpack in the way of my hands.

'How are you, my beautiful,' he whispered in my ears. 'It's going to be okay today.'

Melvin didn't look at me. When we embraced briefly, his arms barely touched me.

'Shall we,' Dad asked.

I nodded. He started walking.

'I came a little earlier. There are lots of nice places,' he continued, turning briefly to us while taking his legs out in a wide stride.

I expected Mum to be wired up, chatty. It was strange walking with her quietly after the gush of words the previous day. She put her arm around me pulling me along. I wanted to lean into her body, get carried away by her presence.

We walked in silence toward the river, then the few steps to the path that ran alongside it. Mum let go of my arm in order for us to walk in front of each other on the narrow steps. She took my hand when we were on the path. Dad and Melvin walked behind us talking. Melvin asked Dad about his work. It was slow but enough was coming in; he had carved out a niche for himself with local news from London and Kent, and some human-interest stories. As if anything we did was not of interest to humans. That was the usual answer Dad gave. That the framing was all wrong. How you looked at things, how you brought them onto paper.

'How are you?' Mum asked me, tuning out their conversation.

'Sad,' I replied.

'Me too,' she said.

'And happy that we are together,' I offered.

The woven bag scratched my arm as Mum put her arm around me again. She sighed.

'One day we should talk. Properly. Or rather more. More what's under the surface.'

I wanted to shout at her but her voice was steady. I had nothing to level against. How did she do that? Climb up so high that I, that we, thought doctors and medication needed to get involved, and then be present. Totally there. The manic rush on pause, or disappeared.

Melvin and Dad had stopped and were now a few paces behind us. I couldn't hear what they were talking about.

'Melvin said I never talk about Johari. It's not true,' I said to Mum.

'Mmh.' It didn't sound like she wasn't believing me.

'I don't mean just about Johari, dear,' she continued. 'We should talk about your father and me. About me.'

She looked at me and smiled, her arm heavy on my shoulder. It made me warm.

'And about you,' she added. It sounded like a question she wanted to ask me. As if to say, will you let me in. I wasn't sure I would. There was the matter of her sharpness that could cut through anything I had put in place as a buffer between myself and her interpretations. The problem was her questions were so piercing they usually cut far beyond her intentions, or what I thought she had intended. I knew Mum cared deeply. On favourable days, she could sit and analyse with me in a way that always blew my friends' minds, and scared me. The stopping was difficult for her. Knowing what not to say, or that not every thought had a valid footing. Some things were just your own anxiety.

'Sounds like a family overhaul?' I wanted to be funny, get out of this now because this day was already too concentrated. I had already worked a whole shift; I should have taken the day off but it was too late when I finally decided that I was up for our small memorial. It had been fairly quiet at work. Still, I was tired. And there was still some work left. The work of this. Of sitting with the memory of Johari. Seeing it gnaw on the ones who loved her. Although the river was full of water it did not dilute the fact that it carried my sister, at some point, somewhere along its course. There wasn't much that could dissipate it. Time made it seem distant. And that made it feel treacherous. We had lived far beyond her memory. She was not central to our lives anymore yet all evolved around her.

Mum didn't respond for a while. She looked back to Melvin and Dad who were talking animatedly. Dad put his hand on Melvin's arm. Melvin was looking down. Dad turned towards us, looked at Mum. Mum raised her eyebrows.

I looked at Mum. She had gotten plumper over the years. It added to her beauty. It was the carelessness in her body. Like she belonged in the world without needing anyone to confirm it. Her body was her vehicle to announce that she intended to occupy the space she entered. I admired that.

Most of the time her face was quick to glow. She could be cheeky, and enjoyed herself that way. Making inappropriate comments was one of her things, she said herself.

'People get shocked so easily. We need to speak more,' she would say.

Her barbered hair was neater than the previous week. Maybe she had gone in the morning to have it cut. It was mostly grey now with some patches of black remaining at the nape of her neck and close to her temples. A bit of short fluffy hair had appeared on the sides of her face a few years ago. It suited her. In the same way that her body was content with its presence. It accentuated her face. Her eyes were still dark, the white a little yellow. When she opened her mouth, her teeth contrasted her dark lips, the dark skin, her dark eyes. All of it, opening mouth and eyes together, was startling. It seemed an ordinary face, good looking but not intimidating, an older Black woman, friendly looking, nice looking, features that told you she turned more than a few heads in her time but that it had been a while. Then she laughed and threw her head back and you would feel unsteady, thrown off your balance. If she walked over to you, you noticed the magnitude. Someone who didn't care about your opinion on her body or looks. *She* liked it. It threw most people, including me. Dad had confessed that she could still catch him off-guard like that. There was so much light in her.

When she was not in a depression.

Dad had both of his hands on Melvin's arms now, holding him firmly while speaking. Melvin bit his lips and kept nodding.

'Looks like they are in the middle of something. How is Melvin?' Mum turned to me.

'Okay,' my eyes were on the two men, 'I think. I'm sure today is hard.'

Mum used her free hand to signal for them to come closer. Melvin looked up and our eyes met. He was guarded. I could see the wound deeper in his eyes. He would have preferred not to look at me, I was sure. But Mum was calling now.

'Are you still deep in conversation? We should get going. It's going to get cold and we won't have more time.'

They walked now, Dad's hand had moved from arm to back, gently pushing Melvin along. Was it me they were talking about? How screwed up I was that I could not treat Melvin right? Was Melvin saying he couldn't see me anymore and the rest of the family either so that it could work, this severing of our strange bond. We were not unhealthy; we were not co-dependent. We had talked about this before. Finding each other's bodies again and again when it felt right. Was that something you were not supposed to do? Thinking back sometimes Melvin had left things unsaid. As if he didn't want to probe too far unless I was offering a view myself. Or was I imagining it now? Mum wrapped her fingers around my hand again.

'Where did you say, Ben?'

'It's a ten-minute walk from here. There is a bit of clearing and a lovely tree to sit under. If we're lucky it's free.'

'Okay,' Mum responded.

Only now did I notice how busy it was. We were coming to a little bridge we had to walk under, the path was narrow here and people were out in droves. Behind us a cyclist pinged her bell. I turned and Melvin looked at me for the first time. His eyes annoyed but not with me. *Not here,* they said. *I dare you. Get off the bike and push.* After the bridge a group of joggers came towards us in uneven formation. They were flanked by an instructor in long dreadlocks, dressed in black shorts and a black top who shouted encouragement.

'It's your time - take it. Yes to challenging your limits, yes to your own capacity and yes for coming out to tell yourself I'll do a little more today. I'll run a little further. I'll stay with it. And reach further still and further. And a little more. I'll go all the way.'

I looked at the eight or so runners. Two of them smiled appreciatively at the coach. All were sweaty, most of them concentrating hard. One was power walking. When she passed me she said, 'Living my best walking life. All the way. I stay with that.' She winked. I laughed. What would Rahul and Crystal say? Did they run in groups, or was theirs a strictly lovers-related hobby? I would call them, I thought. Not today, maybe tomorrow. Maybe on the weekend. It felt like a new beginning today. Something was different. There was water everywhere, the whole river was full of it. And I was on the dry path where my feet kicked up dust without meaning to because the last few days had been hot with a steady sun hitting the ground. Water and dust, primordial. Together it would make mud, which clung to you like I felt Mum sometimes did. Messy, not uncomfortable but unwanted in that quantity. It felt good but I was worried about the aftermath. How to loosen it, her, how not to be so tightly attached. This was when she called too often, shared too much, climbed on tables to throw things that could land on me.

Today she was anything but heavy. She was airy, a cool breeze and it reminded me to step forward one foot at a time. There was lightness in that.

We walked again without speaking but I had not felt this together with her for a while. There was a purpose here. We agreed. Not just Mum and I, but Dad and Melvin too.

The spot Dad had suggested was under a large plane tree. Two people were packing up their picnic.

'It's all yours. We're on our way anyway,' they said.

'Thanks,' Dad replied. Mum took a blanket out of her bag. Once we'd spread it she added a framed picture of Johari and leaned it against the tree trunk. It was from Johari's twentieth birthday. Six months before she died. She was in Barcelona with her friends Jada and Imani. They had gone to a cheap hotel to celebrate. Jada and Imani were older than the rest of the year and had taken her under their wings. The pictures Johari had sent were all with captions but no other text or messages. She was having the time of her life.

In this photo Johari was by herself, sitting on a sun lounger by the pool, posing with a drink and a silver bracelet Jada and Imani had given her for her birthday dangling from her wrist. It had small afro combs alternating with fists and what looked like Adinkra symbols. The latter had nothing to do with Mum's, and therefore our, heritage but they had tried. As Mum would have said. I had it at home, in a small box in the bedroom. Once in a while, usually once a year, I took it out. It was still cool, ten years on but I couldn't bring myself to wear it. It wasn't the losing that worried me but breaking it. How would I feel if it snapped while I was moving boxes at *We Are The Earth*? Or when I was fucking Temi? I knew I wouldn't remember to take it off when I needed to. So I kept it in the box. With a note she had written me.

In the photo Johari was wearing the hat Mum was wearing. Or Mum was wearing hers. I couldn't remember seeing it before. Maybe Johari had bought it there and Mum had kept it in one of her boxes.

'I love that picture of her,' Dad said. 'She is happy. She looks like she feels free.'

'Did you see her much then?' I asked Melvin. I couldn't remember. We were going out then but it wasn't an all-day every-day situation. Johari was still his unspoken number one.

'We did. Although I went dancing mostly, I was already in *Intricate* and she hung out with the two friends…'

'Imani and Jada,' Mum replied.

'We must get in touch with them,' Dad said. 'They were really close then.'

'Why?' I replied. 'What is there to say? She's still dead.'

Melvin looked at me. Now he was angry with me again. There was no reason to. Yes, they had been good friends, the way you were when you saw each other every day because of proximity. They were their best allies, they lived on campus. Not that I doubted that they liked each other but it wasn't like Melvin and her. It hadn't yet found its own form. Three young women who had enjoyed things that most young people like: a few drinks in the sun with some good music and no authority in sight.

Imani had come by a couple of times after Johari's death. Both had been at the funeral and the memorial a year later. Jada had even sent cards for the next two birthdays. The 'would have been' birthdays. Heartfelt words and we had all thanked her for her thoughtful messages, touched. How was it that we could be so moved by people's love for Johari, when Johari hadn't been able to feel that same connection? Was that it? That she hadn't felt it? That she didn't know how much we needed her, how loved she was?

I didn't say anything but I looked at Melvin. How do you hold death ten years on when you knew the person for two years, I wanted to say? What memories do you unearth? What do you make of their personality, how do you project anything? If Imani and Jada needed to, they would get in touch with Mum. Her landline number was still the same. So was my mobile number and Dad's. It wasn't their burden. It was ours.

Dad was kneeling on the blanket ignoring the tension that was building up. He was unpacking the food. Dolma, manakish, baba ghanouj, falafel and some bread. Melvin added two large bottles of

Lucozade. Mum had wrapped a scarf over the hat and tied it under her chin. There wasn't enough of a breeze, no danger of it flying away.

'In case,' she said, smiling.

'In case of what?' I replied. My voice was calm but I was fed up. Dad was getting out real plates he had wrapped in bright kitchen towels. He hated throwaway stuff and was not one to fall for clever but pricey eco-friendly alternatives.

'If I can carry some food, I can bring a plate. At worst, we'll share one.'

'In case of anything. Everything can happen, Nia. Anything at all,' Mum replied.

Melvin laughed. 'Anything and everything. Yes. At any time.'

25

The Climber

The sweat was running into the gap between SuSu's buttocks, trickling down. She wanted to hold Ben's hand but he was focusing hard on the ground. The group had split up. Ben, his colleague, SuSu, and the interpreter had visited a family whose son had been beaten up and was now in hospital. They had sat in the backyard. Yameena had stayed in the car to catch her breath. Everything reminded her of things she hadn't seen herself, things that had happened before she was born, her parents' country. Things she had not been present for. But that she knew nonetheless. In her tissues. The separating. The severing.

Violence echoed.

Afterwards, SuSu and Ben and walked for a bit alone in Gaza city. The street was dusty, the walk was not strenuous, if not for the heat. At one end they came to an area with a few shops.

26

The Dancer

They had found her the next morning. The emergency services. Her foot had caught on a tree root and kept her under water.

Melvin sat on Nia's bed, arms hanging. All air had left his body. Nia sat on the floor with a note.

I had my diagnosis almost three years ago, when I started uni. I didn't tell you, I made Mum promise no-one had to know. Cyclothymic disorder. Look it up. The lows Nia, you don't even know... I don't know how you can live with that and go to work, not have people be weirded out by you, disgusted even, that you are so much work. I can't do it like Mum, make a whole life out of it. Hers started late. Mine just couldn't wait.

You and Melvin are good together. And cute. Be good to Mum. None of this is on you, or anyone. I just feel like giving in is easier. Be good to you! I'll watch you, anyway. J.

27

The Swimmer

Mum brought out a prosecco bottle with a small cooler bag wrapped around it.

'I thought we could toast.'

'You don't want any Lucozade?' Dad teased her.

'Of course I do. But you know, a real glass for her doesn't hurt.'

The high voice was there. It felt calming. The walk here had confused me although her presence was cooling and refreshing. For a minute it had felt like there was someone, she, who understood what I needed better than I did. It was delicious, rare, and true. But there was pain there. The weeks and sometimes months when I needed to understand too many things. Know what to do and when. Things about Mum.

Mum started talking and I nodded. *Okay, she's here. She's not trying to be different, to be un-manic-ed.* I didn't mind. She was telling Dad about the bar she wanted to open outside her building. That the downstairs neighbour wasn't for it but some of the younger tenants were behind her.

'Why not,' they had said, 'leave her alone. She's not loud.'

The man had shouted back with hands clasped over his head.

'She's so loud. You know that!'

Mum laid out cloth napkins next to the plates Dad had brought. They were white with red stitching in the corners and edges.

'These are pretty,' Melvin said. I took one. The fabric was much sturdier than I thought, smooth but the stitching added weight and resistance.

'Are they new?'

Dad stopped placing the cutlery next to the plates. 'I have not seen these... for a very long time. How is it that you have them and not me? They were a gift from you. Remember?'

'I do remember. I got them at the small shop in Gaza city. We felt so terrible that day. All of us.'

'Who?' I had stopped helping with distributing the food and drinks at one end of the large banket. I wanted to scream, *Will I ever get that story?* I don't know why I never asked Dad. He was not one to switch the topic as abruptly as Mum but he would talk you out of a conversation if he didn't want to share too much. Segues that you realised only later made no sense.

'We were a group of writers and journalists. We had visited Gaza to report on the first Intifada. I think it was our first day there.' Dad said.

'Yes, the first day in that prison. We all felt we were suffocating. The Israeli military was everywhere. Young people couldn't walk around freely without being questioned. Then there were the beatings, so many were beaten without any reason. It was a tactic, to deter them from protesting in the first place. Yameena was coughing. She couldn't breathe properly. It affected her. You found it hard to keep the tears back.'

They were quiet. I looked at Melvin with my brows raised. He shook his head. Mum was still smiling but her eyes looked sad. She helped Dad unwrap the glasses, then she put her hand on his arm. They hugged.

Melvin and I jumped a bit at the same time. I didn't know where to look. What was going on with this day? I didn't need them to get back together, I didn't want it. They were fine apart, we were fine. We needed to get this day, that was now late afternoon and would soon be evening, over with. Honour Johari, honour ourselves. Maybe that was what they were doing, relishing in the connection that couldn't be severed, not completely.

'So you bought napkins?' I asked, trying to restart the moment that had come to an abrupt halt.

They let go of each other.

'The white looked so refreshing, it was so hot that day. We had walked along this street for a while until we got to a little outside market. Not really a market. A woman sitting outside a small shop. These were inside it. As soon as I saw them, I wanted them. It was the white in the dark shop, it caught my attention.'

My parents were smiling, resting their eyes on each other comfortably, as if they were somewhere else.

'You thought I needed something to freshen up,' Dad said.

'You did! You wiped your face with it. No snot, mind you, they're all safe for eating.' Mum laughed her funny laugh again, slightly off pitch.

'Mainly I used it to cover up the fact that I was crying. I couldn't take it. We had prepared for this, we had researched, I knew what I was coming to. Only in real life it was harder because it wasn't the picture that was the most troubling. Not just what you saw and what not. It was what you felt. How restricting it was, how isolating, how impossible. I wanted to run away, back to the airport, leave for London. The woman, from the shop, she was just sitting there. In the square life was going on but we had seen other things, the day had taken a toll on us.'

'The morning of our flight I had taken a pregnancy test.' Mum looked at Dad. 'I didn't want to, I thought whether it is true or not, we didn't need the information. I knew it would be harder to go knowing that I was pregnant.'

They were addressing us but speaking to each other, their eyes keeping the other company.

'I wanted to know. I needed to know. And that way we could be careful on the trip.' Dad's eyes were soft. If ever there was love between them this is how it looked or had looked. Letting each other go in front of the other, the other one holding, waiting to see, not reacting, not rushing, not needing anything. A standstill. In the most caring way.

'It wasn't possible to be careful,' Mum replied.

'Not emotionally, no,' Dad said.

'That's what I mean.'

Melvin and I had sat down to watch them. I missed Johari. This was her conception story. Well, the early days of her being carried story. I wondered if they knew when she would have been conceived. I hoped not. That would have meant a sparse sex life if you could single out when exactly you made a baby. They had been hot for each other. They hadn't split up because of lack of attraction. More because of a lack of a lot else. Mostly they had needed different things. Dad needed to hold on to his job at the newspaper for a little longer. Until it felt safe enough to leave because I was on my way, as he said. On my way to independence. He probably needed a different space for his grief, although we had never talked about that. Mum needed to fall apart after that first year. She needed to feel the shame but during the time she was in the psychiatric hospital she had some respite. She was unaccountable. No one treated her like she should have known. Not in the way they did with Dad. Everything was his fault. The dead daughter, if he couldn't help the living daughter with uni, if that daughter turned out to have mental health issues, if that daughter, the living one, didn't cope well. My happiness, down to every smile, became Dad's responsibility. Sometimes it felt like people watched over me to look for signs. Dad was hovering nearby when he could. How could you fall apart to put yourself back together like that? And if you couldn't do that, the breaking open, how would you ever heal?

The day Mum had come to the newspaper that Dad worked for and declared her undying support for Palestine, Dad had changed. He had gone into his own survival mode. He agreed about the need for a *Free Palestine*. He did not agree about Mum being the centre of it at his job. He needed to be the centre of his own life. For me. For himself. I had heard those words from their room.

When I went to uni, he went to rent his own flat.

Johari as a not yet something other than rapidly dividing cells in Mum's uterus had been shaken around in Gaza no less. Johari who sometimes felt our parents were too righteous. Right, yes, but you didn't need to get that distraught over everything, just write the article. That Johari. Johari who had checked out completely, after she returned from Barcelona. It wasn't the trip. None of us thought that. There wasn't a hint of guilt or regret in Imani and Jada, not in that way. They came back on a high that lasted two weeks where they could talk about nothing but their amazing time. The whole five amazing days of it. It felt more that it was the end of childhood that was worrying my sister. That felt inescapable, an abyss to jump into that she didn't know how to navigate. Uni was ending. Barcelona was the *before the results come in* trip. After that adulthood. Responsibilities. Going out in a world I think she couldn't imagine as allowing her the space she needed.

I leaned closer to Melvin. Mum and Dad were still telepathically communicating. I whispered, 'Get a room? You think?'

'I hope not. It would be weird, no?' he replied.

'Terrible! It would be cheating,' I said.

'Require a breakup? Or do you think Ben and Aisha have an arrangement?' Melvin asked.

'Probably not. As the daughter I don't get the exact details of their sexual contracts.'

They finally broke their stare and Mum handed me a glass, then Melvin and Dad. She took the prosecco bottle and started pulling the cork. She stopped.

'I bought the napkins from that woman and you sobbed your eyes out, Ben. I think because life is so fragile and it dawned on us that we would have to protect the babies we'd make. Johari. You, Nia, who was not yet on the horizon but the possibility for you was already there.'

Dad was surprised. Perhaps they had not talked about it like that. Perhaps he felt seen. Perhaps the memory made him feel vulnerable and close to her at the same time.

'You need help with the bottle?' he asked.

'No, I just need a moment to think about the toast,' she replied.

The three of us dished up the food on the blue plates with the tiny white spots that Dad liked to bring out to picnics. Everything looked good that way, he would say. It pops. It did. The greens and browns, the reds.

When Mum finally pulled the cork out, the prosecco gushed out in a big fountain spilling over the grass.

'I guess the ancestors are thirsty.'

'Maybe Johari is,' I said. I raised my glass.

'Thirty. You would have been thirty already. Which means I'm not far from it. You are making me old. Stop it!'

The others laughed but Melvin was already wiping away tears and Dad looked too closely onto his plate.

'I miss you. The worst part is I miss knowing who you are. Then and mostly now. I've been without you my whole adult life. Move well my sister, move, like you always did.'

Mum hugged me and continued.

'My precious, beautiful dancer. You were always good with your legs. Swimming wasn't your strong suit. I always wondered why the river. But then there is water everywhere.'

Dad nodded, Melvin put an arm on his shoulder.

'Every day I miss you. Every day I wonder how I did not take care of you the way you needed me to. Or perhaps there wasn't anything to do. Thirty, like your sister said. You would have been thirty. I will accept it. It's your decision. I love you Johari, my jewel.'

Melvin's face was pressed together and his head rotated and moved, he could not focus anywhere, he could not calm it down. When he spoke the tears were running down his cheeks as if to meet the river that was a few metres down the slope.

'To dance is to be with your emotions. To let some of them run free, wild even, to direct some of them elsewhere so that the form translates what is felt. I'm still dancing with you. Following. Thanks for finding me the day that you did.'

Mum poured some prosecco onto the grass. Nodding, Dad followed suit, Melvin said *Ashe*. We nodded. We clunked glasses and drank. I lay on the grass and closed my eyes. It was warm from the sun. I moved my arms up and down like I was making snow angels. The thin grass blades tickled my fingers as I stroked them, gently. I pressed my palms onto the grass. The sun trickled through my eyelids in bright yellow, there were stars that popped. The way the ground pressed against me I knew I had nowhere to drown. Not here. Not me.

Like Water Like Sea

1

The Swimmer

'I never asked what the bus driver said. Your trainers were making that squishing sound. They were so wet!'

Rahul laughed. He was in his element. He needed to be the life of the party. Especially this one. The first one in their new place. They didn't buy the flat – who wanted that kind of responsibility? they chimed in unison when asked – but rented a two-storey affair they had nonetheless thrown everything they had at. It looked great. There was no reason to deny them the compliment.

Crystal laughed too. The two of them were so weird I didn't know how I had managed to be in their lives for ten years. They wanted me, each of them in their own way. And we had explored that, in all sorts of ways. At least in the beginning.

They were intertwined so tightly that when you separated them too long, or allowed them to present only their individual selves, you would have to rip them apart. The person talking to them was caught off-guard. This well-together couple? These people who communicated so well? These people could make you fall flat on your ass, from the sudden give. They were inconsistent. And to some extent, non-existent. I had said it to Crystal once. The non-existent part. That I still wanted her too, romantically, but that I wasn't sure if I could make out who she was. Where she started, where Rahul ended.

'Was the bus driver hostile to you?' Be had held my attention from when I had entered the house earlier. Despite the terrible name, their quiet confidence had drawn me in immediately. They had been standing in the hallway when I arrived, having rung the bell only a couple of minutes before me. Their shoes were off, the long coat hanging on the wall hook. Rahul had squeezed by them, back into the living room, with a, 'You know where everything is, I'll need to help Crystal real quick. Everyone is here already. So lovely to see you, hon.'

Be was taller than me. The long black shirt they were wearing over dark jeans stopped just short of the knee. Their angular face was framed by close-cropped hair. They smiled, nodded and said, 'I'd shake hands with you but it's not something I returned to doing.' The voice was warm, with no trace of mockery.

I laughed. 'You could have just not done it.'

'I know but then you wouldn't know that I would otherwise make this a more formal hello. Well, not formal.'

'Okay.' The laugh escaped on my exhale. I had to push it back in. 'And this is not clear?' It came out breathless.

'Now it is.' And they laughed.

They were not trying to be funny, although it was funny as hell.

I straightened up and abandoned the boot zipper, which I had been tugging at, midway. I was still by the door. I stood up, scratched my arm, smiled, and nodded. They nodded and said, 'I'm Be.'

The sitting room was already full and I waved to the people I knew. Dominic's eyes flashed brightly when he saw me. I almost missed him with the new beard. It sparkled. Probably beard oil that lit up when the light hit just right. I chuckled. This was a maintaining at the barbers beard, nothing scruffy or accidental about it. I hadn't seen him in two years. What else was new with him? I knew I would be entertained sitting next to him, his laughter was always generous, and his comments thoughtful. Chatting with him at parties had a good balance of entertainment and meaningful observations. It was hard to get hold of him, he only answered his phone when he was in the mood. It was infuriating at first. How could you be friends with someone who was hardly ever available? But when he did call back or even better, when you were able to meet with him you had his full attention.

Mid-conversation, Crystal asked us all to come sit on the other side. There were two steps that ran the length of the middle separating the two rooms. The lower area had the open plan kitchen where Rahul was putting finishing touches to the sautéed long-stem broccoli he was dishing up. The kitchen was sunken in, on the same level with the garden. The new dining table was by the French doors. It gave a view out on the back garden. I ended up sitting opposite Be, Dominic next to them. The reused scaffolding boards serving as a tabletop were covered with a sheet of glass. It was so East London I had to hold back a laugh. We could have been in one of the hipster coffee shops, especially with the planters that hung on the side of the wall, greenery spilling down onto the wall.

I would have asked Be about their name if we had had more time to speak alone. I hoped Be was short for something and not a spiritual affirmation. It was a terrible thing to question a name but it was too tempting to not try. Their perfect introduction. The way they had amplified their weirdness to make sure I would not miss it. Right at the door. I didn't want the name to be a motto. I looked at them. There were several birthmarks on their forehead. Uneven black circles on dark brown skin. One above one of the brows, two closer to the hairline. The one above the brow lifted when they spoke. It looked like their attention was fully engaged.

The jokes at the table drifted around until they were talking about me and my wet clothes. I wasn't sure how we had even ended up here.

I didn't know whether Be could tell. That Rahul was using something intimate to set their party alight. I was the fire lighter. The tinder that would give a sparkling glow to the whole setting. The first party in their new home. Where everything would be even better than it already was. The ignition would match the metaphor: the discarded lover, although of course it was the other way around, my dignity burned up here for entertainment until the ashes cooled with the end of the night.

Rahul didn't know what to do with me. Crystal and I existed in that blurry area of ex-lovers who had never been in a real relationship. But unlike Rahul, who was lost in what my role was in his life and more importantly in Crystal's, mine and Crystal's friendship worked. I didn't care who Crystal slept with, which was mostly Rahul, or very clearly no-one else but Rahul, but neither of us said that this fact was obvious. Crystal and I had seen each other cry during a night together that had opened something in us. One carrying the other, while the fucking opened a door we hadn't planned on opening. That intimacy stayed and it didn't cloud over when I said I couldn't continue because Rahul was too present and I didn't want both of them. I didn't want Rahul. Not after the first few months. He never got a say in it. Not with what our friendship would be like, not what Crystal made of the connection with me. He stood on the sidelines waving *let me in*. Let me be part of this. And I had already been bored with him.

Be was holding my eyes with theirs, the mark high up. It helped to not put my head on the table. If I did, I wouldn't move it again. I would lie there accepting that it was my own fault, coming here. I couldn't move. It was easier to remain seated with my head up and wait it out.

'I do remember'.

Be nodded. They didn't ask anything else.

It is where it started. The intimacy. When I was lying on the River Lea. Them seeing me trying to drown myself. That's what they said, Crystal and Rahul. How worrying it had been to see me in the water. They had turned around as soon as they'd realised what had taken place. Rahul pushing much more than Crystal, who only wanted to call the emergency services. It had been Rahul convincing her that they should check on me in person. To make sure no drowning was taking place.

I had corrected them. 'Actually, I was never going to do that. I wanted to explore what drowning might feel like. I didn't want to experience it. In fact, I only wanted to lie on the water to float.'

This is how we became friends. Ten years ago. At the ten-year anniversary of my dead sister. The one who had drowned herself.

Pemba, who sat at the far end, grabbed a glass and tapped it with her spoon. 'Yeah, you know. The inevitable.' Everyone raised theirs. 'I know some of you do but I don't know why anyone would want to fall into the capitalist trap of owning their own place and upholding a corrupt system while owing the bank indefinitely. So... I am happy, very, that you two trust your landlord to do that for you.'

Everyone laughed. I was sending Pemba an internal thank-you card. Her exit route and the way she executed the diversion was impeccable.

After dinner, I helped clear the table and managed to get Pemba alone at the sink.

'You! I can't even.' I hugged her. 'Thank you.'

'Don't mention it. I don't know what it is with him sometimes.'

She returned to soaping the plates and rinsed them once they had been washed. Her *Supply-and-Demand* business, as she had called it, was going even better than the last time we had talked. It was a mobile office assistant service. You needed some help with light admin? You worked from home? You had enough to pay her day rate? She would scoot, as in electric scooter, to your place, with a laptop and some office supplies in her backpack. She even came with her own Wi-Fi because some clients' connections were too slow for her liking. Five people were working for her by now, and they were busy. Dominic had started right after she had conceived the idea.

Mostly it was about company.

'People work better when they have a colleague present.'

'I get it. I'm just surprised how many people can afford it.'

'I know! We're recruiting again. I guess they like my outspoken associates.' She smiled.

'I can't get over that you called it a capitalist concept.'

She hugged me again, her wet hands leaving prints on my top.

'That's the beauty. We humans, entirely conflicted.'

People had settled outside in the garden. Of course, there were fairy lights. I had nothing against them. Just the burning Rahul wanted to do. Why was I here?

Light drizzle had left the garden furniture damp. Guests were wiping off seats and armrests. Rahul was carrying four mugs of coffee from the kitchen. Balancing them took all his concentration, eyes darting from hands to his feet to make sure he didn't stumble.

'You okay? I haven't spoken to you all evening.' I didn't like how Crystal's hand felt on my arm. A gesture of care needed consistency.

Two years ago, I asked her why I was still in the picture when Rahul found it so difficult to be decent at times. She had said, 'You know how it is.'

'I do know how it is. I don't know why,' I had answered. I did know why. I just didn't know why it didn't change.

That morning when I had got out of the water, my sweatpants dripping, we had walked to the bus stop, all of us cold. They were sweaty and the chill was making it through their clothes. I had been so cold my lips had felt frozen from lying in the water for a good twenty minutes. Their run had been cut short when they had seen me lying there, my arms moving slowly as if I were conducting an orchestra under the water. I remembered the sensation. My fingers playing with the surface, small leaves touching my skin, then sliding off. The way the water was soft touched something inside me. My body felt as if it blended in, the water and me interacting. Inside me, I was trying to locate the release and bring meaning to it. Did it tell me something about my sister? Did it tell me something about me?

By the time they had turned around from their morning run to check on me, someone they had never seen before, I had climbed back out onto the bank of the river.

Crystal shouted, 'Second drawer' to Pemba who was still in the kitchen. To me, she said, 'Let's meet next week. We haven't seen each other. Properly.'

I found Be at the end of the garden by a newly planted Elderflower shrub. 'Apparently, they've done a lot of the garden. They hired someone.'

'Yes, Crystal told me.'

Pemba came out with Dominic, talking animatedly. I admired how she could throw herself completely into her laugh, even while walking. Her head went back, her hand found Dominic's shoulder, then slid around until her arm was holding him, her whole body moving. Dominic had his mouth wide open, his lips barely visible with the new beard, laughing too.

'Do you know them?' Be asked. It tickled me. That they were distracted by others rather than immersed in the moment with me.

'The artist? Pemba? Or both of them?' I replied. It was hard not to be unaffected by Be's enquiry. When people asked about Pemba they seldom remembered to pay any attention to me. She was interesting, charismatic, and too damn nice. You had to work very hard not to get swept away in admiration. I wanted an opening here, find out who Be was, have them ask about me, not fill in details about other, more exciting people.

'Pemba. I know Dominic,' Be said. Somehow, I thought this was Be's first encounter with Crystal and Rahul's friends. I had never heard of them.

'What did they do with the plants they no longer wanted?' I tried. I wanted Be's attention for myself. The air around my body was charged, eager to close in, closer to their body. Not for sex, for comfort. To relax me enough so that I could leave.

'What?' Be was confused.

I pointed to the new beds. 'I'm wondering what happened to the stuff that was there before. I assume they had lots of roots to dig up.'

'Garden waste?'

I nodded. 'Pemba is a fantastic sculptor,' I said. I tried to not let my reluctance enter my voice. 'She can make things out of anything. Cement, wood, stone, plastic. Dominic works for her. She has a mobile office service. She doesn't do the jobs anymore, she's much too successful now. Sometimes she still fills in if one of her associates, as she calls them, is sick last minute. The website for the online bookings is still hers and she organises the timetables. I think despite her anti-capitalist notions she likes being a boss. And she must be good at it. Dom's been working with her for many years now.'

'Ah, this is where all of that came from. The scooter-by-demand secretary. I was wondering why Dominic didn't look for anything else.' Be smiled.

'It's easy perhaps. You have to do good work but you don't have to commit.' Why did I feel like I had to defend the business? 'They have interesting clients. It's not just typing emails for someone.'

'Of course,' they said.

I wanted them to ask about me. To return to the question they had asked earlier.

'The bus driver asked me whether I needed help. A Sunday morning in London and the driver felt concern for me,' I said.

'Did you need help?' Be had turned their attention back to the shrub. They were holding a leaf between their fingers, rubbing it.

'Elderflower,' I said. 'It'll bloom as soon as it gets warmer.'

Be nodded absentmindedly. They hadn't really paid attention to the plant.

I continued, 'Not in the way people thought.'

I had got on the bus and waved to Crystal and Rahul, whose names I had just learned, the piece of paper with their numbers in my hand. They had waved back with encouraging smiles. I had to sneeze and wiped my face with the back of my hand, the sleeve of my hoodie pulled over it. When we drove off she had asked me. I could still see the hunched-over torso of the bus driver, the hands that were holding on to the steering wheel as if they needed to go in for a hug.

She had looked at me closely as if she realised that something had taken place this morning, with me at the centre of it.

'Are you okay?,' she had asked.

'You must be so tired and now I am making your seat dirty,' I had answered.

My clothes had dried by now but they were muddy, and small green leaves were sticking to the sweatpants.

'Don't worry.' That seemed to be the end of it but then she added, 'Don't vomit though.' I had smiled, my body still cold. The bus driver had given me a tissue. I sneezed again.

The next day I texted Crystal to thank them for the concern. I reiterated that I was okay, that lots was going on but I wasn't really as lost as it had looked.

The movement brought me back. Be was pressing on the leaf, still without paying attention to it.

'What did you need?'

I noticed the pattern cut into the back of their hair. I had only seen them from the front until now. They turned to meet my eyes and the lines disappeared out of my view.

'What did I need?' I took a moment to find the right words. 'To fall apart.' I tried to see Be's reaction but they weren't looking at my face. 'Rahul couldn't forgive himself that they kept running for a few minutes before they returned to check on me. If I had wanted to drown myself, I would have been long dead.'

Our hands were close now, Be's and mine. I looked at the brown fingers. There were scratches on one side, where the pinkie met the rest of the hand. I wondered if they were working with their hands, or if this was accidental.

'Rahul can't let go because he feels guilty. If I leave them, for good, he has only himself to look at. For some reason he can't move on from having gone on to run further, although he steered them back to me.'

'Most people wouldn't have stopped at all.'

'I know.'

'He cares.'

I put my hands in my pocket. They were dry and cold. 'It used to be care. And shock. That he was so distracted that morning. It became something else. I didn't need saving. Not in the water, not afterwards.'

'Maybe that's all he has.'

'Yeah.' I took my hands out again to rub them together and looked at Be. 'Your name.'

'My name?'

The speakers had been turned up on the inside and a few people started dancing both in the lounge and outside. 'Is it a proclamation? Be?'

'B for back off, none of your damn business.'

I nodded. I had known better. They turned toward the building swaying along to the dancers. After a while they said, 'People find it difficult.'

'What?'

'The falling apart. To witness it.'

I nodded.

'You could talk to Rahul, find out why he's so angry with you.'

'I've tried.'

'You can try again.'

'I could.' I could tell him what had mattered that weekend. It would hurt him because it had nothing to do with him. All that had happened between us after the water was good sex and spare time. Then over the months, a bond had formed. Perhaps he needed me to need him. Perhaps he had realised that his guilt had nothing to do with me at all. However hard he came for me he was still not who he thought he was.

I had put the tissue on the seat but before I could sit the bus driver had opened the glass partition, her head facing the inside of the bus.

'It's for you! Blow your nose. Who cares about the seats? You have no idea what they've been through tonight. Your clothes...' She paused, then sucked her teeth, '...that's nothing. No problem at all. Sit,' she had continued. 'Sit down. It will be okay.'

Her words were so apt I wanted to follow her to the bus garage and take her out for breakfast. Instead I got off at the bus stop close to Mum's, let myself in and climbed into the bath.

2

Crystal held me too tight. You couldn't invite me to your party and allow your partner to offer me up as entertainment and expect everything to be cosy with me a week later. I broke away, standing in front of her.

'I saw you talking with Be,' she said.

I didn't answer. Crystal cared who I slept with. Not in an obvious way, not in a *she couldn't be friends with me* way, but I suspected it panged her to know.

We did have a threesome once, Crystal, Rahul, me. Crystal had looked at Rahul touching me and her eyes went wild. I thought one day she would have to come out in an entirely different way. She didn't want it, him touching me, him touching her, me doing anything but lie under her and give myself to her while Rahul did not participate. We never did it again. Soon after it fizzled out between Rahul and me, and Crystal and I messed around a few more times. She never talked about that night and why it had been full of explosive tension instead of us just stopping. I had tried to speak to her about it.

I had asked her, 'What was that all about? You and Rahul are happy, yeah?'

Nothing came of it. I also probed more generally.

'How many women have you been with? Do you consider yourself bi, pan?'

She did that very annoying thing that people who held on too tightly to heteronormativity did: 'All good. Rahul and I are very happy. I'm just into you babe.'

She pretended she wasn't as far on the queer spectrum as she seemed to be that night. That I hadn't seen jealousy in her eyes. And not about me with Rahul.

'Nothing to name here, Nia,' she said. 'We are free. People are free to do and sleep with whom they want to.'

I hadn't answered. It bored me when people claimed a freedom they were denying themselves.

We were meeting at a bar in Shoreditch. It was too trendy for me but Crystal loved the atmosphere.

'The small table in the back is free, I think,' she said.

We made our way through the crowded front room where tables had been pushed back to three sides of the room and stood against one wall.

'There is live music sometimes,' Crystal said.

'We've been here before, Crystal,' I answered.

I didn't feel like being here. We hadn't seen each other for a proper catch up in months. If not for Rahul being Rahul, being his insecure self, who needed his confidence boosted at my expense, we wouldn't be having drinks or whatever it was that we were doing. If she wanted to catch up, like she had said, we could have met in my kitchen for freshly brewed hibiscus tea.

The table was free only because it was in the narrow hallway that led to the toilets.

'How have you been?' I started. Crystal's hair was a burnt orange on the top, her roots black still. She wasn't wearing any earrings, which was rare for her.

'The new flat, life... Is everything living up to its promise?' I continued.

Crystal took the menu and slid it towards me.

'Get a drink, babe. Tonight's on me,' she said.

'I told you I have a full day tomorrow. I can't stay out late,' I replied.

It took a while until the server came. I had offered to go to the bar but Crystal said this was the joy of this table. Away from the crowd and exclusive table service. She rose up to hug the server when he came.

'Nia, this is Rocco. I know his sister from choir.'

I ordered a fresh ginger lemon mocktail. Crystal went for a prosecco cocktail with raspberry cordial and basil.

'Rocco is a sweetheart,' she said.

'Okay,' I replied.

There was enough noise to keep us entertained without making the silence between us awkward. Crystal was still looking closely at the menu, although Rocco had told us the kitchen was closed.

'What's going on, Crystal. It's not like you to be so evasive.'

'What do you mean?' she asked.

'Come on, we've been sitting here for a while and you haven't answered a simple "How is it going?" '

She shut the menu and placed it neatly at the corner of the table.

'Rahul wants to get married.'

I nodded. They had been together for sixteen years. It was almost redundant now. What other commitment did he want? What could the formality add to their relationship? Had he always held out, knowing one day he would propose?

'And you don't want to?' I asked.

'No, Nia, I don't want to get married. Why should I?'

It was a calm exclamation; she wasn't pushing against something. She was stating a fact. Rahul wanted to, she didn't.

'I get it,' I replied. 'And please don't take it the wrong way but you do usually end up on the conventional route. At some point.'

She couldn't be angry with that. I had asked her the previous year if she had had any other lovers like me. Women, non-binary, trans folks, anyone other than Rahul and cis-men. It was my way of asking how the queer awakening was coming along. There had been a longer affair, a woman she had seen on and off for two years. It had hurt me a bit. Not that she had been seeing someone, but that she hadn't told me. Two years was a long time. What had we talked about during that time? Rahul. Work. Family. Politics. But not matters of the heart, it seemed.

Rocco came with our drinks and left with an 'I'll check later if you want anything else.'

Crystal thanked him.

'What happened with that woman you were seeing?'

She wasn't forthcoming with anything. This extracting her thoughts was hard. She was the one who had wanted this catch-up. She had said, 'It won't be late, I promise.'

Now we were sitting here, her in satisfied self-reflection, me tired of the observations I had made. We were in the hallway nonetheless, Crystal sat facing towards the bar and the large room. I could see nothing other than the people going to and coming from the toilet.

'It's a colleague of Be. That's how I met her,' Crystal said.

'I've never heard you speak of her, or Be.'

I took the last swig of a ginger mocktail that had too much lemon and too much ice in it.

'Some things take time to make sense.'

'I'm surprised she never came up at all.'

Crystal got up to go to the toilet. I pushed my glass over the table where a bit of ice had melted into a thin film. It swished from on end to the other where I caught it with my other hand. When she came back Crystal hugged me. Her fingers were still damp and cold from washing her hands.

'I had some things to figure out. I wasn't ready to share it.'

Her cheek pressed against mine, reminded me of nights where we had sat looking out of the window, a blanket wrapped around us. I had asked her about what she wanted from life, whether she intended to keep working for the police. She had looked at me hurt.

'And if I do?' she had asked, annoyed.

I had shrugged my shoulders. It was good work she was doing. Yet, I imagined work differently, for all sectors of society, where good was measured in transforming structures rather than doing good.

It had been a complicated closeness with us. Our skin warm and porous to each other, our minds somewhat aligned but our actions differing drastically. It was better when we were friends. Although there was that nostalgia of what could have been if we had met differently, with different convictions about how life should be lived hanging in the air. And yet I had never been too bothered about a relationship with her. They came as a package, Rahul and Crystal. I always knew that sooner rather than later they would fade into the friend zone or disappear out of my life altogether. When Temi and I decided we were going to be in a monogamous relationship, I stopped our once in a while affair.

Crystal said she didn't want my opinion on Carmen, the woman she had sometimes slept with. I had so many opinions then. I still had them but we never saw each other anymore. Rahul had known about her, of course, but she had kept any details away from him too. It was casual, not serious. That was their arrangement. Play but don't date. Tell only about the fact not the details, meaning 'inform me but leave out all that could make this come alive in my mind.'

'I wanted something that was mine. When you're so long with a person and you share the kind of openness Rahul and I have, it can get confusing. How do I know what I want anymore? I only know what works between us, how it works best. I wanted to see what connections I might have with other people.'

I didn't respond that we also had had a connection. She wasn't doing much to figure it out.

'Has Rahul ever had anything with anyone else?' I asked.

Crystal looked at me. 'I don't think so.' She needed to think for a moment. 'Just you, of course. Whatever that was.'

I was glad she put it like that.

'What was it, Crystal?' I wanted to know. Maybe she had an answer.

'What do you mean?'

'It's been ten years since we met and Rahul goes off the rails as if I did something very very bad to him. You invited me in, that is how it all started. And you, the both of you, were adamant friendship was fine when we stopped sleeping together. I don't need to be in your lives if it's not working. You haven't even apologised!'

'For what?'

I laughed and shook my head. 'The party last week? What was that?'

'He was just reliving some old stories. You were busy with Be anyway.'

For a moment there was a hole in my perception. Time collapsed; no here nor there, just a deep, empty fall. Then a hot stream left my body. It was the fury that built up with her words. I fished for some money in my pocket and put it on the table.

'I said it's on me, Nia,' Crystal said, her tone annoyed as if I was a badly behaved child.

'You needed me as your pet project. I always knew that. It was okay because I didn't think you were doing any harm. We were young, not terribly but still young enough to try out some things. But you don't get to sacrifice me because neither of you know what they want from the other. Or I suspect Rahul knows. And you don't quite want him the same way. It's not for me to carry. You are accountable, whether you rise to it or not.'

I hadn't gotten up yet. I was trying to hold on to something here and Crystal gave me little reason to.

'Your party. The biggest farce in the world of parties. You couldn't be more normative with your flat that you didn't buy but desperately want to. Why not be honest? You surround yourself with people who are more interesting than you so you can feel you are a different person than you are. This is how we became friends: you thinking I was more needy than you when I was only more honest. We've been friends for ten years! You know I didn't need a saviour then and certainly not Rahul. Worse, what if I had needed someone and that same person is someone who is capable of offering me up as kindling just so he can get a party going?'

The words came out steady and measured. All the fury had left me. I had nothing left for Crystal. It had deflated me. I was so tired that the thought of getting up and out of the bar was pushing me further into the seat. I needed to learn this. To walk away, quicker, without a catapult other than my own knowledge. Intuition was knowing, yet it stalled me.

'We've always had a connection. I thought it was a good one. I don't know who you are today. I don't know why I am here,' I said.

I heard myself and it echoed back to me in another voice. Temi had said it to me, a year into our relationship, when we had already fallen on different sides of the same wall. 'I don't know why I am here.'

Crystal closed her eyes before she spoke.

'I'm not trying to be more interesting.'

I wanted to laugh again because I knew she didn't even believe it herself. I hadn't intended to say something like that. I wanted to speak about the party and how she had participated.

'Complicity. If you don't act against, if you don't speak out for the person being attacked you are complicit. You worry about me talking to Be? Be was the person I could count on. And I don't even know them.'

'You knew everyone else. Pemba tried to stop Rahul.'

'Crystal are you hearing me? Where were you?'

Her eyes were still closed when she spoke again.

'I used to try and figure out why Rahul was coming for you so hard. Especially after such a long time. I think we had a few good years of friendship and then it started one day. I think it has to do with Carmen. When I messed around with her. He never met her but she was the second one.'

'The second what?' I asked.

'The second person I had feelings for other than him.'

The tension made me shake my legs. Something else arrived inside of me. It was more tender than I had prepared for.

'What feelings Crystal?'

I wasn't trying to be cold, or mean. Yes, there was that look that had told me she wanted to take Rahul apart if he didn't stop touching me that night. And still, after that we had only been intimate a few more times, not enough to make it a big story. It was over before it was anything. The way you see someone very attractive and think *wow* and at the same time know their type of attraction does nothing for you personally. I thought it was only significant for her because I was her first queer encounter.

'I didn't realise it until Carmen. And maybe it was the same for Rahul.'

Rocco came and asked whether we wanted more drinks. We paid instead.

'Can we walk for a bit?' Crystal asked.

It was not as busy as I had expected outside. Maybe everyone was inside a bar, or home already. We walked towards Hoxton. Crystal folded her arms in front of her.

'I did confront him. Before. We had arguments over this,' she said.

My legs were searching the ground with each step because there was a divide here. We would either make it to a common ground or this would be our last walk. I could feel it. We had left things too late; the trajectory of our friendship had always been off because of that skewed first meeting. It had me locked in as troubled, never to be fully acknowledged. Now we found ourselves with years of missing conversations.

'Over what?' I was opening the field for her.

'Why he brought up old stuff with you. Things that weren't relevant.'

I thought of Rahul. Out with friends and someone talking about the tide at Southbank, and how the sand artists always made such beautiful sculptures. And Rahul launching into a tangent about people and rivers and how this good friend of theirs had sought out a river, albeit not the Thames, and this is how they met, her drenched in jogging clothes, they, the actual joggers, standing at the riverbank. How they had extended their hands, metaphorically, and pulled her out of the streaming water, she, so grateful that they had taken the time. And out of this gratitude a friendship had developed. Crystal, quiet at the other end of the table, with questions in her face, searching for a reason for this narrative twist. Looking up from her phone, a text from Carmen on the display, to Rahul's need to dominate the conversation.

'Things that weren't entirely true,' Crystal interrupted my thoughts. 'He thought that you hadn't dealt with it...'

'With what?'

'Your sister's death. That it was obvious. Melvin. Temi. Alicia.'

'What was wrong with Temi or Alicia. Or Melvin?'

'That you couldn't stay with anybody because you were not dealing with the loss.'

'Crystal. I was with Alicia for seven years. Melvin is still in my life.'

Crystal laughed. 'I know.'

'What did *you* think?' I asked.

We had stopped by a bus stop.

'Walk some more?' Crystal asked.

'The irony,' I replied pointing at the bus stop and the seat, but Crystal didn't get it.

Crystal's eyes widened like a landscape of brown, with some specks of black thrown about. For the first time this evening it felt like she was present without a diversion, without trying to cover our conversation up, making it blend into something that felt less confronting to her, something that she had no responsibility over.

'I knew it was us. Not in the beginning. But once I saw you and Melvin.'

Melvin and I had gone to sit by the river again, a few months after our family ritual. Another picnic. Not to honour Johari but to take time for us. Talk about some real and maybe difficult truths. It was not near where Crystal and Rahul had found me. Crystal said later she started taking a different route. She and Rahul had been out for a run when they saw us. Crystal stayed for a bit while Rahul had to get back to work.

'The first time we met, in that gluten-free cafe, do you remember?' Crystal asked.

'I do,' I replied.

'You had said you had people. I didn't believe you. I didn't think you would reach out to anyone and we were strangers, it was easier,' she continued.

'It is easier sometimes,' I agreed.

'When we bumped into you, that time… You and Melvin were so in tune. You said something like he is family and I felt ashamed.'

'Why?'

'Because I had built this whole story around you, the drowning sister that was left behind, struggling to make it onto solid ground.'

'You should become a writer. So many metaphors,' I said.

She smiled.

'You have to let people feel their pain without writing them off,' I continued.

'I know Nia. I know that now.'

Her head was lowered.

'I was also ashamed because I had so overestimated our significance in your life. When I met Melvin, I thought what could we bring? We were newcomers to your life. Those sexcapades,' she waved her hand around, 'they were fun but it didn't feel real. There was nowhere to go with it. Not for me.'

'What do you mean?'

'I wasn't going to leave Rahul. We were very much in love. But it wasn't casual enough between us. You touched more in me than I did in you, I think.'

Her eyes were scanning me while avoiding meeting mine directly. I was avoiding her look and concentrated on the wooden-clad facade of the bar we were passing by.

Crystal waited for me to say something. I couldn't contradict her. I was never in. I had simply not walked away from the situation. Not out of coercion but because it was an experience. Like others. I imagined it would be valuable. I went along with it until Temi and I said we wanted to be exclusive.

'It was less complicated when we became friends. We weren't lovers, you were very capable. You had a complicated life but so did we. It levelled out,' Crystal continued.

'Until Carmen?'

'I had to confront some truth then. Not even about you. It was more about dependency. How much I depended on the stories I told myself. About Rahul and me. About how things go in life. How things look. And I got it!'

'What?'

'Nia, I wanted to lie on the water and float. All of a sudden it was so clear what you had been doing. And so clear that we couldn't get it. That I didn't have the guts, and Rahul certainly didn't.'

'When did Rahul ask you to marry him?' I asked.

'Before the party.'

I nodded. It made sense now.

'I don't want to be with him for the rest of my life. I want to be with someone that can do the falling apart. Otherwise there will always be someone who is offered up for entertainment like you were last week.'

I finally turned towards her and we both stopped.

'Rahul will never have the guts. I don't think so,' Crystal said.

'Are you going to leave him?' I asked.

'I don't really have a reason to. I love him. We are good together.'

'Okay.' I couldn't say more. She was covering for a helpless man who sometimes turned this helplessness to attack others, a man she did not want to take into her future. Yet the present was too fragile to be upset by a breakup. 'Have you given him an answer?' I asked.

'I have. Watch me ablaze at our next social.'

3

The Swimmer

Temi and I fell apart, quickly, after the dinner with her parents. Her father had been in town, a rare occasion, she said. He lived in Saudi Arabia. Her mother wanted us to eat together. I had met her once before where she had eyed me up and down, lingering on the bulky boots I was wearing with jeans and an oversized shirt. She wanted to say something, her mouth was open but Temi told her that I did herbal medicine, which her mother seemed to think of very highly. I surely knew some herbs that could help with her stiff ankles.

'Oh, my grandmother in the village, she used to know which things were good for the health.' Her face nostalgic. 'Come, Nia, please come. You are welcome.'

That first meeting had been light and informal, Temi's brother Layo was home from university and we had eaten in the living room, each sitting on the couch or an armchair, a small side table in front of us.

Temi's Mum beamed my way, pleased with the fact that I already knew jollof rice and had done so long before Temi's arrival in my life. She carefully wrote down my suggestion to start with turmeric extract to help ease stiffness and to let me know if there was any change.

'Are you like girlfriends now?' Layo had asked when their mother retreated to her bedroom.

Temi had laughed and looked at me. 'Maybe. I don't think we've spoken about this. It's early.'

Layo had nodded and gone for a second plate while telling Temi and me about the decolonising curriculum group at university.

'Are you part of it?' Temi asked.

'Are you kidding me? Try telling Dad.'

'I don't think that would bother him. Of course, there is also no way he could actually know.'

I asked Temi later about that and about her Dad. Where was he, what was he doing. She answered but I could tell she didn't want to talk about it. Her replies were short and not inviting. Instead she told me that her mother had been a midwife and was now teaching. A few weeks after our first meeting her mother sent messages that the turmeric was working, and little questions for close friends of hers needing help. I liked her messages. She didn't have my number, I only got them when I saw Temi. They started with 'Tell your girlfriend what she suggested worked/did not work. If she can get a higher dose for my friend...' We joked that I would ceremoniously pass on my number directly to her when I next saw her. Maybe that would be after we had our official one-year anniversary. One year since the clearing up of the misunderstanding, not one year since we'd met or first kissed.

Her father came to visit just before our weekend away to celebrate our anniversary.

His voice boomed across the dining room table and he laughed frequently. I found out he worked for SEC-T Aerospace Systems as a technician supervisor.

'Everything is chill there, Nia, as you young people like to say,' he laughed. 'Except the heat.'

The joke put him in an even better mood. Layo had come to London too and tried to force a smile but he didn't find it funny and it was obvious. Temi watched me from the corner of her eyes. There was more laughter and more jokes than the time I had met her mother. But I felt more uncomfortable.

I was living at Mum's then, saving for a deposit for the next flat. When I got home later I told her about the evening. The loud father. The quiet family.

Mum asked, 'Why does he live in Saudi Arabia? Alone, without them?'

'He works for a company called SEC-T aero something, I didn't quite get it. As a technician supervisor.'

Mum and I had found a good balance with each other. Living with her was better than I could have imagined. We often found ourselves chatting late into the night. About mania, and how it felt. About the life that didn't quite feel like it was hers. About the threat of hospitalisation. About my plans to open a small clinic on Saturdays. And mostly how glad she was that I was in her life. I felt cocooned. Different. This was the mother I knew. Knowledgeable, generous. Full of laughter. Even if there was a discord in our relationship and my ears were always paying attention. I was sharing more with her than I had my whole adult life.

Mum stopped abruptly, still holding the mugs she had in hand and which she had intended to put in the kitchen sink.

'SEC-T you say?'

'I think so.'

She put the mugs back on the living room table and went to her bedroom to get her laptop. Bent over the coffee table, her face was tense. She called me over to show me the website. It was an airspace security company. I didn't really know what that meant but Mum showed me articles that exposed companies that supplied arms and weapons. SEC-T was featured prominently on many of the blog posts. Technician had a whole different meaning in this context.

I confronted Temi the next day. 'What does he actually do, your father, what is he supervising?'

Temi looked at me with a *no, don't do this* expression.

'I don't know the details. You've met him, he talks a lot but is not forthcoming to other peoples' questions, certainly not ours.'

'But you know what the company does?'

We were in her flat. As soon as I walked through the door my body had expanded. It found room here. It felt like floating with just the right amount of gravity, the optiMum balance between being held and letting go. Temi looked like she was being pushed against the wall. Her hands touched the painted hallway surfaces, trailing up and down as if there were better answers to extract.

'I know now. I didn't always know. The story used to be that Dad did business. He was abroad a lot. Life was mostly Mum and Layo and me.'

I leaned on the doorframe. I even stepped back with one foot, inside the kitchen, to make space. To show there were exit routes if she needed or wanted them. Maybe for me to retreat and close the door. I wasn't sure.

'How did you find out?' I asked.

'I don't speak much with my father. It wasn't a thing. One day there was a file lying around. I just caught the name. I thought it was something religious at first. It surprised me. What church group would call themselves "sect"? Dad was on the phone and had walked into the bedroom.'

'Did you know the company before?'

'No. Google. SEC-T ... secure transnational,' she said flatly.

It felt like a stalemate. Temi with her hands behind her body on the wall. Me with half my body trying to leave.

Was it her fault? Her father's involvement in things I believed should be opposed? In the production of war. In the money-making of man produced death.

'Layo and I confronted him together. Mum wasn't having it, she shut the conversation down. Said we should be ashamed. Dad had paid for our education, provided for the family. We were living a good life because of him. That we didn't know the details. Protection was needed against certain things, and sometimes that involved certain people. Even if it included armed conflict.'

Her eyes were pleading with me. It wasn't her fault, I knew it.

'We didn't stop. Layo didn't want to stop talking about it to make sense of it all, to find out what Dad was thinking about all of this or if he just divorced himself from the facts. I was too scared, admittedly.'

'You? The one who doesn't care about other people's opinions?'

'Nia, he's my Dad. Either way, I was not going to escape him. Even if I never spoke to him again.'

I nodded. You couldn't break free from your family. Not like that. You would still feel implicated. Like when Temi had talked to me about the one who had rearranged someone's living room while the person went to get beers. It was personal for me, the knowledge that it could have been light sensitivity related to mania, that again someone was misunderstood, judged on terms that did not include them. It was so personal for me that I had to run from her afterwards.

But war...

To play with war to raise a family? There was a line to how much innocence you could claim. To where complicity started. I couldn't see it otherwise.

We stood, our eyes in each other's hold. My body had contracted. I was still hovering, but it wasn't the holding anymore, it was indecision.

'Nia. I don't like it.' She looked away now. 'I hate it...I am ashamed of it. Shame I learned doesn't do any work. It just holds you somewhere where nothing happens. It's terror that freezes you.'

'What do you want to do about it?' I asked.

'I don't know what I can do. Other than talking to him which makes no difference,' she replied.

I thought about my parents. The *Free Palestine* protests we had gone to. The anti-war protests we had attended. My mother who was too loud for many at times but who insisted people had a voice, needed their voice heard. And she would shout for that. My mother, who many didn't take seriously but who had known straight away that something was up when she had heard the name of the company Temi's Dad worked for.

I was trying to fill her shoes. Being deliberate about what I chose. Who I engaged with. What work I did, and who was implicated.

'Temi, there is terror at the other end of it.'

I pushed away from the wooden door frame and stood inside the kitchen. I was ready to go. Not because of her but because the balance was off in the flat. In a whole year of our relationship we had not engaged with the world. Not the world outside of London, outside of British racism, outside of things that affected us personally. We had spoken about politics but not about the world. The world that did not have us in it. Not even figuratively. It wouldn't be enough, not for another year. Not when Mum still had to tell me more details of her visit to Palestine. When she knew straight away that the company supplied equipment there too.

I couldn't do it. I was finding a family thread, something beyond mental health and dead siblings. I felt an allegiance to the issue at hand bound to my own lineage.

'That is what I am talking about.'

'What is?' I asked.

'That there is also terror that comes from shame. I'm not equating the two, don't misunderstand me. It's just... you are making me ashamed about something that I don't agree with either. I already feel so.'

I was wondering if my bag was still at the door, where I had hung my jacket. I couldn't see it from where I was. We could talk some more but I wouldn't be staying over. Not tonight. There was nowhere to go here for us, not at this moment.

'I'm not making you anything.' My voice was soft. 'I can't even.'

She pushed herself off the wall and walked towards me. Her hands stretched out, waiting for me to take them.

I hugged her, my face on hers and her arms wrapped around me, pulling me close.

'I'm not staying tonight,' I said.

'I know,' she replied.

We were open to each other. Careful but clear. Two sides that didn't belong to each other.

We didn't kiss before I left.

4

The Swimmer

I was still justifying the breakup with Temi. It was months after but once in a while the guilt swept me away. I knew Temi wasn't the problem, I just wasn't prepared to stay in such close proximity to a serious issue that came with her Dad. I was walking to a new gallery when on the left I saw the street that led to the arches we had passed through on our way to the club. That night, long ago, when I ran out on her, then to Mum's and later ended up on the River Lea. I had passed the street many times before but not since we stopped seeing each other. I found myself thinking, *I did that*, running out on her, and not taking the time to find out about the things that lay underneath. I ran for good reasons but still. I hadn't stayed. Not the first instance and not when it got significant. By now both Temi and I knew, firmly, that I wasn't as invested in her as I had thought. You stayed with people, through the hard times. Even when they were problematic. Because all of us were. There wasn't much I could say about Temi that put her at fault. She was smart and deliberate, exact and thorough. She was not her father. She would confront him if that was what I wanted. It wouldn't make him change. But I couldn't quite make her responsible for that.

The street had been empty but suddenly a group of tourists appeared taking pictures of each other under the arches. Their voices echoed and I had to laugh. I couldn't understand them from the distance, and I don't think I recognised the language, but it sounded careless. Unattached and free. The way we are when we are in the middle of something new that we don't have to commit to. It was weightless in a meaningful way. The wind picked up and I hurried to the next side street where the entrance to the gallery was illuminated by a spotlight on each side. I showed my ticket and walked down the steps into the basement while taking off my jacket. At the bottom was the door to the exhibition space. My jacket in one hand, I opened it. The door hit someone and the person jumped back.

'Sorry! I didn't see… I didn't know someone was…'

The woman held her head where the door had grazed her. She looked around. Her glasses had slid off. I rushed to bend down and pick them up.

'I'm so sorry. They should probably have a sign or something. It's so dark in the hallway,' I said.

'It almost happened when I entered. Although I do remember they warned me upstairs.'

She had bangs. Black hair in a straight line covering half of her forehead. The rest of her hair fell over her shoulders, her ears exposed. I hated bangs, at least I would have said so. I didn't understand the precision of it. It seemed unnecessary to draw the attention to the face in such a sharp manner. Hers framed her face and made it difficult to look away. The dark eyes, the open look, the cheeks that pulled upwards in a smile. She was in a flamboyant suit, a dark green material, cut well, with a flowery corduroy shirt underneath. She had one of those smart backpacks over one of her shoulders. The ones that had the stiff material with the top part that needed to be rolled up to close it. I handed her the glasses and she thanked me.

'Are you okay?' I asked.

She put her arm on my shoulder, very briefly, as if she realised immediately what she had done, that she didn't know me. It had been an automatic gesture. 'It didn't really hurt. It startled me more.'

I asked her about the exhibition. It was a small space. In the middle was a freestanding wall onto which a video was projected. The walls on the side seemed to have drawings on them, all the way to the back. A Peruvian artist Pemba had recommended when I had run into her earlier in the week. Something about suspending things in the air in an unusual manner. Pemba thought it was fascinating.

'It's really good. You should take your time. I came during my break and am annoyed. I haven't taken everything in.' She swept her hand from one side to the other, highlighting the work on the walls.

'The sculptures in the back are particularly interesting,' she continued.

I nodded. I couldn't see anything with the wall in the way.

'You could come back,' I said.

'I will. I'm meeting a client nearby, which is how I ended up here.'

'I understand,' I replied and moved to the side so she could get the door, open it, and make her way out like she had intended to. There was a beat, as if she forgotten for a moment what was supposed to happen and I had stepped into that moment and we hovered there, together, not yet moving forward with our day, not changing anything either. Then she looked at her phone.

'Shit, okay, that's very late now.'

She nodded and smiled and run up the stairs.

The exhibition was good. She was right. The sculptures she had talked about were made of an array of twigs that got increasingly bigger until it became a canopy that sheltered half of the space. The bottom looked like a miniature bird's nest, balancing on a single stone. I looked for hidden strings and saw one secured to the back wall. But I couldn't make out how the whole stayed up.

My phone rang. It was Mum. She was upset because there were air raids on Gaza and she had stayed up all night following various news sites.

I went outside and stood under a large tree talking to her. I liked her like this. Not that she was upset but the sincerity. That some things had so much weight on her that her heart ached and she looked for compassion, that she needed to connect with people to know that we cared about life, still. That it mattered. That names were called. I touched the bark. It was a horse chestnut. I looked up to see whether this one was also plagued by the leaf-miner moth that attacked half of its species. It was a large tree. I couldn't be sure; the leaves were too high up.

'I know,' I said. 'It's awful! I don't know what we can do.'

I sat down with my back against the tree and listened to her crying. It was soft. It didn't need anything from me, other than me being there because I think she trusted that I found it as upsetting. Once when Johari was thirteen and I had been eleven we had been on a march and a Palestinian woman had been on a megaphone calling the names of her family that had been killed. Only the names, over and over again. Mum had nodded and cried. When Johari tugged on her sleeve, embarrassed, she said you must never shove yourself back into a box just to keep a lid on when that lid was meant to keep you away from humanity. There were too many people who couldn't feel anything at all. Johari had looked sceptical but others around us had overheard and agreed. The woman was still reciting names, not only her family members at that point, but others too.

When we hung up I went back inside. On the stairs the woman with the bangs called from behind me.

'You're still here?'

I turned around. 'Yes, I had my own distractions. Although I guess work is not a distraction. Not like that.'

'Oh it is but what can we do?'

We smiled and went down. Inside she asked me what I thought of the sculptures.

Afterwards we exchanged numbers. 'If ever you want to go see something with someone. I'm in the area quite often.'

That was that. I don't think either of us had planned to get in touch. It was a nice afternoon. She had looked interesting; we had enjoyed a bit of small talk about the art. And we had our lives to attend to.

A few weeks later I got a text from her.

Not sure if you remember me but I couldn't resist. A friend invited me to a gallery. I was late and rushed down some stairs, opened a door and banged into someone. She was not as friendly as you were or as me. I had to laugh, which didn't help the situation. I mean, am I not supposed to see art? Can I not manage an accident-free viewing? Anyway, I had no one to share this with so here you go. It's Alicia. We met briefly at the Fine Tuning show.

Melvin was washing up the dishes, I had invited him for a meal. He had hardly been in my flat since I moved in. I was sitting at the kitchen table and laughed out loud.

'What is it,' Melvin asked.

'This woman I bumped into, literally.'

It was like a bad film. This is how we started, heads colliding, or almost as mine had been on the other side of the door. We met to see the show she had wanted to see before the grumpy encounter because I was intrigued. A few weeks later we became a thing. Alicia the statistician. I liked to say that.

Crystal had teased me, 'You are reducing her to her job.'

I answered, 'No, hon, I'm telling you how good she is at maths.'

But it wasn't the maths. It was the applying and modelling findings. Alicia was good at figuring out paths. Hers were with numbers, and through the data, but it was still a position of a seeker.

5

The Climber

SuSu found Nia on the bed, the curtains drawn. The room smelled as if the windows had not been opened for days. It was almost evening. Nia was lying on the bed. The skin on her face taut, the mouth pulling. It looked like her blood was standing guard to prevent an invasion, the skin alert, ready. Her body was still. SuSu looked for the eyes to move.

SuSu had returned from a day out in Epping Forest. A day of walking in nature. It ended with a picnic with Denise, a young woman she had befriended in her support group for people with bipolar disorder. They enjoyed each other's company, the younger asking the older one about her experiences, the older asking the younger about her environment, whether things had changed, whether there was more acceptance of her in her world. SuSu felt full of life. Nia had been living with her for months now after losing her flat. The first time in years that they had lived together. She was not having episodes, not manic ones, no depression. They were spending time like they were supposed to. Talking, living. Both things equally distributed between them. She enjoyed her daughter's seriousness. The way she would sit in her bedroom with the door wide open, looking over papers that had her writing on them. Thinking through options, for her next flat, how to secure one, for opportunities to open a naturopath clinic. The open door an invitation, sometimes for her to enter, other times to keep company from a distance while Nia worked something out on her notepad or laptop. SuSu didn't know why there was so much ease between them, all of a sudden. Like they were getting closer in age, the gap shrinking with each small mundane gesture. Maybe it was the living together, maybe they needed each other in close proximity to overcome the scales that had often been tipped towards SuSu. It wouldn't last forever, so she tried to absorb as much of their daily gestures, as much of her daughter as she could. Her scent, her voice, her daughter's way of doing and looking at things, of looking at her, which had almost lost the careful twitch that tried to suss out whether she was travelling towards a manic episode.

Nia was about to break up with Temi. The past week they had talked about it. What she should do and how. SuSu stayed away from the *should*, listened more than making statements, asking about the woman that Nia got on so well with. And Nia kept asking 'Tell me about what drew you to go. To Palestine. Was it sudden?' SuSu had responded that it wasn't good to mix the two, SuSu's political decisions and her daughter's love life. SuSu didn't add that she thought Nia had already made her decision the moment she walked out of Temi's. If she wanted to stay in the relationship she would have stayed that night. It was not for SuSu to say. Sometimes SuSu would say too much, ask too much. She had seen Nia cover her ears when she couldn't stop herself, when her mouth had run away from her. Nia would retreat and could be gone for months at a time, speaking to her in short sentences that were meant to keep her mother in line. SuSu had said that too, during an episode, how she didn't need her daughter to keep watch just to keep her in line.

'In line with what, Mum?' Nia had fought back.

Once, SuSu had accused her of admitting her to the hospital.

Things were good, she wasn't going to make the same mistake by giving too many opinions on Nia's love life. Her sometimes very serious daughter could make her own decisions. She had been making them for a long time.

SuSu was standing by the bedroom door waiting for Nia to acknowledge her. She hadn't moved at all, other than her eyelids, which closed and opened infrequently.

This couldn't be because of Temi, surely this was something else? Melvin perhaps? Any time they fell out of favour with each other Nia was shaken to the core, although she did not admit it, not even to herself. If something had happened to Melvin?

'What is it, baby?' SuSu asked, walking into the room.

'A torrent. Pressing me down. Like hail, striking my face.'

SuSu sat on the bed pulling the blanket up to cover Nia. Nia was staring straight ahead, not acknowledging her other than the words that came out, directed at no-one, just there in case there was a witness to catch them.

'My skin's ripping.'

'What, baby? What's going on?'

Her daughter finally moved. She pulled the blanket over her face.

'I'm getting flooded. It doesn't stop at my skin.' Her muffled voice struggled to make it through the duvet.

'Everything is hitting me, all at the same time. I can make out every detail.'

SuSu put her hand under the blanket and stroked her arm.

'I can't protect myself. It is so loud.'

She waited for her to continue. Nia gripped her hand, squeezing herself back into the room it seemed. She lifted the blanket off her face with her other hand, panting. She started talking.

There was the texture of the sweets. Gooey, drenched in sugar syrup. A faint memory of dough rather than pastry. So much sugar her gums started humming. An almost imperceptible breeze. Her skin detected the hint of fresh air, which was welcome. The voices were soft and polite. *So* polite. The woman's voice pressed through a small opening, as if the chest was turned off, the sound had to originate *and* travel through the nose. It had sounded breathy. Nia exhaled and continued. The surface of the seat they had offered. A chair. The couple on the sofa across from the broker. Nia by the side, already turned away before the words were uttered. The wood of the chair welcome against her skin. It was worn, sat in, you could fit into it. If the space was offered.

'Where are you, baby?' SuSu asked.

'I don't know.' Nia was holding her head with both hands now, pressing against the sides of her face.

SuSu held the blanket higher in order to look at her daughter.

'Where was this?'

'Everywhere.' Nia coughed while she spoke.

'The wind. I don't think there was any. Just the air whipped up by me cycling. So fast. So so fast. I flew through the streets although I was peddling. It was on the ground. I could hear things cracking, things the bike cycled over. Sweat dripping from neck down my spine. It was hot. And cold. I couldn't wait until I got to Melvin that night. I couldn't see anything until I reached him.'

'Which night?' SuSu asked. Her daughter was still pressing the sides of her head with her palms. 'Tell me all the details. Everything you remember.'

Nia's hands shifted to the front, the pressure easing until she was merely covering her face.

She told SuSu of the time she was on an extended work holiday with friends in India and the owner of the flat she had rented while still in the UK wouldn't let her stay when she uncovered her hair. Her skin had been fine, fair enough to be celebrated, but when he saw the curly, Afro-textured hair, he retracted. The person handling the sublet had diverted the conversation into Maharathi to spare her the details. The owner and his wife had sat her down, offering her sweets while speaking in low voices to the broker. She couldn't know what was said, and he wouldn't say why she couldn't stay there. It had all been arranged, him coming along was the last formality, only an introduction. He wouldn't give her the details. She needed to take her luggage that she had left at the entrance somewhere else. The couple looked at her apologetically but as if she would understand, as if she would know why, and surely would agree. As sad as it was. The order of things. The who was included and who needed to be excluded, needed to know their place in the hierarchy of racial markers. The broker looked at her with compassion and suggested a nearby hotel until he found another suitable place. The sweets had been the bribe. They were supposed to make up for the harm caused. Like fattening her up for the slaughter that took place. Only after they had left did she unravel what had happened. When she took off her headscarf, their attitude had changed. She had dutifully eaten the sweets because she thought they were a welcome gesture.

She had felt so unsafe that a hotel seemed like walking into a warzone. The friends, who were not Black, who had secured an apartment a few weeks before, let her stay for a couple of nights. She relaxed there, slept for the first two days as if she was recovering from a physical exertion so deep it demanded her horizontal, off her feet. They did not talk about it, the friends and her. After a week they urged her to find something of her own, they couldn't share the large room for the duration of their stay. Out into the hostile world where her skin was only good enough if it did not come with traces of African hair. She had swallowed it, barely enough time to acknowledge what had happened.

Then, the time three Black footballers missed penalties during a Euro Cup game. She hadn't even watched the game. She didn't care for football. This would have gone right over her head. If they hadn't missed... Two friends had texted anxiously, already spinning out in fear. The next day would not be easy for the footballers or any Black person. When she cycled to Melvin she didn't see the traffic or people. She sat in Melvin's kitchen, when she made it there in one piece, trembling. Melvin aware of what was to come, was already happening, sat with his knees and his pressed together. His face bent to one side, then the other as if he was trying to pull meaning from somewhere.

Nia was shivering now.

'The time when I was six and you picked me up from school and that old man spat on the new shoes you had bought me. The one that lit up. When you complained, he called us the N word. Me, your little N bastard.'

SuSu nodded.

Nia's grip was from her arm but her breathing was slower now, deepening.

'It's coming down on me, Mum. Real hard. I don't know how to make it stop.'

SuSu kicked off her house shoes and climbed under the blanket with her. She pulled it back over both their heads and held it up so there was room to breathe. Nia covered her face with her arms. SuSu remembered these things. The flashbacks. One of the best things she and Ben had done for each other. Acknowledged that it was real. The way the trauma found a way to hold your body captive.

You felt free, like your brain was controlling your limbs, your body parts, your movement. It was all your doing, you had choices, you made decisions based on your thoughts. You decided on your actions. Then, in a split second, everything changed without a conscious knowing. You were overcome with forceful sensations. The memories drenching you, from inside out. The body, your body, washed away, not knowing where it would end, how you could stop it.

They had talked about it. Ben and SuSu. The day when Ben had quit the job at a paper he was working for. He had come to drop something off, something for Nia. He was angry that day and had said, 'I get it. I understand. You had to do it. You had to stand on that table and shout, I get it now. Sometimes you have to, otherwise it will dilute you until you are nothing but the constant reverberation of this.'

Ben's understanding came a few years after their relationship had ended. He had wanted quieter complaints before that. A quiet reaching for something that resembled "just" approaches. He didn't have the courage to risk everything. When he said, 'I get it. Nothing is gained by politely asking. Stand on that table! Every time,' she loved him more than she had ever before. It had given her strength. The confirmation that she wasn't *just* bipolar, that not all came from inside her. She was also trying to save herself from a world that she was asked to carry in her body. A world that demanded her disintegration. And she couldn't carry that.

'It's real,' SuSu said to Nia. 'I'm here. I will sit with you. I will watch you. Until it's done.'

SuSu dropped the blanket on one side and stroked her daughter's face. Nia turned toward her, her legs pulled up. SuSu's other arm was getting tired from holding the duvet up but she wanted this cocoon. Life on halt for a brief moment. You had to stop it sometimes. Bring it right down to what happened on the skin, inside the flesh, in your bones.

'What made it start?'

'Nothing particularly bad. Two bus drivers were slowing down in the street yesterday. They opened the window and greeted each other. It was barely a few seconds. One laughed. An older white man was standing by the side of the road. His face... His face made my stomach tighten. He wiggled his stick and hit a bin with it while saying "You people". You could have missed it. It was a small moment.'

SuSu nodded. They were holding hands now. SuSu watched Nia's face, following closely the pooling in the corner of her daughter's eyes, the way the tears built up until it looked like they burst from the face, suspended for an instant between outside and internal world. The fall, the silent trace of horror. The body's shedding.

They were quiet for a while.

Nia folded the blanket back. 'I'm done,' she said, and blew air out of her mouth.

'Okay,' SuSu answered. She stretched out her legs.

'What did you do today? Before this?' Her daughter's voice was lighter now. Open.

'I met Denise, that young woman I became friends with.'

They both sat up and at the edge of the bed, their legs feeling for the floor until they touched the rug in front of the bed. Nia hugged her mother.

'How is she?'

'She is fine. It's always a delight to see her. It is precious, talking to her. Like it is with you.'

Nia walked to the wardrobe to pick up a cardigan.

'What should we do after this?' SuSu asked.

It was abrupt, the way Nia turned around.

'That's the most important thing, isn't it,' she asked her. 'What we do.'

'Our world, the one we make. Yes,' SuSu responded.

Her daughter tried on the cardigan then put it back. She took out a light jumper, oversized and yellow. She pulled it over her head.

'Shall we meet Melvin in the park? I'll call to see if he has time. He can bring a take-away.'

It wouldn't be dark for at least another couple of hours.

'Food outside in beautiful surroundings with my favourite people? Absolutely!' SuSu said and pushed herself off the bed.

Her daughter's hands were already on the phone and Melvin picked up after a few rings. Nia nodded towards SuSu, smiling.

'Any stew they have left but extra big portions p l e a s e.'

The please was drawn out, it had an arc to its delivery. SuSu could hear Melvin laughing on the other end.

6

The Swimmer

In bed, I was thinking about Crystal's words.

'Watch me ablaze...'

I assume she had accepted Rahul's proposal. She had said, there was no reason to break up. Even if, which is what I thought, she didn't love him much in that sense anymore. It was comfortable and convenient. Those were good reasons.

'... at the next social...'

I was going to avoid any get-togethers that involved Rahul and friends. It was time to let it go. This entangled three-way friendship where I was carrying the heaviest load.

In the years since I had known them I had had two relationships. The stormy one with Temi, and the quietly content one with Alicia. Alicia and I had been a good match. Six years of working well. We never moved in together and maybe that was the secret. Visiting when we wanted, enough space to not do so when we had other plans, or needed a bit of time to ourselves. It worked without a fanfare. Steady, tender, understanding. Why would Rahul bring up Alicia? We, as a couple, only changed when she was offered a position at a gallery in Bogotá. It was such a chance offer; she had been working with psychologists at the time. Something to take her out of her routine, an adventure. We had said, 'Let's give it a year to make a decision.' It would have been our seventh year. The first time I visited I stayed for three weeks. I enjoyed it but the trip was overshadowed by assessments. Did I like the weather? The food? The surroundings? Did I want to be here full-time? Was I excited enough? By her, by everything around her?

Alicia was happy there. It reminded her of something she had never had: a big culture around her. Her Colombian mother had died when she was eight. Her Irish father had moved them to Dublin where she stayed until she ran back to London for uni. She had missed community. She was diving into a world of intellectuals and artists in a way that London didn't offer her. I liked seeing her in it. The world she had found in such a short amount of time. The glow that had attached to her body when she left the house. I knew this change in vibrancy. It was inhabiting the body differently. I felt the same when I visited Kenya and hung out with relatives. When everywhere I looked, bodies like mine were the norm. I decompressed, physically. I could feel the edges and curves, the corners of myself, which made me feel awkward sometimes and as if I was entirely new to my own being. It freed me too, that I was able to breathe into myself and to leave my own shape hanging, which meant letting go of the tension of entering a world where the way I moved was always already explaining, or defying, where I negotiated the normality of hostility, where your body, and your mind, meaning mine, were, was, never neutral. The hostility itself being a burden, the normality of it, the impossible feat.

It moved me, in those three weeks, to see Alicia occupying all of herself. She came to London for a visit and to tie up loose ends. I visited again, for ten days only because that was how much annual leave I had left. I loved it for her. But it wasn't the same for me. We both knew, even after the first time I came, that I was not going to follow. It wasn't my decompression. It was hers. And despite the matter of the holding I had to do, holding myself together, disappearing parts of myself at times, in ways I could hardly detect, I loved London. I thought I would never tire of it. The harshness that enabled things that couldn't be created elsewhere. The beauty within the cracks.

We let each other go. Our seventh year was that: a release back into lives that didn't include the other. A year in which we wished each other well. Where we hardly spoke because there wasn't anything to say. When you let go you have to do it. Otherwise the connection isn't anything but prolonged stifling. After a year we started calling for birthdays, sometimes just to check in. It was a loose bond, like a faint memory with someone you always wanted to be closer with but had never known. Only with us it was the reverse. We had related to each other respectfully, thoughtfully. When we started calling again sporadically, we laughed and said, 'This adulting, we're very good at it, don't you think?'

What was Raul's concern with Alicia? When I asked Crystal she said he was just lashing out. Finding things to say. But why, I said. Why am I so important? That he mentioned Temi was unfair. Was it jealousy because Temi had been around when we met? Because I chose a relationship with her and not with them, not with him? Temi and I had a long 'in' and a very quick 'out'. The relationship itself was fine. When I thought of her, I thought of the day when my senses were flooded by old racist wounds.

First the dinner with the parents. Then a week later the Major Assault. Assaulted by memories and sensations. The echo ringing to its own rhythm, without an exit route. Mum had brought me back. She didn't leave my side for the next week. I was supposed to call Temi that week. I needed to. I had left things too open to disappear without a word. When I finally picked up the phone, Temi's response was sharp.

'If you had needed me, or wanted me for that matter, you would have at least texted,' she said.

I was still at Mum's and in awe of her. She was my newfound cocoon. Sheltering away from discomfort. Although she did not encourage it. Mum. The avoidance.

Temi and I did talk. Albeit not that first time I called. But in truth, our relationship was finalised with her analysis.

'You would have at least texted.'

It included the unspoken *if there was any significant space for me.*

Even Temi. I didn't think there was anything to blame me for. We had not made it beyond our first year. Most of my friends didn't consider the first year to be a relationship. Not in that real sense.

I couldn't sleep. Crystal hadn't apologised. Rahul's comments on my past relationships had got to me. I got up and sat in the kitchen that looked out over other houses. Coming up to nine years and I still couldn't believe that I got the flat. It was around the same time of the breakup with Temi that I was invited to a viewing. Six weeks later I held the keys in my hand. We painted, Mum and me. Taking two weeks to make an extended decoration party out of it. I think both of us needed the transition. My tiny kitchen was dark for most of the day but it was so calming that the dark only helped the feeling of being tucked in. I sat at the small oval table, the side leaf dropped and pushed right up to the wall. I could reach the kettle from it. The chamomile tea on the counter, still out from earlier. I loved the view over the roofs below. Even at four in the morning. The darkness was not complete, it never was in London. Lights sneaked up from windows, and streetlamps, bus stops, from displays left on overnight. The trees were visible in a darker colour, more than a silhouette but all dipped in a cooling blue. The blue-ish darkness would lift soon, if I sat here long enough I would see the orange that made promises and that was soon washed away in a little too much hectic for a regular weekday morning.

Crystal without Rahul. Was that possible? What kind of friends would we be if it was just me and her?

She had rushed off earlier. I had shouted after her, 'Don't be so mysterious, it doesn't suit you.'

She had answered, 'And yet you are intrigued.'

It was news but I think Crystal knew it wasn't that exciting if she just told me all of it. Rahul and Crystal, the semi-boring institution amongst our circles, would marry. They had always been like an old married couple anyway, even if they performed it younger. It was simply a generational thing, the facts of married life hadn't changed. They spoke in we's exclusively and the sharing of interests and friends, extended to points that felt forced. I suspected we would get a secret invitation. Secret, as in the particulars would be revealed at a later point. Just date and time, and perhaps dress code for now.

The kettle pinged. I dropped the sieve with chamomile buds into the mug and poured water over it. The smell alone was soothing.

I thought of Be. We had walked in the same direction for a while. I found out that they were a speech therapist.

'What drew you to that, anything in particular?' I had asked.

'Communication,' they responded.

I laughed, I couldn't help myself, and it made me cough. It was such a non-answer. Be wasn't annoyed but they hadn't intended to make a joke. Not that much of a joke. When I couldn't stop and the coughing became laughing again, they joined in.

How to communicate. How to say things. How to produce sound in your vocal cords, how to transport them out of your throat into your mouth, onto your lips, out into the world. It was a metaphor and also a plain description. It struck me as an odd choice for them. Be came across as an observer. Someone who didn't waste words. Then again, maybe that worked in their favour. Listening, not taking over, helping to correct others' utterings. We had been walking for twenty minutes when they said they would jump on the bus as they had work to do the next day. I offered my number. They gave me theirs in return. They said they were busy for the next couple of weeks but we should text after that and arrange to meet.

It had been ten days. I could sneak a message in but it couldn't be at 4am. It had to have some meaning. Some relation to our conversation. Something that had come up and that was relevant to our meeting, to something we had talked about.

I remembered their fingers. I had watched the scratches on the side move as they typed their number into my phone. Those scratches, had they healed? Surely, they had disappeared by now. It was not enough of a reason to get in touch. It was ridiculous that I remembered them. That I could recall so many things, insignificant, fleeting details. The hairline, the barbered shapes. Those too would have grown out by now.

The city was starting to lift itself out of the darkness. It made me feel lonely. The appearance of life outside. I didn't need to see the houses properly. Houses with flats inside, people who lived in those. People who might not be alone, like I was. The blue of the night was comforting, it had me in a protective hold. I took the mug and went back to bed, placing it on the bedside table.

It had stung. Crystal and Carmen. I wasn't jealous. I had merely thought that we were different kinds of friends because we had slept together. That we had a kind of intimacy that afforded me special insights into her emotional life. I was thrust into realising that I was not as exclusive in her life as I had imagined.

The bedsheets were cold but I rolled myself into the duvet, packing my feet in. To see the sun made me sleepy but I couldn't stop the thoughts. Lovers, friends, those who were family or like family... The solitude that living alone afforded suited me. Yet it was loud at times. Absence can roar, announce itself over and over in a deafening silence. No-one to fill the gaps, no-one to disperse the moods. There were those slivers too. Where light poured in but illuminated the questions. The longings. The missing.

I texted Mum and was glad when she didn't text back. It was just after five. Good to know she was asleep. At least, I hoped she was. I hadn't seen her in a couple of weeks, the last time she had just come back from a den-building workshop in Highgate Wood with a group of Black women. She had gone with Denise. They were a good pair. Friends across age differences who enjoyed outdoor activities. I was grateful that Denise had so much time to spend with her. Being outside suited Mum.

'Nature, Nia, it speaks so much. I find myself communicating with the trees, especially with the leaves.'

I had laughed. And agreed. Agreed because Mum was glowing when she talked about their outings. In another time it would have put me on edge. Talking to leaves would have been a 'oh-oh' moment. Put the hairs on the back of my neck on alert, searching for traces of fluctuations in her mood. I had stopped doing that. The looking, the watching out as if I was already expecting it. It meant that we got lost in the present, in each other's company, in whatever we were doing or talking about without me trying to foreshadow a trajectory that might or might not occur. I couldn't be entirely sure that leaves did not communicate. Clearly and directly with those able to hear them. I was open to the possibility that even if it turned out that she meant a literal speaking, Mum knew what she was talking about, and I simply lacked the knowledge to hear them.

I had joined them once and they had taken me to Hampstead Heath where we meditated under a big oak tree. Both of their faces had instantly changed. They were attuned to each other and attuned to recharging from their surroundings. Mum's mouth was playing with the idea of a smile, her eyes closed. They had settled quickly into a quiet that reflected outwards. I had peeked at the treetop, at the branches and yes at the leaves. It was hard to keep myself from laughing. Not because of the meditation but because I was waiting for the leaves to start a conversation. I shuffled on my bum and closed my eyes again until Denise's timer went off on her phone. When Mum returned from adventures with Denise she was excited but not agitated. I looked at her last text. It said *good night my beautiful. I love you too.* It was her reply to my *have arrived home safe, as expected. Love you Mum.*

It was bright now, clear, with a few clouds that made the sky look more vivid even. I pulled the blanket up to my chin and stared at the ceiling. I would wait for sleep. Or a reply. Whatever came first.

7

The Swimmer

Be and I arranged to meet at Hackney Wick. We wanted to walk in the Olympic Park.

The River Lea. Sometimes it was everywhere. Lately it felt more like an ordinary river, unrelated to me. Not one that carried traces of Johari's body, the memory of my sister. Be had suggested it. It took six weeks for us to find a couple of hours outside together. They were still vivid in my mind but I wondered what impression I had made. What were they expecting? Were they nervous like I was? Had they deliberated about their clothes in the way I had? We were going walking but I wanted to look good. Worthy perhaps. My jeans were paired with an asymmetrical jumper that had studding on one of the seams. It felt appropriate for the weather and was something I could have worn to a casual bar meet.

Be was locking up their bike when I spotted them. They had loose trousers and a long top on and smiled at me while pulling the key out of the lock.

'How are you?' they asked.

We didn't hug. It was too early for that. And we had talked about the shaking of hands already. I answered, 'Well, actually. How are you?'

I had gotten over Crystal and her secrets. We hadn't managed to speak to each other in person but had texted a few times. She was evasive, not taking up my repeated request to come clean with the details. Two days ago she had asked to meet as soon as I was free. *Sorry I haven't been saying much. Life is hitting me over the head at the moment. Or knocking me off my feet. I'll let you decide when we see each other.*

We were meeting the following day for breakfast.

'I'm good,' Be replied. 'Cycling was fun today. The wind is warm. Very pleasant on the skin.'

None of their skin was showing, I wanted to say. Other than their face and hands. But then, I was already answering myself, that was enough skin to make such an observation, surely.

'Cool. Lovely, I mean. Do you cycle a lot?'

'Yes. I do. Almost everywhere in London, if I can. How about you?'

They shouldered their backpack and we started towards the park. We were a similar height, and my body expanded. There was something steady about them that made me think they were reliable. It made me feel that I would be cared for. I didn't know in what instances I imagined that I might need their care. It was a general thought that came without warning and that made me want to walk a little closer to them.

'Sometimes, not regularly. More when I do things in my borough,' I replied.

We chatted about bikes and distances in London. About the useless bike lanes and the helmet Be was carrying. It was made out of lacquered wood, with no air holes, the inside padded in protective casing. A small visor/peak finished it off in the front. They had gotten it on a trip to Portugal. It was the most stylish thing I had seen in a long time. As we entered the park the helmet conversation finished and we didn't say anything for a while. I eyed them from the side. They seemed to be content in the silence, pointing left with a question mark on their face to decide which way we should go. I opted for the route that took us straight to the water. I wanted to see the river, and what reflection it might hold today when the sun was elusive although it was warm. And I wanted to know how it would feel, standing by it, with them. It had been a long time since I had wanted to lose myself, let go of everything and watch what that would be like. Especially by a river. I was glad about that. The shift that had placed me in another body. A body that felt differently about rivers, certainly this one, a body which cells had renewed in their entirety so it was factually new.

There was gravel on the otherwise smooth path. Stray stones that had found their way onto it. The sound our shoes made when walking over them was relaxing. Like short bursts of release. Repetitive and unobtrusive.

I asked them how they knew Crystal.

'Her great-aunt had a stroke a few years ago and she was referred to me. Crystal brought her sometimes and waited to take her home afterwards. Once we walked in the same direction and started chatting.'

'And how did you start hanging out?'

I was wondering if there had been a different start here. One that included some of the feelings I was having for Be. Feelings of exclusivity. That I wanted to matter to them differently than other people did. At the party, six weeks ago now, they had been the unexpected anchor. Reminding me that it wasn't the truth, the atmosphere Rahul was invoking. And that all that I was feeling was not because of me but because of his shortcomings. Since then all the other questions had found a lot of space and few answers. They all revolved around the same central quest: who were they? My interest had multiplied and made this more than it was. I was careful, today was about navigating away from this trap I had built. The fantasy that had built its own sequel.

Over the years Crystal and Rahul had managed to attract many interesting friends. I was always amazed that a couple that was to some extent so straight and narrow could have a circle filled with artists like Pemba, gentle and free spirits like Dom, people who sought out unconventional routes. Be was more interesting than all of us, I thought. It was the way they had observed at the party and intervened. The quiet way they had spoken to me was not to evade Raul's radar but to create a line between me and them to shut the rest out. I was impressed with how self-assuredly they had held themselves in that scenario.

'Her great-aunt always had the last appointment of the day and we walked together to the end of the street where I lock my bike in one of the cycle pods. One day she asked whether I wanted to meet for coffee. She was in the area the following day, without the aunt.'

Crystal and her coffee dates, I wanted to say. Nothing came out of my mouth. What was I basing such an observation on? The fact that I wanted Crystal only as the person who had delivered Be into my life but who had never otherwise encountered them in any significance? I didn't want to know about the unfolding relationship but Be continued.

'She had just re-trained, I think. The new office was near my work. We started meeting for lunch.'

The path took a sharp bend and a row of bushes blocked the view to where we had come from. It was quieter here, as if it took guts to come here, sheltered away by shrubbery.

'Ah,' I said. I struggled to find anything appropriate to respond. We fell quiet and the crunching noise of the path returned to my attention.

'We could sit there,' I finally offered. A bridge led to a gathering of trees. A good spot to rest for a while.

'What made you choose herbal medicine?' they asked.

'Mum quite likes her home remedies and I grew up with that. I liked the idea that I could mix something in my own kitchen which could make you better without big pharma involved. I think we used to know some of these things anyway and adjust our cooking or what teas we were drinking. At least for common things.'

'That's true. I grew up with my Mum mixing potions for colds and fevers. She also had these magic soups.'

'Exactly. Common knowledge. Obviously my studying went a lot further than those but it is the same principle.'

'Did you always want your own clinic?' Be asked.

'No!' My reaction was stronger than I had intended. It made me laugh. 'Sorry! It's not a bad question. I just didn't want the hassle. But where do you get employed as a herbal practitioner?'

'I don't know. Are there no established places?'

'It's not enough of a business model. Once they've paid all the overheads no-one wants an employee to look after on top of that. You can rent a room in a shared clinic. Or rent by the hour or day to make it sustainable.'

'That makes sense,' Be said.

'Or work in a health food store, which is what I did for a long time. But you're basically giving away your degree-certified knowledge for a normal shop-floor hourly rate. What I studied is valuable. It just doesn't pay the bills.'

We both followed our own thoughts and I noticed the many times we had fallen silent in the last hour. Unlike with other people whom I had just met it felt quieter, without the need to fill the space. Be looked comfortable too, their face turned toward the river. The trees were on a slope and we could see the water below and the commotion on the other side. Beyond the bushes we had passed not long ago there were play areas for children, and it seemed there was a gathering of dog owners. Or dog walkers. I was glad we were away from the noise. I caught Be's eyes.

'I don't know why I am still friends with them,' I said.

'With Crystal and Rahul?' they asked.

'Yes.'

'I don't know Rahul. I was surprised that no one stopped him. I would like to think if they were real friends, they would point out how he had gone down a dark road,' Be said.

'You've not met him before?'

'I've seen him twice when Crystal had forgotten something from home and he was off and able to drop it while we were out at lunch together. Crystal is my lunchtime buddy. We don't meet outside of that often. She never brings him.'

'Mmh,' I replied. Another exclusivity I hadn't known about. Of course, Crystal didn't owe me a detailed outline of all her friendships. I wanted Be to add that they knew why now. Why Crystal wouldn't bring Rahul because you couldn't bring him anywhere. But it wasn't true. And Be wouldn't know that. Rahul used to be caring, which is what Be had picked up on at the party. He probably still cared. It had been about Crystal. It didn't make me feel any better. I didn't feel like speaking about them any more than we already had. Instead, we talked about the flow of a house. Be was redecorating their flat.

'I've emptied everything out.'

'There is nothing in your home?' I asked.

They laughed. 'There's a bed and some clothes. A table to sit on. The essentials. I've stored the rest with my neighbour. He had several burst pipes and that doesn't work very well with tenants. He decided to replumb the whole flat in one go. He agreed to keep my things in the living room for two weeks.'

'When did they start?'

'The two weeks?'

I pulled my jumper around me. 'Yes.' This was one of these conversations I wanted to stumble upon. Something you couldn't foresee, that would take you down an unexpected route. It was like playing along to something that wasn't entirely true. Who had a completely empty flat but had all the things to put in, if they wanted to? Right in the next house?

'You must be close for him to agree to this.'

'An old client,' Be replied.

'How far have you got?' I wanted to know.

'I've gotten to: I love empty rooms. I just don't know where to put my things.'

We both laughed. It was easier, the conversation from here on. The silences had been comfortable but I wanted to get to know them. I also wanted to make an impression to cement future meetings. I offered help. Interior design wasn't a specialty of mine but my eye could certainly help. An outsider's opinion. Someone who couldn't cater to their taste and therefore gave a fresh perspective. To my surprise Be agreed.

'We could eat at mine. If you want?' they offered.

'You didn't outsource your kitchen?' I asked.

'I absolutely did. I meant take-away.'

They hadn't exaggerated. They gave me the tour to show me how empty really was. There were a few files next to an oversized cushion and a tea mug on a ceramic coaster on the wooden floor in the living room. Plants on the windowsill and nothing else. The bedroom had the bed, a chair with folded clothes, and a small carry-on suitcase which I assumed had the rest of their wardrobe. The bathroom was the busiest. The cabinet was missing. Instead a yellow rectangle stood out in the middle of the dusty white walls. Nail clippers, toothpaste, a bottle of shower gel, lotion. A comb, a loofah. More plants next to the window. The kitchen had a table and three chairs. The same number plates.

'How little are you trying to live with?' I asked.

'I don't know. As little as possible,' they replied, and plated the vegan medley they had ordered from the local Caribbean.

'It's not about the little. It's about what to fill it with,' they continued.

'What do you mean?'

'I enjoy thinking. Sitting in my home and following my thoughts,' they said.

'I do that. I still have lots of stuff.'

And I needed it, I wanted to add. Even when I liked space for my thoughts. It gave me comfort. That I had things available when I wanted them. That I could pull out the chamomile tea during an unsettled day or a sleepless night although I hadn't made tea for weeks. It was a selection, I felt. It was about *the* selection.

I suspected Be had thought about this more than I had. They were not going to live in a completely empty flat. They were off work the following week to re-introduce things into the home. Or find a new home for it. I asked about the natural light and where it entered. I told them how I put things according to my needs. I like reading on the couch with the sun hitting my face. Even when a couch didn't belong in that spot. I also liked dark bedrooms, they helped me sleep. If there was a lot of light I would make a reading nook and separate it from where the bed was.

I wanted to offer more help. To be there and say 'Yes that fits well there,' or 'Are you sure you need all of that?' somewhere else. But it was desperate. Our afternoon was easy. I had invited myself over and Be had agreed. It was for them to ask for our next meeting.

When we said bye, Be hugged me briefly, then stepped back.

'I hope that was okay?'

'Yes sure,' I said.

I was startled by the sudden contact and by the fast separation.

'It was nice. Better than not shaking hands,' I continued.

'My thoughts exactly,' Be replied.

I took two buses and walked the rest of the way home. I was wondering how long it would take. Hearing from Be. To rearrange the whole house in two weeks? To sort through all your possessions? My tummy felt like it was weighed down by a block of metal when I realised it was unlikely I would be seeing them again until they had finished their project.

8

The Climber

The trip to Palestine was a beginning. SuSu knew it, although she couldn't say what was beginning, what was ending. It was uncertain where the shift was but it was there. And she wasn't talking about the pregnancy. Ben was struggling since they had returned. He became withdrawn and overprotective, constantly telling her to rest, to concentrate on her body, to be quieter, still even. A couple of times she lashed out, yelling, 'Easy for you to say. You are not throwing up for weeks on end. There is nothing else I do than my body. Leave me to do something, anything else. Sometimes!'

One time she stormed out straight after her outburst, only to return five minutes later to shower and get dressed. She left him standing by the bedroom door, informing him to not stay up. She went out dancing with some of her friends.

SuSu was following all the doctor's orders. It could happen, this severe nausea, this frequent vomiting. It was bad luck. That night she challenged her stomach to settle, she wanted to dance. As if it was an agreed pact she managed to keep her food down by snacking every fifteen minutes. The music lifted her spirits and she was the first of her group to dance. She had nothing else to hold on to. No drink to spice up the night so she gave herself to the music. It was soulful house, not her usual favourite. The foetus that would become Johari seemed to like it, rolling about to the beat, exercising. Her midsection had gone from making her retch to stretching the limitations of a womb. There was kicking and extending, roly-polys. She stopped and laughed with her mouth wide open. It was joyous. Her body, the things that were happening inside of her. Her hands traced the movements. Makena, her closest friend, came running.

'Are you okay? Is something going on with the baby?'

SuSu laughed again and took Makena's hand to let her feel. 'It's okay,' she said. 'It's nothing. The baby is feeling the music.'

Makena replied, 'That's one at least.' They walked back arm in arm to where they had snatched a table and seats earlier.

Makena dropped her back home late in the night. They were still animated about the child who had not yet been born that had its own taste. That liked the music that the adults, and particularly the mother, felt lukewarm about. It had shifted their moods and they had started to dance. In the car, in front of SuSu's building, where Ben stayed most of the time, Makena hugged her and kissed the belly that was a bump but hardly so. She whispered into SuSu's dress, willing it to travel beyond the skin, through the water.

'You show your parents how to feel the things that need feeling, where the music is, where to catch it, you move them like you did today. Promise me that.'

SuSu had kissed Makena on the cheek when she sat up. She couldn't say anything, she was moved, by her own body which was doing things that seemed beyond her comprehension and by her friend who she loved and who blessed her child with the vision of feeling and movement.

When she came up the stairs she opened the door to the flat as quietly as possible. Ben was still there. She had expected him. He was lying on the sofa, there was a cup on the floor next to him with wine in it, the radio was still on. She showered and returned to the living room. She slipped a hand under the throw he had pulled up to his chin. She squeezed his arm to get him to wake up enough to come to bed with her.

'You're back,' he said, half-asleep and followed her, her hand pulling him along.

It changed after that night. For a while, Ben was less obvious with his panic. There were moments when he seemed to forget that the world was hostile and he wasn't yet sure what position he wanted to take in it. How much standing he wanted to do, how much hiding. That he would have the capacity to protect the child that was to come, and SuSu who was growing it. Tenderness returned, not the strained watchfulness. After a few weeks, she could feel him watching her everywhere in the flat again. SuSu closed her eyes when she felt crowded. She wanted to send him home and say,

'I can't do it like this, you need to let me breathe, both of us.'

But she couldn't bring herself to. He was trying. He wanted to be cheerful, light-touched. He was going through something.

The nausea wouldn't stop. Not in the second trimester as everyone had promised. It wasn't severe enough for her to stay in hospital but she was off her feet most of the day. Work was out of the question. It was a welcome excuse. Since their trip to Palestine she found it hard to concentrate. It seemed too small, her efforts, the things the charities she was fundraising for could achieve.

Ben worked like he was in a trance. He didn't register anything. He went through the motions and returned home to pretend he wasn't watching SuSu.

Once she asked him,

'Why, Ben? People have been doing this since the beginning of time, really. Why this level of fear?'

He wanted to get angry, she could see it, but he had sat on the rug in front of the couch and put his head on her lap.

'I don't know,' he said.

She was grateful that he was giving in, not pushing her away.

'Maybe we shouldn't have gone on the trip. But we didn't know. We only knew the day of our flight. It was too late to call it off. No one else could take over our places at such short notice,' she replied.

She had stroked his face and when he looked up his eyes were clear and present. He got up, kissed her and went to the kitchen to make food. It got lighter between them. Lighter than the weeks after the dancing. More playful. Sex returned. He moved her body decisively when they were intimate, hungry as if he wanted to fill up from the months when they had hardly touched each other. Makena called her lucky.

'My friend Tulu's man is always careful, she says, so careful that it feels like they're doing nothing at all.'

SuSu laughed. The same Ben that would have kept her on the sofa for the duration of her pregnancy was the one pulling up her dress while she was standing at the kitchen sink. He'd whispered breathlessly, 'now? And she did want it then and there even if the bile pushed up into her mouth and she would have to 'quickly visit the bathroom' in between to spit. Later they would laugh and revel in the fact that they didn't have to wait for a sleeping baby to have sex yet, just for a generous reflux to give them a break. SuSu watched his body, careless after so many weeks of tension. Ben pulling up trousers in the kitchen, his smile sheepish and content. Or shaking them off to meet her on the couch. Or naked and warm, one leg thrown over the other, his penis falling to one side, when they were in the bedroom with the heating on, lying on the duvet to look at each other. His colour was the same. From his neck to the calves. It was an even dark brown except for the scars and scratches he had accumulated. SuSu would trail the edge of his hair, first on his face, then on his belly until she arrived at his crotch. They were happy. In a bubble. When Ben wasn't at work.

One day Yameena called.

'Darling, I had to tell you first. I've decided. I'm leaving. I can't...'

SuSu lifted her head to get Ben's attention. She had picked up the phone from the stool beside the bed. Ben stood up, in front of the bed, picking up a hoodie he slipped on. Yameena, SuSu mouthed while her friend was telling her she was taking the redundancy that had been on offer at the newspaper. The lack of subscribers, the lack of people buying paper copies, the availability of news anywhere at any time for free, seemingly free, meant that they had eventually run into a financial tight pass.

'You know, why not me? Take a bit of money, have some sanity. Think about what I want from my life now.'

SuSu could hear it. The stifled parts that were neatly folded away like laundry in a basket. They must be at the bottom of her stomach, she thought, the packed-away emotions. The silent parts trying to crawl into Yameena's voice. The things she didn't say, that were already seeping through. Ben was looking at her, asking with his eyes, leaping ahead in his mind because he would be the only one of their circle left working for the paper. SuSu wanted to hear Yameena. She had always liked her breathless honesty, which is how they had become friends when Ben had introduced her years earlier. Her voice carried more than it would name. Maybe more than she could express. Ben scratched his face, smoothed over the stubble he had intended to shave a couple of days earlier, scratched again. SuSu went to the kitchen where she closed the door behind her. Yameena had taught her things in Palestine. How to hold her breath so she would not suffocate.

'Inhale sharply, SuSu,' she had said when she came to her room the first night they were there. 'Do it like you are shocked. Like there is a big surprise and you were not expecting it.'

She demonstrated how to suck the air in so that the whole body was implicated in the intake. The movement was quick, then just as quickly you had to close off any outward movement. It stayed inside, the air. SuSu had followed her instructions, nodding.

'Close your eyes. You can feel how it is filling you up, how you have to hold it, so it does not escape.'

SuSu's hands became fists, involuntarily but she let go of her fingers when Yameena continued.

'Let a bit of air leave your nose. A bit at a time. Make it steady and even. It should not escape in one go.'

It had become a regulator. Not only for their time in Gaza. Holding, releasing, finding an even flow. The first part opened her chest. The second part showed her the depth of her feelings.

SuSu was doing the breathing exercise listening to Yameena because it was a shock. If she wasn't at the paper, would she be in London? It was the work that had kept her, SuSu and Ben had thought for a while because they had noticed the restlessness in Yameena's voice. The way her eyes were searching for something that wasn't in view. Even when she focused on their faces, she looked somewhere else. SuSu was holding Yameena's words, letting them expand inside her stomach, examining it from all slides.

'Are you leaving?'

'Yes darling, there is no use working there...'

'No. The country,' SuSu interrupted. 'Are you leaving the country?'

SuSu could hear Yameena's breath but there was no holding.

'Darling...' Her voice trailed off. She sighed. 'SuSu. Darling...'

The kitchen door opened and Ben appeared. SuSu shook her head. She pushed him out of the room, closed the door behind him and stood with her back against it.

'When are you going?' SuSu asked.

'Nothing is decided yet. It's not like *that*.' Yameena sounded tired. 'I'm not giving up my flat. I'm not moving anywhere. It's not like that.'

SuSu nodded. Of course Yameena couldn't see it. Her confirmation that things weren't like that. They hadn't been for a while. Her life had changed and no one seemed to notice. There was no ground. Nothing steady under her feet. She was holding on to ropes that were strung along ceilings, that reached from lamp posts to trees, sometimes they simply hung in the air. She moved with her hands, dangling with one arm, heaving herself forward to reach the next rope with her other hand. Others seemed oblivious. She could see her friends, Ben, everyone, placing their feet confidently as if they knew they would be met with resistance that kept them upright. As if streets, floors, meadows didn't disappear into thin air once touched.

The pregnancy test had been the first clue. Nothing worked quite like it was supposed to. Why would she be pregnant? With condom-worshipping Ben and her reluctance to let him come anywhere near her body?

Accidents happened, she understood that. The timing of the test, that Ben would produce one, on the morning of their departure was not an accident. It was a sign that someone was taking the hinges off the door frame and still asking her to shut the door. She couldn't find the leverage.

'You're not usually late. You've been nauseous,' Ben whispered to her that morning.

She had looked at him. Their bags were already by the front door. They were going to leave in a couple of hours, by tube to the airport to meet Yameena, and the others. Some she already knew; some she had met at the meetings to prepare them for the journey. They were on the cusp. Things would never be the same again. They both knew it. They had talked about it the previous night, Ben and her.

'You cannot unsee things. Whatever it is we witness we will have to carry it with us.' She loved this about Ben. He wasn't one to withhold his intuition. Not with her. Later, when she was already dozing off, he had spoken softly into her ear.

'I need to do something; I'll be right back baby. Do you need anything from the shops?'

She was sleeping by the time he came back and had only woken up to push herself into him so that he could wrap his arms around her.

The following morning, the day of their departure to Tel Aviv, she had been on the phone with Makena who was in Kenya and couldn't see her off in person. SuSu was in the hallway, Ben by the living room, blocking the light. There were two important conversations going on. The one with Makena, about her late father. And the one without words with Ben. When SuSu asked him what he was doing, he whispered,

'In a minute, when you're done with the call.'

SuSu demanded, 'Tell me now, it's almost time to go.'

When he didn't answer she went over to see what he was hiding in the plastic bag in his hand.

'I'll call you back Makena,' she had said.

She and Makena had things to talk about. The trip to Palestine was because of her. Because of her father. It was through Makena that SuSu learned about Palestine when they were both undergrads. Makena had said then,

'I feel it, so deeply, I feel for the Palestinians. It was bad luck. It could have been in my father's country.'

One time at uni they had sat in the middle of a party at the kitchen table that was full of drinks, spilled and in bottles, crisps, and bowls with half-eaten food. People were coming and going, laughing and talking at the top of their voices, the music from another room was loud. Makena and SuSu sat at the table cut off from the noise around them.

'Maybe if he hadn't died when I was young. Maybe I would not think about it as if it was a personal request for me. Maybe it wouldn't feel it so deeply inside me. But I remember how he talked about it, every time the subject came up.'

SuSu had used the napkin to wipe the edge of the table and Makena had given her one of her sad smiles. She had put her head on the table. SuSu had put hers next to her.

'He said, it could have been us. That's all he thought of. It could have been us.'

That morning she had things to talk through with Makena. Yet there was Ben with the pregnancy test. She couldn't believe it, that he would buy one without asking her.

'I don't know. This trip. I need to know things. I need certainty. Some things need to feel like they make sense,' he said.

SuSu had looked at him.

'And pregnancy does?' she asked him.

'You don't know that you are,' he replied.

'But you think I might be, otherwise why am I doing this?'

She took the test out of his hand and went to the toilet. She wanted to call Makena back. She stayed in the toilet while she waited for the results. She couldn't face Ben. Something was different this morning. She knew he was nervous. So was she. She was scared. She didn't know how to prepare for this trip. But until a few minutes ago they had been in it together. The last-minute purchase late the night before separated them and it felt like she had been forced under a cold shower. She was awake, everything was sharp, but her skin was tingling. Ben knocked at the door.

'Not yet,' she said.

She could see the double lines. She wanted to be shocked. She wanted to say to Ben that she couldn't believe it. Instead, she nodded. It felt right. Different. Not making sense. But right. She sat on the toilet and called Makena back.

'Yameena. If you leave without saying goodbye, I won't forgive you.'

'I won't, SuSu. Where would I be going without telling you?'

They ended the call with a promise to have dinner together that Friday. They did. And the Friday after. It became a thing. For a while.

9

The Swimmer

Crystal rang the bell ten minutes before eleven.

'I'm making you Trini-style scrambled eggs and you'll have this new gluten-free bread I've discovered because it's out of this world. You gluten-tolerant people can learn! This is how you make delicious bread that all can eat.'

I had overslept and was still in my pyjamas. The night before I had been out with friends from *We Are The Earth*. When Jackie, my co-worker, commented on how often I checked my phone I ordered an extra rum and coke. My body was reminding me now that I hadn't needed that one. Nor the late-night karaoke singing improvised and supported by sheepish bar staff who were entertained by our drunken antics.

'Can I shower first, hon?' I asked.

I kissed her on the cheek. I wanted to be ready for the big reveal. Fresh and clean. Ready to hear the news and, more importantly, the details of it.

'I was going to kick you out of the kitchen anyway,' she replied.

We hugged and Crystal shushed me into the bathroom.

The hot water relaxed my muscles and signalled to my body that it wasn't all bad. I had drunk water too; I was not stupidly hungover. The tension in my muscles eased, draining with the flowing water. Crystal was singing along to a song on her phone. She didn't have a good voice but I loved that it didn't stop her from going all in, signing at top volume with conviction and drama. She wasn't going to be deterred by a few notes she couldn't reach. Where was the fun in being restricted like that?

When I came back into the kitchen, Crystal was placing two plates on the table.

'Nowhere near the toilet this time. And less noise,' she said.

'And more talking?' I teased.

I sat down smiling. The Saturday was starting well if I was being cooked for in my own home. I needed to find a way to keep Crystal here for the day so she could do dinner too. She wasn't one needing to cook to express herself but, as she had said to me a few times, sometimes she couldn't help herself wanting to spoil me. She had said 'take care of me' but I hoped that was now no longer in the saviour category and more a general notion. Maybe if she felt guilty enough about the party and for withholding important things about her life I could persuade her to be my personal chef for the day.

We ate and as usual time slowed down when I watched Crystal. She packed some egg in a buttered slice of gluten-free bread and folded it over, bent her head and went in.

She nodded.

'Mmmh. Not outstanding, still good. So good. I was hungry.'

I missed her. I didn't want her but sex with her was like her eating. No polite etiquette, no holding back her pleasure or her narration. Sometimes it had been exposing, feeling like it was too open for what we were. But it was tempting, this knowing where she was in the moment, where we were in relation to each other. Crystal was good at making devouring feel like a tender confession. I loved being loved by her, even if I didn't want the rest of that love.

The egg was spicy and I could feel a little burn in my mouth triggering another response in my body.

Crystal had also made fresh ginger tea and I poured us both a cup. We shared a spoon to stir in the honey.

'So. Are you ready?' Crystal asked.

I was putting the last piece of bread into my mouth and nodded. Her eyes looked as if she wanted to soothe me.

'No wedding,' she said calmly.

I had expected it and still it sounded wrong.

'Why?' I said.

'I said no. We are officially no longer a couple.'

She took the plates and went to the sink to wash them.

'What? Since when?' I asked.

'Since I went home after our drinks,' she replied.

'I don't understand. I thought no marriage but yes Rahul, definitely Rahul,' I said.

'It wasn't going to work,' Crystal said.

I was confused. Yes, she had said things about their relationship. It had sounded like a moment, of which there were many along the way. Something you explored, where you took some time, then eventually found a new connection.

'Rahul doesn't *want* this. He *needs* this. We can't recover from me not wanting it. The last few weeks have made that clear,' she said.

Crystal had explained herself. They had talked, and fought, made up and talked some more. She said they hadn't found the same sense of togetherness. Rahul was freaking out about everything and Crystal couldn't reach him, not at this point. It wasn't good for her, let alone other people who came into the crossfire.

'It's not about you, how he treats you, but yeah, I'm aware of these things too. I mean Nia, really, I'm with a man who ridicules your pain in front of others,' Crystal said.

I was looking for words and not much came to mind. I didn't think this was possible. This institution walking in the world as two separate people. That Crystal took so long to speak up for me wasn't a consolation.

'Did he do that to you?' I asked.

'Firing away at me? No. He's sweet to me. Even if he doesn't understand me,' she replied.

Crystal had said no when Rahul eventually agreed that their relationship was all it could ever be. That marriage wouldn't change anything, it wouldn't usher them into a new phase, a better one. She no longer wanted to continue like they were before. She wasn't sure how good they were for each other at this point in their lives.

'You're really going to leave him?' I asked.

Crystal seemed sure, very sure, it shocked me. I hadn't taken her *I don't want this* seriously. As much as I understood and liked her more I also saw how she had needed Rahul. How much she wanted him to enable her and how much she was part of the creation that shone a good light on her and a problematic one on Rahul. He slightly ditzy, if not offensive, to her thoughtful manner. He made her look good. She had hid behind him for a long time and not in the way you expected. They were a pair that worked well together because they had divided their roles.

'I know. It's a surprise. To me too. But it feels so right. I can't explain it,' she replied.

I was puzzled.

'But the flat and the new chapter?' I continued.

'Will just have to look very different,' she replied. She washed some grapes and took me by the hand, pulling me to the living room. We sat on the couch, our shoulders touching.

She was going to stay with an aunt of hers who was in TriniDad half of the year. She and Rahul were still speaking, talking things through. He was taking things hard. He couldn't believe that things could change like this. I found it hard too. I suspected I wasn't going to be the only one in our circles who would find this unsettling. When certainties exposed their fractures without a sufficient build-up, you were confronted with the reality that nothing was really as it seemed. Stability was an illusion we had to keep rebuilding, day after day. Crystal and Rahul had done some of that work for us. They had been Fact and Truth, with capital letters. Not the truth but the Truthfully Together, however awkward at times.

'Are you going to try it with Carmen?'

I didn't know why it came out of my mouth. I didn't know why it was still on my mind. It had been a few weeks since our drinks and I had forgotten about the initial pang. Crystal looked at me.

'Why?' she asked.

I didn't know why. Maybe it was her eating. Seeing how sensual she was and that Carmen had been the one she had eventually opened up to. Maybe I was disappointed that it felt like I hadn't left that kind of a mark.

'I'm just curious. I was surprised that I'd never heard about her before,' I replied.

'It wasn't really a thing.'

'That's kind of *not* what you said, Crystal. Anyway, you don't owe me a rundown of all your relationships. I was just surprised,' I said.

Her head hadn't moved and her eyes were burning into my skin.

'You didn't really want me like that. You don't get to pout when I take your word for it,' she said.

'You were with Rahul!' I exclaimed.

The volume of my voice stopped our conversation. It embarrassed me. Rahul was the excuse. She was right, I didn't want her. It was vanity. I wanted to be wanted. Especially now when I was waiting for Be to reach out. It wasn't fair to Crystal and I knew it. She knew it too.

'Honey, you definitely didn't want me then,' she said. 'Rahul or no Rahul.'

It was a question even if she didn't pose it as such. Maybe she had seen me watch her eat although that was not a secret. That I liked the way she was all present, unashamed of showing how much pleasure she was experiencing. Maybe she could sense something I wasn't ready to admit. I met her eyes and kissed her on the cheek.

'And I'm sorry I didn't,' I replied. 'I suspected you had a little more feelings for me than you let on.'

She laughed and nodded.

'I did. I think it was obvious. I would have never left Rahul then. I was in love with him. I liked you. A lot. I wasn't ready for it but if I had the feeling that it was about me for you I would have gotten into trouble.'

'Trouble? What do you mean?' I asked.

'My feelings. It would have been hard. In a way it made it easier. You didn't really want me. We got a friendship out of it, hell, it is sometimes more than that. Some days it's like we are connected. Then we don't speak for weeks and it's not a thing that we're not in touch. We are weird. Not best friends, but sometimes more intimate.'

She was right. I felt embarrassed. I was needy. I was waiting for a sign from Be. I wanted to know that I was desired. That it was hard for people when I didn't give them the attention they needed. I was the one waiting for it.

We sat for a while without speaking. I wanted to tell her about Be. Ask her about them. Find out whether Crystal thought I'd stand a chance. Crystal moved to the end of the couch and stretched her feet out over my lap.

'Are you at your aunt's tonight?' I asked.

'I've been there since we broke up,' she replied.

'Don't say it like that. I'm still processing.'

'How else do you want me to say it? I know it's sudden but it's also true.'

'You could stay here tonight? The sofa pulls out,' I offered.

'It does?'

It wasn't the prospect of another home-cooked meal. Crystal was right, we did have a special relationship. Only we hardly enjoyed it. I was off for the whole weekend and we could keep each other company.

'I could do,' she said.

'Yeah, why not? As you've said, sometimes we don't see each other for months. I don't think we've spent a weekend together since...' I was thinking about when would have been the last time.

'Since we recruited you for mutual sex pleasures?' Crystal said.

We laughed. I took her feet in my hands and started massaging them.

'It's nice, me and you.'

Crystal mmhed. Her eyes were closed and she had folded her arms over her chest. I took her socks off and pressed her feet and calves.

At night I tossed and turned. I had to go to the toilet a few times because of all the water I had drunk. I peeked into the living room. Crystal was sleeping peacefully. I was happy for her. Break-ups were hard. She seemed fine with it. In the morning I offered to make breakfast but Crystal had pre-soaked oats and grated apple the previous night and we had a healthy muesli. Rahul called while we were sitting in the kitchen. I showed Crystal the display when his name appeared on my phone. She shrugged. I picked it up.

'Hi Nia. How are you?' he said.

'I'm okay, how are you?'

I wasn't sure whether to say that I knew. That Crystal was sitting next to me although she was getting up to wash the bowls and to put on more tea. I couldn't get her eyes to give me a clue.

'Good, good. I was wondering if you have spoken to Crystal? She was supposed to be at her aunt's but I couldn't reach her there and she's not picking up,' Rahul continued.

I'm sure Crystal could hear his anxious voice coming through the mobile. She didn't turn around and instead walked out of the kitchen.

'No idea,' I answered. 'I've spoken to her recently but I don't know where she is.'

If Crystal wanted to speak to him, she would have let me know. I was friends with both of them but only on paper. My friendship with Rahul had long ended. I didn't owe him anything. Not even honesty.

10

The Climber

SuSu could hear music but it didn't sound like it was coming from the living room but from a building much further down the street. As if other people were in the middle of activities and she and Makena cut off from their surroundings, frozen in their spot in the kitchen, frozen in a moment that would mark the turn of their friendship. Their student friends had finally stopped coming in, the change of music in the living room getting most people up to dance and others to stand at the side shouting encouraging words, discussing heated topics or laughing with each other.

SuSu and Makena had met at one of the first student mixers. It was a public relations event; an attempt to cement the university's reputation around diversity and SuSu had been reluctant to go. It felt like they were trying to make the university look more inclusive than it was, without committing to any internal changes. But the speaker was a woman from an organisation that worked with people with lived experience: migrants, care leavers, disabled people. SuSu had been intrigued to hear her. They were supporting projects led by people who knew the communities they were working with because they were part of them. Soraya, the woman from the organisation, talked about representation and storytelling, the way narratives shaped the thinking and how important it was to break the contract that dominated public discourse on how one had to speak, what credentials one had to bring to the plate, who was an expert. It was challenging what knowledge was, who had it, and how one acquired it.

SuSu shuffled in her seat, listening to the examples Soraya was giving, to testimonials. She wondered whether she should switch majors from journalism to media and communications. She realised that maybe she didn't want to write articles but she did want to help facilitate opening up the space for people to speak up. The talk ended with a spoken-word performance with participants from several of their partners. Afterwards they were asked to fold up and move their chairs away for the dancing that would follow. SuSu watched Soraya who was speaking with people on stage, several others waiting in line for their turn. The chair caught her hand when she closed it.

'Shit,' she said.

'Are you okay,' a woman from a couple of rows behind asked, walking towards her.

She picked up the chair that had clattered to the ground.

'Yes,' SuSu replied, rubbing her hand with the other one. 'It hurts a little but it's nothing.' She tried to take the chair out of the woman's hand, but she refused.

'Let me do that.' And she brought it to the side where they were stacked behind the speakers.

When she came back she asked SuSu what she had thought of the event.

'I loved what she said about the construction of narratives and how we're bound by a contract we didn't sign. Well, not bound by but abide to it.'

'Yes, that was amazing. So much politics in "just telling a story", don't you think?'

'Absolutely,' SuSu replied. She looked at the woman with the short dreadlocks who was smiling at her, in no rush to leave or join friends in another part of the hall.

'It makes me want to change my subject,' SuSu said.

'Really? What are you studying?'

SuSu sighed. 'Journalism. I thought I wanted to uncover *truths*, you know.' She raised her fingers to make inverted commas when she said 'truths', drawing out the word as if it was a fallacy that needed to be exposed.

'And you don't?'

'I do but she made me think. Obviously, you can do your own reporting or investigative journalism but I don't think I would be good at that. I think I would be stuck in some newspaper job having to keep the editor's line. Maybe there is another way for me...'

The woman nodded.

'I understand, completely.' She offered her hand to SuSu. 'Makena. International student, political science.'

SuSu laughed. 'SuSu, home student, undecided.'

They had danced the rest of the night between conversations about the politics of words.

At the party in one of the student's flats a year into their friendship, Makena had told SuSu about her father whose birthday was the following week. He had died when she was nine and the lead up to the date was difficult.

SuSu asked about her father. His name, his way of being. Things Makena could remember. How she perceived him when she was that little. What stuck from those childhood days and translated into the adult she was now?

'My father loved to laugh. He loved the house full of people and full of laughter.'

SuSu had taken her hand, listening and waiting out the gaps when Makena drifted off to places SuSu couldn't follow and Makena couldn't explain. It wasn't necessary to say everything, you couldn't follow someone like that, with the sheer information of things. You needed the spaces, the silences, the things that hovered between people, the memories that pushed out of them but that couldn't find words. That is how you reached closer.

'He also liked to speak about the state of the world, you know. It's probably why I decided to study politics, it was something that would have pleased him. He was always discussing this, that or the other with his friends.'

SuSu nodded. 'It suits you too though, I think it's in your nature, political analysis.'

She was still holding Makena's hand. A lanky guy came into the kitchen to get another drink.

'Oh, am I interrupting? Don't want to spoil your...' He was drunk and loud, sure of himself in the way that alcohol made you feel like you were in charge, pointing at their hands.

'Piss off,' SuSu replied. She kept Makena's hand in hers and followed suit when Makena put her head on the table. The table was wet with spilled drinks but it felt right to be this close with her friend, to take the pressure off holding your head up to make sense of the world. Or loss.

'Everyone says that about me, that it suits me. But is it nature or nurture?' Makena laughed but it sounded sad. 'Who knows what would have been my nature if I had different parents?'

She told SuSu about her father who kept coming back to the people of Palestine, not just Palestine as a place but the people. For him it was personal. Something everyone needed to pay attention to in Kenya because it could have been them.

'There was a proposal at the beginning of the 20th century for a Uganda scheme. The British had offered an area in the so-called East African protectorate to relocate Jews because there were so many problems and pogroms in Europe at the time. It wasn't actually

Uganda but Kenya, which is where my father's personal vendetta comes from.'

'What do you mean,' SuSu asked.

'At a Zionist congress in 19-something, right at the beginning of the 20th century, they offered an area for a resettlement of Jews and it would have been in today's Kenya.'

SuSu was stunned and lifted her head briefly.

'In Africa, really?' she said.

'Well, East Africa,' Makena replied. 'Maybe it was the climate. Probably it was the Brits. Carving out what they thought they could distribute. Their usual.'

Makena had looked at her, her head so close to SuSu's that she could smell the wine she had drunk earlier.

'In a different version, I could have been like the Palestinians. That's what my father said.'

11

The Swimmer

Mum watched over me, the week after The Assault. The day when all had rained down on me, all things racial abuse, and I couldn't stop it. It was new to me, Mum taking care of me, like truly tuning in for more than a couple of days at a time without herself appearing anywhere in the exchange. I couldn't stop myself asking, 'Has this happened to you? How did you deal with it? What is this even, do I need to call a professional?'

She kept her answers short, smiling and diverting the trajectory. We could talk about her another time. First we needed to get me back to safety, physically speaking, in terms of muscle memory, in terms of sensations. There was no need to rush, it wasn't good to speed it up, she knew this better than anyone. The process took time and she had that time.

I had been living with her for months and things were steady and in sync between us. I spent a week on the couch, or in bed, and only left the flat when I absolutely had to. Mum had called in sick for me at *We Are The Earth*. I had a nasty intestinal bug, which she said to me wasn't a lie. My insides needed purging. Just an entirely different version of the word. She held my hand so often that week I was thrown back to my childhood, when we had loved walking hand in hand, me chatting away while Johari sped off in front of us, too old, as she said, to be walking with her mother still. To hold hands, to feel Mum's skin on mine, to melt away in her presence and feel that there was an end to it, I would not disappear, I would not be overwhelmed. I would end up right here, on the couch, or wherever I was, returning from this feeling of a continuous strike with her looking at me, calmly.

A friend of mine had given her mother a card for one of the Mothers' Days years back that had said 'I am Mum, what's your superpower?' I had complimented her with a high five, it was the perfect card, brilliant choice but I couldn't really relate. I didn't understand it, not in myself. It was something other people said, a feeling others had access to. For me it was different. I had a mother and she was there. And she was not there. Often, I wouldn't know which was which, which version I would get. Someone I could talk to or someone who was in a different world to me, one that I had no access to. Often both came at the same time. The having a mother and having to run for cover because what came my way was too much of a challenge for me to lean into.

Mum was home most of that week, fussing over me. I could feel that our flesh had once been one, the way my breathing slowed as soon as she sat next to me, falling into a rhythm that contained my anxieties. Things loosened, without much noise but it was there, an overwhelming sense of physical relief.

When I emerged from the blur that the processing had put me in, if that was what it needed to be called, I called Melvin. I was confused about Mum. It was good, so good, and it left me disoriented. Were things different or was this a phase? Melvin was free the following day and I cycled over, very slowly, mindful that I had not participated in the world, that my body had questioned all that happened in my life until then. I left the front door and entered into the unpredictable free fall of the city. The city in which I was living while Black. I was aware of my skin. It was hypervigilant. It was guarding me against what could come my way, what could make it past my skin's defences. The purging had detoxed me and made me supple and relaxed. Now that I was outside again I could feel the hairs standing on my body, at the back of my neck, on my arms, even the ones on top of my head, like they were antennas that were there to make sure that my being stayed intact. They would alert me, I felt, as soon as something seemed like it was going into the wrong direction and signal loudly to my brain: get out of there. Use a different route, exit, leave these surroundings as soon as you can and get back home, home, home. To safety.

It was the first time I could feel how much work my body was doing, and my brain, receiving, decoding and adjusting, constantly. And this was on a normal day, when there was no cause to be alert. Then again, what was normal?

I had to get off the bike and push it the last mile to Melvin's. My head was so heavy I found it difficult to watch the streets attentively.

Melvin was standing at the kitchen window and raised his hand when he caught sight of me. His face was gentle. There wasn't a border, like that other time, when I had crossed one and wanted him to remain open. That time he was also standing by his kitchen window but as if he was slamming his front door in my face.

I didn't quite deserve it, his bottomless care.

We hugged at his flat door. I said, 'Can I stay for a second longer, in your arms I mean?'

He kept his thin arms around me, his body taut and supple at the same time. There was attention there, in his embrace. He was standing there for me, waiting to find out what exactly had happened. I loved his balance of steadfastness and suspension. I let go and patted his lower arms briefly, releasing away from him.

'I didn't bring anything; I came straight from Mum's. I haven't been out in a week,' I said.

Melvin made some mint tea and we sat in the kitchen. I could see what he was seeing earlier. The view extended until a couple of lampposts down the road if you got close to the window. From the table it was mainly the street and pavement right outside the house. I wondered who else he had watched approaching, how his face changed according to his visitor. I explained what had been going on.

'Mum is an expert in this. I don't know how. She was brilliant, I can't even tell you how she did it,' I said, both proud and stunned.

Melvin nodded as if he had been expecting it.

'I came undone. I think that is the only way of saying it,' I continued. 'I don't know if it is finished. Have you ever had that?'

I detailed the symptoms, how sometimes I couldn't even read anything because a blinding headache had appeared suddenly and taken over making it impossible to use my eyes. How Mum had made a hot bath, the lights low. She had guided me back to my bed, in the half-dark so that nothing would trigger more pain. Was this something we needed to do? This unfolding into each other? Find ways we could fall apart and let someone else set a framework for it to happen in?

Melvin replied that he hadn't ever had it quite like that. He wasn't surprised about Mum. He was happy but it seemed he knew that of her.

'I think it's hard to see what is there sometimes,' he said, 'with her. There is so much failure in her behaviour, in your eyes. So much neglect, maybe? So much that she hasn't done for you or couldn't do or wouldn't do. The talents she has, the uniqueness, gets lost under the noise she can make.'

I agreed with him. He had known us for so long, maybe he had seen it better than I could. With a bit of distance.

'Are you better now?' he asked.

'I think so,' I replied. 'I'm back to work the day after tomorrow. I think I'm ready.'

We talked some more and decided to order food and watch a movie. Melvin was sitting on the rug in front of the couch that I was lying on. After the film, I kissed him on his head.

'Boring, no?'

'Wasted our time,' he agreed. 'Why didn't you say anything?'

'Why didn't you?' I asked.

We laughed.

'I wanted time with you. I don't care about the movie,' I said.

He twisted his head to look up at me.

'We're good, you know. You don't have to worry about that.'

'Sometimes I'm mean...' I interrupted.

'Yes, Nia, sometimes you're mean.'

He left it there. I wanted to hear that it was okay but Melvin wasn't going to lie to make me feel better.

'We never talked it through.'

'What,' he asked.

'You know, Johari's anniversary...'

'You could have brought it up,' he said.

'I should have.'

Again he stayed quiet. That time we had re-patched our friendship after my callous 'We need to speak about your twin' outburst because I had been in the middle of my Johari's ten-year anniversary downward spiral. Then there was the beautiful celebration that brought us back together. Mum, Dad, Melvin and me by the river. Everything heavy in the heart, certainly in mine, but also good, and meaningful. We did find each other, the ones that loved her still. In the end, we always managed to return to a place where we were a unit, belonging, grieving and celebrating together.

I had assumed Melvin had forgiven me. Hoped, rather. He hadn't. A few weeks after our impromptu memorial at the river, he had said, 'I know this was hard for you. Next time remember it's hard for others too,' he had said.

I had wanted to go into a longer explanation but he had put his fingers on my lips.

'Others miss her too. Maybe more than you, like you said. We can't find any answers, ten years later and none the wiser. I miss her, Nia. When you lash out, make sure there is somewhere for it to land if you don't want to break things for good.'

His fingers had stayed on my lips and his eyes had looked as if they wanted to drill into my insides, making sure they reached every part of me. As usual, he was composed, not calm but his anger was quiet. He didn't need to unload it on me. He had done what was important to him, put a boundary in place. I knew about this limit, it was obvious and probably the same for everyone. I just couldn't help myself sometimes. We had left it that evening. He had said he had to prepare for something and asked me to go home. A week later he had to go on tour. When he came back I was experimenting with Crystal and Rahul. Soon after, Temi and I embarked on our relationship. I threw myself into my romantic connections. I needed something good to happen. Something magical. As it was, these things didn't always turn out magical.

Melvin and I didn't see each other much that year, other than for birthdays and family celebrations. Now it was another ten years later. Johari's twentieth anniversary. I only knew because it had come and gone a couple of months ago. Mum and I had marked it with a candle. There wasn't the same type of messiness inside of me. She was dead for as long as she had lived. It almost cancelled itself out. It was difficult to imagine her at forty. What do you do with a person if they never change but remain a fixed version from a time long ago? How do you meet them, even in your fantasy, when you have been steadily changing for twenty years? That was the thing about time and how it progressed, and some things remained the same.

Mum loved her firstborn.

'It is special. And weird, Nia. I'm being honest because we don't talk about these things. How having a child makes no sense at all. No-one knows what to do, and most of us do our best. And sometimes whatever you do isn't right.'

'Do you blame yourself?' I had asked her.

'All the time,' she had answered. 'I don't think you can keep someone alive. But I wonder. What did I not do? What did I do too much? If only I could have switched off this bipolar and been there all the times she needed me. Told her that she would manage, that she could live a life the way she wanted, she could, with a bit of work, a bit of help maybe. If only I could have been stable enough for that...'

The truth was Mum had been stable in a few things. Her love. Her support. Her belief in us. The things she had passed on to us. The surprises, like last week, where I learned more about my life than in the last ten years thrown together. How funny, what you took away, even from hard circumstances.

Melvin was playing with the rug with one hand and scrolling through his social media feed on his laptop on the other hand.

'Can I ask you something?' I said.

He stopped and pushed the laptop back.

'If you have to ask, I'm worried,' he said.

'I've learnt.'

'Okay,' he answered. He was looking past me, into the hallway.

'Two questions, really,' I said.

'Okay,' he replied. His voice was flat.

'Johari is dead for so long. Do you ever feel it to be surreal? Because she is longer dead than she was alive?'

Melvin dropped his head backwards while he exhaled slowly. He stared at the ceiling.

'I know what you mean. I'm so different now. Would she even like me? Would we be friends?' He asked me back.

'You two? You would always be in each other's lives. I'm sure of it.'

I had jumped in because it was what I believed. If Melvin and Johari were not friends, the world would have to stop spinning. There were universal truths that could not be changed.

'You know, the reason I think so is because you were more *doing* friends than talking.'

'What do you mean,' he asked.

'You did stuff. You showed up for each other. You were by each other's side. You didn't talk everything through. Like your physical presence was the talking.'

'But we hadn't done that for a while,' he said.

'Yes you did! Just not the same way you do it when you are fourteen and there is absolutely nothing else going on in your life. As soon as one needed the other, you turned up.'

He had to think about it and he finally faced me, waiting for what else I had to say.

'What I wanted to ask... do you think she would have not done it if she...' I was looking for the words now. '...if she understood... I mean knew... how much Mum really knows about life? If she could have seen that in the end Mum still gave us all we needed?'

Melvin pulled himself up on the couch and sat next to me.

'I don't know what makes someone take their own life. I think it is about how much you can bear in the moment. I think it was hard for you. And for her, living with your Mum. It wasn't easy when she saw her being sectioned. The times she was away.'

'I know.'

It hurt to admit that. It wouldn't have changed. The experiences were hard and she had been scared of her own hard life.

'You know she felt sorry for Mum.'

'She did?' Melvin asked.

'Yes. She said to me that Mum had to take medication for the rest of her life and she will still end up drawing attention to herself, annoying people.'

'As you said, we didn't always speak with that many words.'

'She hated Mum's manic episodes. And I think she hated thinking that she could be like her, that people could look at her the same way.'

We both got lost in our thoughts.

'Was that all you wanted to ask? I'm not finished talking about her, I'm just wondering.'

This one required courage. I wanted to make good and be truthful. I was grown. Almost forty. Johari hadn't reached that milestone. I didn't feel like I was tripping behind her like I had ten years earlier. I was the only one of us two still making this journey.

'Also Mum has levelled out. Getting older helped her. The mania can't sustain itself in the same ways anymore.'

'Yes, she mentioned something similar to me a while back,' he replied.

'I did want to know.'

'What?'

'Even ten years ago I wanted to know. I was mean but I also wanted to know.'

'What Nia?' Melvin looked alarmed now.

'Do you feel it? Having lost your twin at birth? Do you feel like a piece of you is missing?'

'Do you feel like a piece of you is missing because of Johari?'

'Yes and no. Yes, absolutely, and no, because I don't know who she would be now. I can't imagine it.'

Melvin got up and walked to the window. He put his head on the glass and traced a pattern with his finger.

'I do feel something is missing. That I should have been part of something different and here I am stumbling along trying to find my way when what I am looking for died in my mother's womb.'

'How did your mother take it?'

'She is still depressed. She just doesn't admit it. She was great, attentive, present, stable in all the ways you didn't always have with SuSu. But I felt there was a part that I could not reach, and never will. And I feel guilty. I am the one who is here, my twin sister is not. She must have been the better version. If someone doesn't live to fuck up they become a saint. How do you live in the shadow of a saint? Guilty that if you hadn't been so eager to survive she might have?'

'That guilt, right? It's the worst.'

I got up and walked towards him. I put my head on the other side of the window.

'I was wrong, ten years ago. But I did want to know. Deep down I think I know this kind of guilt.'

I lifted my head again. 'It's bloody cold on this damn window.'

He was amused. 'I wanted to show my emotions.'

'You could dance.'

And we burst out laughing. Melvin stepped closer and hugged me.

'How to live in the shadows? Of a person, of a tragedy, of circumstances that don't entirely make sense?'

'Any answers,' I muffled into his jumper.

'You dance. Tension and release.'

I boxed him. 'Come on, I mean it.'

'Me too,' he replied. 'Seriously, you go all in, and then you let go.'

12

The Swimmer

Crystal stayed. I wanted her to. It was nice having her around. She tried to be a domestic goddess for the duration of her stay and I tried to be appreciative of all her creations. The recipes she followed on YouTube, the table decorations, the homemade room scents in the living room, even the bath bombs she made with things bought online. Rahul kept calling. I only picked up the first couple of times and said, 'No news, I'm afraid.' The next time I saw his name on the phone display, I rejected the call and messaged him instead. *This is between you. You need to leave me out of it.* It was another way of saying I had made my choice. I was going to take sides. He should have known that. I wanted to say much more, things like how dare he reach out to me to help him, but despite having no respect for him I wasn't going to kick him while he was hurting.

Four weeks after starting to sleep on my couch Crystal resigned from her position with Project Guardian.

'I need a fresh start. I can't tell you exactly what but it feels good. Everything feels really right.'

I nodded and smiled, tucking into the vegan millet cakes with carrot and spinach that she was trying out that day. Seeing someone transform in front of your eyes, not knowing how they would come out and whether you would still recognise them was a privilege. What would stick? Who would this new version of Crystal be? What recipes would I be eating a year from now? When I spoke to Dom, he asked me whether I was scared I wouldn't like the new Crystal. It had me burst out in laughter.

'I'm not sure it's about liking.' In a more serious tone I continued, 'It's more allowing, don't you think? Crystal is having a do-over. Who am I to throw my fear into the mix?'

Dom was impressed. 'Very wise words,' he said.

He had started calling me after the party in the new flat which we now called The Ultimatum. The last gathering before the breakdown. When the illusion of the happy couple and being friends with both without complications was still intact. The time things could have gone either way: driving off into the sunset, also known as disappearing into the domestic bliss Rahul and Crystal seemed to have conjured with their flat, or the other version, which was the one that life had thrown at them, the dissolution of that image. Henceforth there were sides to take, decisions to make, parties that required delicate handling of invitations lest they'd be even more awkward than at The Ultimatum. Although of course it was a little easier than that. Most friends followed back in line where they had always been, either Rahul's or Crystal's corner. The first time we spoke, Dom apologised. He said he woke up with a headache and not because of any drinking but because he had dreamt of Rahul. He didn't understand it. He asked me what it was with Crystal, Rahul and me. I answered it wasn't anything but Rahul wanted to make it something. He wanted some significance that wasn't there. I forgave Dom, I couldn't even see what there was to forgive. He had watched something he didn't understand and wasn't part of.

I didn't think I had great insight, not in the way he implied. I enjoyed my friend. Maybe I had learned from Mum, from the week of cracking open while she quietly encouraged me. What greater gift than allowing someone to fall apart, completely and on their own terms. Sometimes you just stayed, or let them stay. You didn't project your own ideas onto them but you enjoyed the fact that you were seeing them. Even if what you saw was difficult, uncomfortable, not to your taste. That was the love.

It took six weeks for Crystal to go out to more than just the local grocery stores. She arranged to have her things moved from Rahul's to her aunt's. They had talked and Rahul decided he was not going to keep the flat. It was too expensive by himself but really it was the debris he could not carry, the aftertaste of their shattered hopes. He had found somewhere he could move in straight away. Their conversations were short, Crystal kept it that way.

'I need my space now, Nia. So many things are clearer. Things weren't good for a long time. Not in the way I pretended they were.'

I didn't agree outright. There was a phase that kicked in after a break-up, where it all made sense. Everything before became funnelled into the logical and unmovable truth that was separation. As if there had been an undertow, suction even, and there had never been the slightest bit of opportunity for it to end up differently. I couldn't agree with Crystal. I thought she wouldn't have left if not for Rahul wanting a particular kind of outward expression of their relationship. I was still surprised that that was the reason she was suddenly so allergic to him.

The evening Crystal moved her last things out of their flat, I met up with Be. They had texted a couple of times but a family emergency had called them away to Leeds. Finally I was sitting across from them, in a quiet restaurant that served only five dishes. I was too nervous to eat and ordered a salad. Be tucked into a vegetable kebab that came in a size suitable for a small family.

'How's your flat? Everything in its right place?' I teased. 'I imagine all the excess thrown off a cliff, or responsibly donated slash recycled?'

I had wanted to go to theirs. Of course I couldn't just ask, 'Let's arrange at your flat, shall we?'

Be wanted to meet after work and suggested the small place. It reminded me of Crystal. How their friendship had developed when meeting during or just after work.

'You know, most of it is actually gone,' Be said.

'What do you mean?' I asked.

Be laughed. 'I decided to go minimalist. The things I want are mostly hidden away. For instance my books. You can't see them anymore. I made a shelf that is hidden. It looks like a painted wood covering for the wall. Most of my things are stored away like this now. It's as clean and sparse as I could manage to keep it.'

'Wow, that's a surprise,' I replied.

It made my cheeks burn. 'In general, I mean. I don't know you enough... Is this something you aspire to? Being minimalist?' I continued.

Be went on to speak about how they were fed up with stuff. All the items that took up space or time. They wanted a clean canvas every day. I felt we'd had part of that conversation the last time we saw each other. I wanted to know how they filled their imagination, their life. How did they decide what to bring in, what to leave out? I was too shy to ask and listened with my face in my hand as if I was totally absorbed by their words. They were talking about their family in Leeds. Their grandfather who'd had a fall and whom they were staying with for a couple of weeks to help around the house. I drifted off watching them. It was warm between us. They liked me, that much was clear. But what kind of liking was it? How was I going to find out? I didn't think I could muster the courage to say anything, or even try anything. Their hands fanned out when they spoke. Mapping the scene in the air. The way their grandfather had fallen twice more when they were there. Once dangerously close to the stairs. I could almost see the top step Be was describing. How the carpet was threadbare and without grip. How easy it was to slip. How they had run up from the kitchen from where they had heard him shout. Be's hand moved again and my eyes followed.

When the grandfather was back on steady ground, in their telling, I asked whether they had heard about the break-up yet. Crystal and Rahul. They had.

'She is at yours, Crystal said,' they continued.

'Only because she wants to be. And I like it. She has a more permanent place at her aunt's.'

'Okay,' they responded.

'You should come for dinner some time. I'm not sure how long Crystal is planning to stay but I'll ask her. She is in a *trying out lots of new recipes* phase. To my own benefit, I have to confess.'

Be laughed. 'Sounds like a plan. Do you want to check with her and suggest some dates?'

It had felt like the best way to get us into a private space. Now I wasn't sure what I had achieved. It sounded like we were going to end this dinner soon and then I'd be meeting Be with Crystal, who had known them for much longer.

'Perhaps we can also do our walk? In nature? My Mum gets a lot out of it,' I continued.

'Do you go with her?' Be asked.

Be was looking around with their arm in the air already, waiting to signal to the server.

'Not really. She has a friend... a much younger friend. They are both bipolar and support each other. Hiking, spending time in woods... that has become their sanctuary.'

I hadn't meant to say that much. I didn't speak about Mum with new people. What was there to say? I couldn't explain it. Unless they knew people who had bipolar disorder themselves it became this abstract notion. Especially for those who met Mum and were taken by her. She was open, outgoing, and interested. Meeting her was always a highlight for my friends.

'That is your mother?' I had heard a few times. 'You're so lucky. Mine is not really that concerned with what my friends think or do. She'll be nice but she wouldn't be as engaged as yours.'

It was true. I could bring anyone home and she'd talk to them like they were old friends. I didn't say that sometimes it was sharing too much, the conversations were too open, where the line blurred between parent and child. Once she had been at mine at the beginning of a birthday get-together I was hosting. She was supposed to leave beforehand but when the first people arrived she stayed in the kitchen while a couple of people organised food and drinks. In the middle of the commotion a new arrival introduced herself and asked her how she was. It was a polite greeting, something you did when you met a friend's mother for the first time. Mum answered, 'It's shit in depression.'

It was the voice that brought all action to halt. As if it was coming from the bottom of a well, cold and dark and unreachable. My friend came to me for help.

'Did I do anything?' she asked.

'No. Nothing to do with you,' I replied.

Mum stayed for dinner and sat in her chair with slumped shoulders, her body withdrawn, while we felt terrible for being merry. She told anyone who engaged her about the way the darkness felt. It was awkward. This chafing of emotional states. How did you bring them together to exist alongside? How could I claim my own life still, not responsible for her even when she was clawing on to me for help. At the end of the evening another friend took her home.

'That sounds great,' Be interrupted my thoughts.

'What? Bipolar?'

While I was lost in thoughts, Be had paid.

'No! Shall we walk for a bit?' they said.

I pulled out my wallet but Be waved it off.

'You can make sure I get an invite to Crystal's new home restaurant. You can buy the ingredients.'

We walked out and Be unlocked their bike. We decided we would walk to mine, so they knew where to come to for the dinner Crystal was going to prepare without knowing about it yet.

'How long has she been ill? Is it like that, I mean did it change one day or was it always part of your life too? Am I making any sense?'

They were spot on and I said that much.

'She says it changed for her during her first pregnancy. But my first years were blissful. Mum had all these ideas about parenting, she was really big on including us.'

'Siblings?' Be asked.

'A sister,' I said.

I didn't want to say more. My body must have given it away. Be hesitated, the words already on their way out of their mouth, then left to dissipate in the air.

'We were allowed to have a lot of opinions. Make decisions. My father wasn't always in favour of so much freedom. He wanted clearer rules,' I explained.

'It changed at one point?'

'It did. I'm only understanding some of it now.'

We had arrived at mine and I pointed to the window that was dark. Crystal must have been out or sleeping. We stood without saying anything. I wasn't ready to keep talking about Mum. Not with Be, not right now. Be opened their arms and I leaned in. We held the embrace for a while.

'I'll let you know what she says,' I said.

'Yes, please. And I'll text you some dates for lying under a tree?'

I laughed. 'I would love that.'

Be cycled off and I opened the front door. Crystal wasn't in. There was a note on the living-room table.

My aunt is in town. Having dinner with her today. Don't wait up in case I stay over.

I had asked Mum how she thought her mental health evolved over her lifetime. She talked to me about Yameena. That trip, the one she didn't like to talk about because it was both the beginning of our family and an ending to other things. It changed her and Dad, they never recovered the carefree way they had been with each other before. It might have not been the trip alone; it was the finding out about her pregnancy and then having to go to the airport straight after. The being pregnant while thinking about death and violence. There was no separation between them and their growing responsibility as parents and their growing responsibility after becoming witnesses in Gaza.

It made her feel she was accountable for meeting the world in a way she couldn't always understand. The feeling would be there, pressing against her heart, urging her to find it, a way to speak out clearly, at all times. In all that turmoil Yameena was the gentle voice that said hold your breath, *then* release.

Yameena had left the country and it had felt like the last link to the before, where all was somewhat steady. It wasn't that she was no longer her friend but Mum couldn't make out what the before looked like.

'That's how I remember it, Nia,' she said. 'That I knew, I had a steadfast belief that I would be okay. I never had that feeling again.'

It was hard to hear that. I looked at her, this woman who was complicated in the easiest way that I could now imagine. Easy because it spilled out of her. It was obvious. I could understand it, I could react to it, and I could run away from it. What I didn't need to do was decipher her. She had put a single flower behind her ear that she had picked up on her morning walk. It was a small purple flower. It fell off. She leaned down and picked it up playing with the short stem.

'Makena though. I thought you have been good friends all of your adult lives,' I said.

I didn't understand the significance, that one person could upend your whole life. Johari didn't count. That was a different upending. Simply moving away?

'Makena left too. She comes once in a while, you're right.' Mum handed me the flower. 'It's pretty, isn't it?'

'It is,' I replied.

'Verbena, I think,' she continued.

I nodded.

'The leaving was just a catalyst. It told me things would never be the same again. Everything can shift at any given time. In the middle of that, how do we know who we are?'

My mother. The one who despite years of medication and several hospital stays was always so much of herself. Recently she had told me how it was to be sectioned. I had asked her and after a while she had opened up.

'When the police came, several times, different times, you know, and I already knew how it was going to end... That they would restrict me, hold me down, take me away. If I didn't comply it would be violent. I danced, Nia. Instead of pushing them away, I moved my feet, my arms, my hips. I focused on my body.'

I had looked at her, not understanding at first.

'What do you mean, danced?'

'It's not a gentle thing when they take you away. If I'm on that kind of a high I don't want to calm down, I don't want to comply with an officer so they can lock me away in some hospital ward for who knows how long. They restrict you. They carry you away. It's not pretty. You must have seen it sometimes.'

I couldn't remember having witnessed it but I was sure Johari had. Maybe she had pushed me back into my room or blocked my view. Maybe Dad had carried me away. Maybe I had been lucky, and those times happened when I was elsewhere.

'In the ward, if you are sectioned, they can inject you whether you want it or not. I would dance again. Throw my arms into the air and feel my body lifted. I didn't want any needles inside of me. But I made a pact with myself, from the first time it happened that I would not be violent. I would resist but I would not strike.'

'You danced?'

'I had to do something. And I had to do it my way.'

I looked at the flower. I had based my whole identity on coming from this woman, who despite how the world saw her, how much she was forced to submit, could not be erased, and until today, I thought she knew what that meant.

I was sitting with my knee high up, the foot on the seat. I put my head on my knee and watched Mum as she sighed and shrugged her shoulders.

'You have to ride the wave. I have learned that,' she said.

'Yeah,' I replied. 'I'm pretty sure you have.'

I handed the flower back and she put it behind her ear again.

She said, 'It's easy when you let it. But it's not always pretty.'

Her hand came back from her ear and found mine, wrapped around my leg.

Everything Makes Mud, Even The Dirt

This

The sun would no longer be reluctant, that day. I would stand for a moment in the middle of the path, hands in the pockets of my thick coat, the sides open as if they were wings. My eyes would be closed, letting all the rays my face could catch hit me. The definite sign that we would be getting out of winter, a full day of sun that had the right yellow. Strong and convincing.

Their voice, out of nowhere, would reach my ears as if it had been seeking me in the crowd. It would make me think of shrubs and leaves. And playful fingers. I would stop. My insides would start to whisper, at least that's what I would want them to do. My whole body to quieten, to stop making any noise. Maybe I would be able to stand there undetected. Disappear in the middle of a path with an electric blue coat that would fall to my ankles. They would not be able to know it was me, not with my long locks. For a younger me, locks had been something I sometimes, rarely, admired on others but that I didn't want, would never want. That version of me liked changing my hair, often. Colouring it, putting it up, braiding it, cornrowing it, shaving intricate patterns into it. The whole spectrum of what my hair afforded me. I couldn't commit to locks. I would look back and think it might have been my lack of interest in the permanence they demanded. But what about next week, when you want to go on this interesting night out? Are you wearing just the same locks? It was my restlessness and I didn't mention it to anyone. When my hair would start greying, I would think of nothing else. I would sometimes have one side shaved, one side silver locks draped over my shoulders when I would wear shoulderless dresses. Other times they would be pinned high on my head with long flowing garments. Or I would cornrow them back with a good suit and do nothing, like on days like this when I would step out to stretch my legs, leaving Dom to take care of the babies. Washing the dogs would not be my idea of a good Saturday. I would even skip walks with them on the days Dom arranged for it for fear that I would become too domesticated. That it would pull me in. Into this life we would create with each other that included taking care of living beings dependent on us. I wouldn't need to do any of these things. We would have an agreement. That would be one of the reasons why I'd love Dom. He would indulge me at all the right times. I would think that I would know him back that way.

Be would be talking about an academic prize that would be going to a friend of theirs. Prestigious and surprising, given that the friend's work would be challenging some of what the prize stood for, it would be arguing that all work was political. In fact, every act was and would be. What happened when we left the house, how the world happened onto us, what it did to us.

Still, the friend would accept it, they would want to share the prize money between their debtors and the free Black university. There would be plans for a gathering, not a full-on party, just a small get-together to celebrate. I wouldn't hear another voice, just Be's, but someone would be there because there would be too much explaining for self-talk. I would know it couldn't be Pemba. They would have broken up years ago and Crystal would have told me that they were not back in any friendly communication.

'Nothing major, they're just not the type to be friends with exes. Or maybe they don't have friendship for each other.'

I wouldn't have asked after Be. Not for years. Still, Crystal would bring me whatever nugget of information came her way. Once I would say, 'I don't care, really, Crystal. I'm not avoiding them but it's been years.'

She would be honest and reply, 'I have nothing else, babe. Give me gossip. I'll be respectful to the subjects, I'll try, but I need to feel like I have something the world needs. You are a big part of my world.'

I would say, 'Of course, hon. Give me all the info, anything you get.'

Rahul and her would have patched it together so that co-parenting wasn't an endless exercise in restraint. I would have told Crystal that I was proud of both of them. Their dynamic would still be obvious and hanging over them, when it was just the two of them. But it would fall away when it came to their daughter. Zaida would be so confident and pleased with her life that she would sometimes show off with having two homes, two rooms, two beds and the two best parents. Crystal would not miss Rahul. She would miss having surprises. Wedged between parenting and organising, she would find it hard to figure out what her life would look like. Things would have moved on, the relationship firmly behind them, and still, what new things would be on the horizon?

'When, tomorrow or next Sunday?' The other person would say.

They would have stopped a couple of metres away from me. I would know, for certain, that I didn't know them. Their voice would be raspy. Perhaps they would be hungover, or they might have smoked recently. Or they would be dehydrated, sick even. Or it would simply be the way they always talked. I wouldn't like it. That I would like the voice. It would make me want to turn around and look. I would want to see who would speak like this; in what body this sexy rasp would originate. Who would produce it? An attractive voice that would talk about Sundays as if it would be an intimate music listening party in the garden on a hot summer night. All the neighbours on holidays elsewhere. Just the voice, the bodies, the warm air and the sky. Would this person, this body match the intrigue?

'Tomorrow. I'll confirm in a bit. Will you come?'

My hair would stand on end and I wouldn't know why. My toes would be looking for even distribution on the ground. I wouldn't want to waver. I would need to be steady.

'I want to lie on the ground and look up at trees with you,' I had said to Be the first day I met them. We were walking home from Crystal and Rahul's new flat, the one that was so fabulous you just knew the relationship would not stand a chance in it. There was too much exterior. Not enough inward reflection.

'What, right now?' Be had replied.

It had made me laugh. Their puzzled look. We had left the party when Rahul climbed on the garden bench to encourage everyone, shouting, 'And I mean everyone,' to fill their new home with their beautiful dancing. Their energies, Rahul wanted it, a blessing to shower their home with. He didn't use the words blessing and showering but it was equally terrible and clichéd. Even Crystal, who was still finding his outbursts mildly attractive then, although not for much longer, had looked anxious. Most of the guests were too tipsy to mind and a couple of old friends had even joined Rahul on the bench. Pemba had laughed so hard at the door to the kitchen that I had whispered, 'Did she smoke a spliff?'

Dom who pecked me on the cheek, replying, 'Don't think so. This is just hilarious. Rahul is in the mood. Are you off already?'

I had nodded.

I had wanted to lie on the ground, rather than water, which was the story Rahul had liked best about me. Disintegrating, floating. Or so he had thought. I wanted hard soil and to still have green leaves filter the sun. I wanted to fall into the ground. Fall and fall and go nowhere. Arrive exactly where I had left off. Knowing that there was nowhere to fall through.

'Not now!' I had replied to Be. 'A walk in the woods sometimes. Hampstead Heath. Something like that.'

'Walking and then lying down somewhere?'

'Why not,' I laughed. 'We've both touched the plants in Rahul and Crystal's garden. Maybe we could look up at some?'

I don't know if I had thought I was being romantic. Clever, even. I really wanted to lie under green foliage. It was a good place to let thoughts run free. Be had seemed intriguing the first time I had met them. Who better to do it with? To talk in soft voices about the fact that I wasn't the person I had seemed to be that summer all those years ago. The summer that Rahul had been replaying, in a condensed and not so hilarious fashion, at my expense, in front of other people, including Be. I wanted to introduce myself on my own terms. Not Rahul's unwelcome interpretation. Be's fingers had moved towards me while I was waiting for an answer. I'd got transfixed on their hand, everything else was fading into the background. I had seen them in the garden we had just left. The scratches on their hands, the skin that had caught somewhere. The long fingers. I had to look away. A friend had once said that when you're not entirely penis-focused when it came to sex, it was like people were carrying their primary sex organs on full show. All the time. We had been in a group of people and most had laughed and agreed. I wanted to put Be's fingers in my mouth. It shook me. This sudden attraction. It hadn't been there in the garden half-an-hour earlier. Even when I had asked to lie under a tree, I had thought I was showing my weirdness to someone who might understand it. It had come from curiosity, not desire. When their hand reached my shoulder, I looked the other way. My face couldn't bear theirs. Their fingers touched my jacket only to snip away a torn piece of paper that had got stuck on it, from where and how I didn't know.

'That sounds nice. I drive. We could go to Epping Forest. It's beautiful.'

I wouldn't want to turn around to see them, or their beautiful fingers, standing there with someone else. Even if it would have been years since we had been together and years since I had seen them.

The raspy voice would answer, 'Sure. I'll come. It will be nice to see Keane and Marc.'

I would have a few seconds. They would move on eventually; we would be in the middle of the path, people would have walked around me, and I would wonder if they had done the same a little further where Be and their companion were standing. I would turn. Hand in the pockets of my coat, flaring it out as I moved. Be would not see me. They would be facing the person with the raspy voice, both of them a similar height. Be would be wearing a thick jumper instead of a jacket, it would be colourful. When I had known them more intimately they had always dressed entirely in black. Top to bottom, even the beanie they wore until the start of summer. The select jewellery, large statement pieces they wore, stood out against it. The jewellery was always bright but their clothes had been monochrome.

Be and their companion's bodies would move close to each other and I would feel it again, the pang inside me. The voice would come from a body bigger than Be's. I would be jealous of how it stood there, smiling, the braids falling to the other side. I would see the dimples. I would feel the ease. Be's hand would be on the other's cheek pulling their face closer. They would kiss, smiling while their lips touched and played with each other. They would look at each other, kissing again with closed eyes. The ache inside me would make me feel embarrassed. That type of kiss had been rare for me, from Be. Slow and deliberate, without a destination.

I would wait. It would be too late to walk away. My day would be full of Be now whether I spoke to them or not.

The last time Be had kissed me I had accused them of wanting Pemba, which they hadn't denied.

'What do you want, Nia?'

'I want you to tell me you want me.' I had been flustered, it sprung out of my mouth without my intention.

'I do want you. I just think not the way you want me to. Not the way you want me.' Be had searched my face. I couldn't return the look.

We had been in Be's living room. The dark grey sofa stood imposing in the near-empty room. Opposite it was a huge canvas that was propped against the wall. It was abstract, navy blue dominated the background. Oranges, brown and green forms and large brush strokes in the forefront. I loved that painting. One time, early on, Be had licked me while I stretched backwards until my head hung a little over the sofa. I had seen the colours swirl when I opened my eyes.

Then I had moved back up, taken Be's head with my hand to bring them back to my mouth. I had tasted of myself. Salty, sticky, with that pungent undertone that made me dizzy whether it came from me or another person. That kiss was the one I measured all others against. We had stayed there, my tummy muscles engaged so I could reach them, their lips and tongue hungry for me. From then, every time it got quiet between us in the living room, when it was clear that something was not there to take up the space between us, when we were close to the abyss, the part where you step over and there is no going back, I looked for that closeness. I had stopped thinking that day, the day we were making love and it felt like it was even, the longing, the desire, the wanting. I had gone places. When I came with their fingers inside me and looked up their head was mingled in with the colours of the painting.

We had stood, on that other day, much later, when we were telling our desires apart, looking at the colours on the canvas. I had wanted to sit on the sofa. If I was sitting, with Be, I could reach out to them, touch them above the ear and have my tongue follow the trail. The coffee table was in the way. I looked around the room. Sofa, coffee table, painting. Speakers on small shelves on each side of the wall. They had a couple of lounger chairs that would go back into the hallway cupboard if there were no visitors. They were still out from the previous night. Two tall Monstera plants in big pots on the floor. Their long arms waving in the breeze, almost inaudible. All their books were on the shelves that followed the wall in the long hallway but they had a covering, a lid if you wanted to call it that. They could be hidden away to make the flat appear as if it was seamless uninterrupted surfaces. Their living room was a room to have your thoughts take form in, to speak with others, to listen. I had been right about lying under a tree with them. They were the ideal person to follow a trail of ideas, to catch glimpses of important connections, make new ones and imagine beautiful things, times, scenarios. Like their room they were just there, not many distractions. So many times I wanted to say Be, the way you spell it, matches you. It's a cliché but there is nothing else I can think of when I am with you. I knew it was short for their first name, which they didn't like and didn't want to share with anyone. When they explained it to me, when we started seeing each other regularly, I had wanted to counter their disappointing explanation.

The way you spell it... you are introducing us to you as a concept.

But I never said it. It seemed out of place, putting them on a pedestal that they did not want for themselves. The intentionality was there and some things did not fall under it, like shortening a name you found boring.

Eventually, I sat on the coffee table while Be remained standing. The pain was already landing on me, making it hard to be upright.

'Are you in love with her?' I was talking about Pemba and I couldn't believe I was letting my anxieties get the better of me.

'I don't even know her!'

'That's not an answer.'

Be had looked at me. They had sat down on the floor, the old floorboards creaking as they folded themselves down into a cross-legged position.

'I am curious about them. I don't know if there is anything else.'

I had nodded. I didn't want to know. Be was not a person of whom I should ask things if I wanted them to lie about them. Especially not when I orchestrated the whole conversation in such a dramatic manner. Our joint dinner, a rare occasion for us, had brought a few friends from our various lives into Be's flat. I had sulked all night after the guests had left although I had been the one flirting with Dom. I had suddenly discovered how still it got when I sat with him. Still and charged. I had seen his eyes catch sight of me several times that evening. And while I sat and talked and felt the energy between Dominic and me, I had seen Be looking at Pemba. In my mind I could already see them kissing. Sometimes when you knew someone, even if you didn't know enough of them but could see them inside the world and the world in response to them, you knew. It was inevitable. Pemba was as straight as they came, as she said of herself.

'Embarrassingly so,' she would confide.

She had tried. Several times. And then there was Be. She hadn't tried it with Be. She hadn't tried it with someone who would meet her unusual mind and challenge her in the right way.

Be sat on the floor and looked at me while I looked away.

Eventually, I had said, 'You're right. I want something that is not there between us.'

Be had said, 'Are you sure we should do this?'

It was months after we had started hanging out regularly that one evening sex stood in the room in a way that neither of us could brush aside without saying something.

'It seems risky. To our friendship,' Be had said.

I hadn't had the courage to say that I wanted them to love me then because their question was already an answer.

I slid from the coffee table to the floor next to Be. They were growing out their hair and I loved the way it stood according to how they had slept in the morning. Before the oils, the comb, the grooming. I ran my hand through it, my face followed. I loved smelling them; I loved the oils in the hair. Knowing that I had recently held on to this same patch while we were doing other things, things that required holding on. My lips found their ear and I kissed it, making their shoulder twitch. They pulled my face closer and we kissed. It made my insides turn; I could hardly hold it. The knowing that I took more pleasure from this than they did. That nothing would change that. It had nothing to do with Pemba.

That evening they had said, 'I think it's better we stop. Take a break. I want you in my life. But I don't think we can hop from one way of being to the other seamlessly.'

I didn't want to go. I didn't want to lose someone again. I stayed. I didn't leave that day or the next. After a week Be said they had enough. They packed my things and stood them by the front door. I called Crystal. Be didn't pick up the phone again when I called the following day. Or the day after. They texted. *I need some time. I think you need some too.*

Pemba and they became an item a year later. I didn't know what Be had done in that year.

They would have stopped kissing. Be's head would be on the other side, their hand still on the cheek. They would be smiling, I would feel it although there was no way to be sure. But the other person would be smiling and leaning in. It hit me in the stomach.

We had talked when they started with Pemba. Be had called me.

'I want you to hear it from me.'

'Where have you been this year?'

'Thinking about things.'

It was closed between us. The connection. I shouldn't have stayed that week when they asked me each day to leave so that we could one day be something to each other again. Instead I had orchestrated one argument after another until we were both worn out. Only I wanted to keep going. I couldn't hear them. I felt only the pain.

'Thanks for letting me know. I appreciate it. You will be good together. I'm not saying this in an ironic way.'

'I know.'

It was quiet on the phone.

'Have you been well?' they had asked.

'I have. Well, after the awkward week and a couple more that followed...' I cleared my throat. 'It was the timing.' I paused thinking about our first meeting at Crystal and Rahul's. 'And how we met. I put more meaning into it than there was at the time.'

'Okay.'

I didn't know whether it was an invitation to talk more.

'We might see each other at Crystal's,' Be said. 'If you'd rather not–'

'No that's fine,' I replied. 'I'm over it. It will be nice to see you.'

It was. I enjoyed seeing them again, although it was always with other people around. And Pemba. They were organic. I had the suspicion that Be turned the volume between them very low when I was around. I was grateful. I hardly ever saw them be affectionate.

They would stop kissing. Be and this other person that would claim a space I hadn't even been able to imagine properly.

Dom and I would have started seeing each other just before Pemba and Be got together. We would have taken it slow. Romantic dates for months. Meeting out in sexy outfits. I would have been a mess when we finally had sex. Melting away before we even touched. We would have laughed about it. How unimaginably stupid it was to hold out for so long just to prove that we were meant to be more than friends. And it would have been hot. So hot.

'What if it had been terrible?'

'Was that an option?' I would have replied.

We would still be laughing four years in. Laughing and being silent and doing all the things that made my inside jump out of my skin while stroking it gently back in. Dom would be hot. I would be hot for him.

Seeing Be would remind me how inadequate I had felt. That I had wanted to force something into happening that hadn't been there. And that it hadn't been a judgment on my person. The faint echo of that time, of how I couldn't resolve my feelings for quite a while, reached me nonetheless.

'Hi,' I would say out loud, aiming to bridge the distance that was still between us. I wouldn't walk any further. Memories would have swept me away; I would need to stay anchored.

Be would turn still holding on to their lover. The raspy voice would turn too.

'Oh...' it would take a moment for the fog to lift from their eyes.

'Hey! Wow. I haven't seen you in... years!'

They would let go and turn towards me.

My legs would make a step forward, I would manage not to stumble. We would meet somewhere in the middle. Be would hug me and I would go from stiff to folding my arms around them. As we let go they would hold onto my arms for a brief moment.

'How are you?'

'I'm good. How are you?'

'I'm good, I'm good!' They would smile, then continue, 'We're out for a walk. The day was too beautiful to stay inside. This is my partner. Yara.'

Yara would come closer and shake my hand. I would laugh.

'I'm sorry! It's nice to meet you. I'm not laughing about you. It's the shaking of hands... that is how I met Be.'

Be would laugh too. Yara would look from my face to Be's. There wouldn't be a hint of panic in their eyes. They wouldn't have the need to have it explained, to be part of this memory between Be and I. I would envy the self-assurance. Yara would smile and wait without any urgency.

Still, I would relay the story of our first encounter at Crystal and Rahul's flat door. How Be had declared that they were no longer shaking hands but still wanted to do a formal introduction. Yara would laugh and the rasp would be better even, this close. It would be filled with warmth.

'I heard a lot about you! Not the funny hello though. I can imagine! Sometimes you're extra Be! In the best way.'

I would have to agree. We would chat a bit about our lives. I would tell them about my practice, how well it was going. How I would be specialising in skin conditions in my herbal medicine practice. Not exclusively but as my main area of expertise. My own clinic, a space I would have opened a few years earlier, would be going well. It would be in a small shop that had belonged to a physiotherapist before. I would rent out the back room to other therapists. Yara would be impressed. They would be an osteopath. There would be this overlap, between us, our professions and interests, but I would not take on another entanglement. I would change the topic before we could end up talking about room-hire prices. Be would be looking at me, really looking. It would feel good to feel their eyes on my face, no holding back, no careful checking whether stalker-me, the one who could not adhere to a boundary, was present. Of course, it wouldn't be. It would have been a *then* thing. I would have lost it. Be was the one I had wanted to fall apart with. Knowing that it meant different things for us, that I wouldn't be the one they would let go with completely, had pushed me over the edge.

We would exchange our new numbers and before I would walk off I would say, waving goodbye already, 'You look good, Be!'

I would want to add, 'I missed you,' but I would walk away. Dom would be in the bathroom when I got back to our flat, kneeling on the tiles. Frieda would be shaking out her fur, her hair hitting his body. I would know how much he enjoyed it. Tulya and Erica would be in the living room on their beds, drying off.

I would lean on the door frame to the bathroom.

'Hey you.'

'Hi.' I would stand for a minute looking at this man, the way I loved him and trusted him. How my body expanded when I was in his orbit. I had no holding on to do, no checking for signs that the time together was starting to expire. He would have eased into our relationship saying, 'Can we be complicated together, and let that be? Endless things to find out and see whether they'll match.' He would have been talking about the weirdness we all carried. He would want more of it. Only it felt too different to name it that.

'I bumped into Be,' I would continue.

Dom would have leaned forward to put his arms around Frieda. His head would turn. 'How are they? And where have they been?'

'I don't know. We didn't talk that long. They have a new partner. Yara.'

'I met Yara! I told you. When I bumped into them at the Southbank.'

I wouldn't remember hearing about Be. Not for years. Crystal and I would no longer be keeping in touch.

'It happens babe. People drift apart. We text once in a while but we never meet. It's probably my fault, kid and all, I've not adapted to her new lifestyle,' she would have said to me when Be came up a couple of years earlier.

Crystal would have a tendency to downplay how involved she was. How much she kept up with her friends' lives. More than those of us who did not have any dependents. I would not remember Dom talking about Be. Maybe I would have blanked it out.

The pang would no longer be there. I would still feel inadequate.

Or this

Be would meet me on most days on the path behind my clinic. We would walk for a bit, seeking out back roads until we would get to one of our favourite green spaces. I would still love to be there, with them, after all this time, lying under a tree, looking at the leaves that I had to agree were communicating. Mum would love that I had finally understood the way the leaves gave her comfort. We would talk about the significance of listening and I would not shudder and back away from any literal meaning.

One day, while lying on the grass somewhere, Be would tell me about Pemba, who had gone back to South Africa. A gallery was representing her now and there were opportunities she didn't have in the UK.

'She said she wanted the audience. Her people. She was tired of showing for a majority who were too privileged to know anything about her work. Not deeply, not in their bodies.'

'She said in their bodies, Be?'

'Yes, the knowing in their body even if you didn't have words for it.'

I would have known what Pemba meant and would think of how our tissues, each cell, needed rest. Renewing. Filling it with new information. I would envy that she had somewhere to go, to find people who could feel her work and reflect it back at her. I would want that. The knowing in bodies that were not my own.

Denise and Mum would be living together. They would have given up their flats for a three-bedroom in an estate in Walthamstow. Mum and Denise would make a home together in a way that would astound the people around them. It would get chaotic if both were caught on either end of the mood spectrum but mostly their moods would not coincide, nor their episodes. Chaos as is, would be, was and is, universal. Life was messy whoever was living it. It would still be that way. Tomorrow, or ten years after. Living, making this thing work, could jerk anyone around, at any time, wavering, trembling until balance was a far-fetched memory.

Mum and Denise would manage to allow the other space for their own journey, while sharing the mundanity of life. The repetition of daily tasks, the steady reiteration of morning, afternoon, evening, night. There were spaces to fill, meaning to impart. There were chunks missing, times they had lost to hospitalisation or recovery. These wanted mourning, acknowledgement. How you can live a life and then be absent for parts of it and still experience it as complete?

The flat would be close to the marshes, which is where their initial and sustained excitement for it would come from. Being close to a green space they could get lost in. Discovery, repetition, always something new to stumble on. The grass would never look quite the same, neither the trees, or the way the light fell onto the water.

Sometimes I would pick them up, wait downstairs until they would both be dressed and ready. We would walk together, chatting and enjoying being in each other's life. Again and again, over and over, in this iteration or another. Sometimes Mum would be in a mild episode, talking politics and care, and I would laugh about how she would put things, impressed by her lucid observations on current affairs. The voice would be off, a permanent grin planted on her face and I would enjoy it, this spirit of my mother, undefeatable. I would hook arms with both of them, walking in the middle, thinking about the state of the mind, and how there was little grasp to it. Sometimes Melvin would meet us, when we came back. He would cook dinner and we would sit and talk in their living room, our voices rising high. Mum would choose the armchair that faced away from the window into the room and she would rest there content, watching us. I would walk over and sit on the floor next to her. She would be wearing a woven jumper, green and brown threads that mingled into each other. A gift from Denise's mother. Her hands would be folded on her lap.

I would ask, 'Are you okay, Mum?'

And she would answer, 'I am, dear. More than okay! I love this, watching you, the younger generation. You bring me joy. And hope.'

I would stay for a while longer, right next to her, putting my head in her lap, and watch Melvin and Denise who would have started a heated debate about a dance show they had recently seen. Denise would find it obvious, not daring. Melvin would think the contribution was in the subject matter and it was speaking to climate justice. Denise would counter that it would take too much work to figure out what they were trying to say. That the merit was lost that way. Mum and I would smile because those two would get into arguments over dancing because they both knew so much about it, challenging each other was rewarding. The challenging was the main part of the enjoyment, not the conclusions they reached. Denise would still be writing reviews from time to time, her dance career having collapsed in her early twenties when the pressure of performing triggered too many episodes and they would not keep her in the dance company. Melvin would be helping with her dance troupe with people with mental health issues. They would devise shows in a way that absences would be visible. A dancer or a couple of them missing would not change a show, it would alter it, leaving the gaps noticeable. Like life, Denise would explain over and over to venues and funders, things are different each day. Not everyone can show up the same way that they did for an event the previous day. It would teach me, her approach. This knowledge that Denise would bring to her work. It would remind me of the way my mother taught me that complexity and contradiction was the only thing to really grasp about living.

'We want to honour that. If need be, we can perform as long as one dancer is available.'

At times their choreography became more impactful the more dancers were missing. A duet performed alone with clear reference to the missing partner allowed both the person who was there and the one who could not make it to be present. It was a standing in, not a replacing, and not a forgetting or silencing. Their team of visual artists would produce atmospheric lighting and sometimes visual storytelling, which would add to their ideas, the conception of the piece. The bodies on stage would be a testament to the unpredictability, the frailty of life. One after another we will leave our structures, eventually, one way or another.

'No-one needs to show up when they are not in the frame of mind to do so,' Denise would proclaim. 'Showing up means something entirely different. It means acknowledging and honouring yourself, your body, the realities of your world, which are different on each day.'

Her dancers would be the most committed I would have come across. They would be there, unless it was impossible to. On several occasions someone would take liberties with the choreography during a manic episode and perform differently. The tension between the rehearsed piece and the live version would be thrilling. There would be that infamous time that Tabitha would halt the performance seven nights in a row. It would start on a rainy evening with a full house and the mist from the drying clothes steaming off into the large hall making the air uncomfortable. Abdullah would be late because of the rain; he would arrive drenched on his bicycle and scramble to make it into costume for the start of the show. About ten minutes in, just before he would have a brief solo part, he would stumble. Maybe his muscles would still be too cold, maybe it would be his concentration, his mood off, not in the right place because cars were careless on wet streets and more than once he would have been sprayed by large puddles because drivers refused to slow down when passing him. I would be in the audience, with Mum. Not in the front row because we would have booked too late, but close enough to the stage to see his face. Mum would tense up and I would move my head briefly, looking at her, wondering what she was thinking. Her lips would be moving but her face would show the concentration, drinking in what was about to come.

Abdullah would stumble, then fall in front of Kofi and Helen who were about to do a synchronised jump. All three of them would stop in their tracks for a second, Kofi looking around. Tabitha, at the back of the stage, behind the curtain, with the rest of the group and crew would look at them, then with her head poked out slightly behind the curtain, at the audience.

I would be taking Mum's hand and she would bring it up to her mouth and kiss mine.

The light in the hall would be dim other than on stage but it would feel misty, too warm and too wet at the same time. Tabitha would see that combination and she would look like it was unbearable. She would look again at her co-dancers. Helen would be pulling Kofi's hand, discreetly, to get him to start moving and their feet would start following the steps, the jump would now have happened already, they wouldn't do it any longer. And Abdullah would fall into his routine. The moment would have been brief, noticeable but uneventful in itself. Tabitha who would have been struggling with feelings that weren't entirely personal but that pertained to the world and how impossible it was that people talked so much about their intentions and never quite acted that way, how the world was falling into the grip of some scary right-wing movements and few people seemed to take it seriously. Tabitha would skip forward, gracefully and end at the very front of the stage with a jump. Her arms outstretched in line with her torso, she would land on her knee and say loudly,

'It's not good enough.'

And Mum would nod.

Tabitha would remain there, a human stop sign, anchored at the front of the stage where a bit of tape signalled to dancers that they should remain behind this part. For several minutes she would repeat, 'Not enough. Not good. It's NOT GOOD. ENOUGH.'

The others would watch her from the corner of her eyes and continue until Denise coaxed Tabitha off the stage from the audience side.

I would be the first to stand up, together with Mum. Clapping. That night the whole audience would stand for the whole duration of their applause. The praise would be louder and ongoing. Most audience members would wait in the foyer for the dancers to come out and break out into rapturous applause. Mum would be listening to people saying how powerful it was, and she would reply, 'So eloquent and convincing.' And I would know I had to listen and feel. That this would have been the falling apart that I had wanted to do. And the whole audience patient to witness it.

The next evening Tabitha would choose that same moment, which would no longer have Abdullah stumbling and do the same thing. Light jumps until she would arrive at the front to end in her open embrace which also meant not any further, here it stops.

'What are you doing? What are we doing?' She would add. 'It's not good enough.'

I would go each night. To support Denise but also because I would want to know how it looked in a different iteration, on a new day.

After the second night Denise would choose a seat in the audience close to the spot. She would wait for Tabitha to make her point, then lead her off. Tabitha would be crying then, large tears, heavy tears, a sorrow that would be deep and consuming. After the fourth night Denise would stand by the spot at the stage to receive her. Her heart would feel heavy too. The performance would change that way until Tabitha felt she had made her point. After their extensive seven-day run they took three days off. They had only agreed to the week-long schedule because they would have been sold out for the very first time, struggling to accommodate those that wanted to see the show. Tabitha would not return from the three-day break. She would have to stay in bed, the world crushing her so hard she would not be able to face it.

The not having to fit into the box, the way dancers sometimes broke free of the choreography, would kindle feelings in the audience. Some would want to shove them away, bury them. This is not how an economy can function, an organisation, an institution. Only dancers can be this untethered. Others would long for the choice, or the courage to be themselves and wonder how this could be achieved, not just in their specific jobs but in life itself.

I would feel that being yourself needed to be negotiated each day. That this was the thing we would have witnessed.

The reviews, when Denise could get people to write about it seriously, would praise the professionalism. *How This is My Mind* held together the tension of expected and improvised.

The funding would be a challenge, and getting the bookings, but they would produce shows when Melvin managed to raise enough money to pay everyone. They would work on getting a bigger organisation to partner with them, for this to gain traction. For spaces and places to change. It would not happen, not in the way they wanted to, not at the speed they had imagined; although the show of Tabitha's refusal would have gained much media attention, it would not have lasted. There would be so much resistance. The loudest one always being, 'But how would we pay them? If they are not performing, it's not fair to keep giving them the same amount as those dancers who show up on the night.'

Fairness being such an elusive concept. Showing up used as its physical representation, not in its caring sense of the word. Denise would be disheartened, retreat, sometimes get depressed by the sheer inability of people to conceive how things could work otherwise.

Melvin would sit in my kitchen sometimes, with Be and me, and talk about losing faith.

'Everyone talks about change, that things need to be different but they want it to look exactly the same, with only the facade painted. They can't see anything else. Everything stays the same, essentially.'

'It's so frightening, that everything is constantly in flux. What you know, and what you feel, drifting in and out of view.'

How This Is My Mind would keep growing a loyal following. The performances would start paying for themselves.

Be and I would lie in bed on days off, late until the morning and I would trace their fingers with mine. They would say,

'Most of what I understand about being I have from Denise. A little from Melvin too.'

'How so?' I would reply.

'Remember when Pemba talked about knowing it in your body? This resonated so deeply for me I tried to think, no feel, this. When Denise started *How This Is My Mind* I understood what it means to step outside. To renew the experience in the body maybe we have to renew what we do with it. And not just physically, as in how we move ourselves but how we move in the structures we build.'

I would snuggle into them, their naked body against mine soft and warm. Their voice muffled because they would be facing the other way. The pillow, with their head in the middle, would come up a little obstructing the full volume of their voice.

'That we let go of expecting the structures to hold us. That is the goal. To untether.'

Be would turn around and we would drift off.

Probably, most likely, this

The tree would hang to one side, as if it was leaning to rest. Perhaps it would be reaching outward towards the gathering of small birches scattered close to the shrubbery by the pond. Its trunk lifted up from the ground in a straight line but sideways. Denise would have selected it for the occasion. She would have asked whether she could oversee proceedings. I would like her unusual and surprising way of doing things. I would have no reason to say no to her offer to be my party planner, I would be excited. What would she come up with? I would trust her with the invites. Mum would know who I would want there. I would be giddy. It would have been sunny all morning and I would be grateful. Denise would be kneeling on the grass facing the tree and she would be rummaging in a blue IKEA bag. Walking down from the path I would see the two of them, Mum and Denise, where the roots of the large tree would have broken through the ground, firmly held by the earth around them. Mum would wave Be and me over.

I would have stayed over at Be's. We would opt out, again and again, of living together in that old sense of the word. Or the old perception of what in relationship might mean and how it could look.

Our life sharing would include the people close to us and I would have chosen to live with Crystal and Zaida, in that physical sense of the word. It would have been a decision that would prompt me to grow. To see Crystal, to spend time leaning back, trying not to insert myself too quickly before I would perceive who she was in that moment, and the next. To meet Crystal as a parent, and Zaida as my younger, so much younger, friend for whom I was an auntie. I would adore that girl and equally adore the fact that I got the easy end of the equation. I hadn't chosen parenting for myself, but I chose Crystal and Zaida. Be would join our household for days on end, or I would stay with them although rarely more than a couple of nights in a row. I enjoyed my platonic domestic bliss, and my extended family, which included Be, who also felt that living together wasn't a prerequisite for close familial ties. I would end up missing Zaida when I was away too long.

Sometimes Rahul would come by and it would be relaxed in that civil kind of way. But he would never stay long, just to pick up or drop Zaida. I would encourage, with my body language, his quick departure, although there would be no reason. He wouldn't be close to any outbursts, his visits would show how much he dedicated his life to Zaida, to her well-being, to her care. To the balance of her needs with the realities of their parenting. Crystal and he would have grown together, and each by themselves, as parents. The way everyone is challenged to extend themselves beyond what they thought possible when they need to care for another human being. Rahul would be quieter, without that many loud outward opinions. He would listen more to his own feelings and the reasons behind it and he would have found that the posturing he had done in the past was a shouting for things he needed to find in himself. He would be part of Zaida's life. And to that extent Crystal's. I would wish him well but I would care little to find out the details of his journey of self-discovery and kindness. Not because I didn't believe in it, but because we hadn't been close enough to recover anything meaningful.

This particular morning, the one that marked my fiftieth birthday, I would have woken up at Be's, in their minimal flat, in the bedroom that was still clean and streamlined except for the plants that trailed down from invisible nooks, fixtures and shelves, and those lining the window. I would have woken up to Be's face bending over on the side I slept on to put down a tray of fresh fruits, and a bottle of champagne. A pot with a new succulent next to the bottle because Be didn't believe in cut flowers.

'It's not ideological. It's just a wasted opportunity. If you don't want to care for the plant you can just pass it on, right?'

I would have refused any other breakfast, knowing Denise, Mum and Dad were probably planning a feast. I was hoping for the grilled vegetarian special sharing platter from the small cafe Dad had discovered recently.

'Good morning.' Mum would hug me and hold me in her arms when Be and I arrived at the spot where she and Denise were standing. I would hear her voice close to my ear. I would sink into her arms for a moment. This person, that was my mother and who sometimes hadn't mothered me at all. Still I would know that I came to be, irrecoverably, through her care. And care would be a complicated word, like mothering, in my book, because it wasn't continuous or guaranteed in certain moments. But mostly because I wouldn't know how to place it within the society I lived in. Mothers who couldn't or wouldn't care for their children in a particular way were still, quickly, demoted as sub-human. Monstrous perhaps, unnatural, would definitely be part of the narrative. Would she be viewed as such? How would one reconcile this with this woman who could command the senses in such powerful fashion? Who knew what warmth was without having to try, and who would seem to have a direct line flowing towards those she cared.

I would know her voice so intimately that I would receive words in shapes and textures. Her words would feel soothing, like her hand that was stroking my hair and then her voice would start to colour until it felt like it was that bright deep yellow that made my heart sing and I could feel her smiling.

'My child. Fifty. How proud I am of you. I love you.'

She would have spent ten days in hospital two weeks previously, but she would be sleeping better. And other than a chirpy mood, laughing a little more and buying things for me even before my birthday which would need to be returned, nothing would seem like she was in a manic phase. She would be fine at home. Of course. She and Denise would have found a good rhythm together. They would have lived together for ten years by then, exploring the edges of their minds and the depths of their moods while being friends. Both would have partners with whom they also did not wish to live. Denise would have finally found someone Mum thought would stick; Mum would have an ongoing affair with a retired carpenter, who in his words was living his best life. I wouldn't see either of the men that morning. Perhaps they would come later.

Mum would give Be a peck on the cheek.

'How are you darling? Your skin is glowing,' she would say.

Be would get shy. They and Mum would have a good relationship, meaning Mum would think the world of them, Be would be lost for words in front of her still, after all those years. When Be was around her the mom knockout effect kicked in. Words halted inside the other's body by one woman's sense of self. Unfaltering, intimidating, undefeated.

Mum would be wearing her hair longer now. The curls, stubborn like her, would fall onto her shoulders and frame her face in a striking salt and pepper look. She would be slower now. Sometimes she would take a cane out to ease the arthritis in her right knee. I would see it lying close to the tree.

I would understand why Be was rendered speechless in Mum's presence. I would be intimidated looking at her. How did she manage to emerge from a life of medication and hospital stays like she was a trendsetter?

'Must be all the water I'm drinking now I gave up on caffeine,' Be would say to Mum, a little breathless.

'You did that? Oh good! You don't really need it, do you,' Mum would answer.

'I could do with it in the morning,' Be would laugh. 'But I'm doing okay.'

They would turn to me. 'I am, right? Or am I deluding myself?'

'Quite all right,' I would say while I would open my arms to Denise to thank her for organising the festivities, if that is what they would be called.

'I'm so looking forward to it.'

Denise would give me a quick squeeze and continue unpacking.

'Be, can you pile up the blankets and cushions? I want to put the old woman on a chair. I can hear her joints squeaking through the walls at home. I don't want to know what sounds they'll make if I let her bend and unpack all this stuff,' Denise said.

Mum would laugh and pick up a stick to wave at her. She would pull out a small camping chair out of the other IKEA bag and unfold it. She would look like she was a conductor with an oversized baton.

'Ben and Aisha are finding better parking. They're bringing the drinks once the car is parked,' Denise would say. She would put her hand over her eyes and wave with the other one.

'Crystal and Zaida,' she would say.

I would see the two figures coming over a hill, the smaller one bobbing up and down. Zaida never got tired of jumping. Why walk when you could skip, she would say and add a twirl just to make her point. Zaida would open her arms wide and with a drawn out "Happy birthday" would run down the hill towards us. I would meet her halfway.

'Thank you, my dear,' I would whisper in her ear. 'The party can get started now you're here.'

She would kiss me and whisper back, 'I will tell you when it starts,' and smile sheepishly. She would let go of me and run to Mum. Crystal would be carrying a backpack. Dom would appear behind her and put his arm around her.

When we had all kissed, Crystal would hand me a card.

'I'll give you this before we start celebrating in case you'd rather not read it. It's from Rahul.'

The purple envelope would have been sealed shut. Inside would be a printed list with names. A post-it attached to it with 'In case this is of interest to you. People ask me for natural ways to support their oral health. I know it's not your specialty but in case you have some suggestions… They've all asked for a referral to support their treatment with natural medicine.'

The card would be plain, blue stars on top of a grey background. It would read:

Dear Nia,

I hope you forgive me for intruding on your birthday.

I just wanted to say that I'm proud of you. Although it's not my place to say that.

I'm glad you remained in Crystal's life. And in Zaida's. You two always had a special connection and I would hate to have destroyed it.

Perhaps in the new year, your new year, we can meet for tea sometime? Or for a walk on the river? I keep returning to it. The spot where we, I, first met you. I look at the water and think about what it means. Swimming. Going places, letting it happen, whatever it is that has to unfold. Not holding it back, not trying to squeeze the life out of it, out of something, just because you don't get it. That it wasn't a jumping into the pain. It was a looking at it and accepting it.

There was so much I did not want to understand.

This is an apology for my behaviour, for failing to acknowledge what meeting you triggered in me.

Happy birthday, Nia. You were always more grounded in this life than I was. I admire you.

Rahul

I wouldn't be able to help myself. I would nod along while I read to affirm the growing we all do, one way or another. I would know that it was likely that I wouldn't meet up with him. Not because I would be full of resentment but simply because Rahul would be someone of such a long time ago that the ten years when we were in each other's lives felt like a passing fast train. But I would know that things had a habit of changing. He was still in my life, after all this time. And he had tried, was trying. I would still know him in ten years because I would still know Crystal and Zaida then. Our connection was coincidental, but it wasn't untethered.

Be, Crystal and Denise would be walking closer to the pond, whispering to each other. Zaida would be playing tag with me, chasing me up and down the hill. Denise would politely order me to take a walk with Zaida to the playground and the other end of the heath.

'We'll call you, have your phone to hand,' Denise would say, completely in her element.

Zaida and I would run around the pond and decide to climb onto the giant tree trunk. Zaida would carefully place one foot in front of the other. In the middle of the trunk she would show me her dancer's pose, which she would have learned from Melvin, or Uncle Mel, as she would call him. She would balance on one foot while her torso folded forward and her leg backward until she formed a human T.

The phone would ring. Denise would say it was time to come back. I would see everyone standing in front of a big banner that would have been attached to the shrubbery by the pond. Pemba and her two kids, Melvin and girlfriend, Mum who would be leaning on her carpenter boyfriend, who would have arrived while Zaida and I had been playing. I would briefly scan the others but not see Denise's partner. Maybe he would have had to work. He would be a nurse for whom shiftwork destroyed many a good socialising opportunity. Ben would be there, his fingers pointing at me, laughing. Aisha would be standing next to him, in her understated beauty, the hair falling to one side of her face. Crystal and Dom would be holding hands. Be would be walking towards me. They would hook arms with me.

Zaida would say, 'I told you it was going to be a surprise. A love bomb.'

I would take her hand.

Be would lead me to the guests who would take me in their middle. I would hug each of the friends I hadn't seen earlier. Then I would notice the blankets and the cushions. They would have been laid out in a fan-like fashion, the cushions close to the tree trunk, the blankets following. The width between one cushion and the next would be smaller than between the blankets. It would look like someone had opened a giant fan that came in various colours, the tree providing extra shade.

Everyone would look for a blanket that suited their taste and make it down to the ground. Mum would need some help, the carpenter holding her arm firmly while she would bend her knees to lie down.

I would be lying next to Be on one side, and Crystal on the other. Denise would ring a bell. She would start to speak.

'I thought it would be nice for us to lie together to connect and be in these beautiful surroundings. Look up for a moment.'

All of us would do so. The sun would be filtering through the leaves and I would need to blink, my nose tickling from the rays that made it through the canopy.

'Spend a few moments thinking about what we love for and about Nia. We are not saying this out loud, although of course you can share it with her later.'

I would hear us breathing, the way everyone did differently. I would hear the carpenter's chest rattling a little, he would be next to Be. I would open my eyes and the sun would be strong now. I would be thinking of myself and everyone else in my life and I would feel lucky. I would close my eyes and return to the love that we were supposed to share among us. I would feel guilty that Johari was not part of my thoughts. I would open my eyes again. I would feel the leaves. I would feel the communication.

And I would know it wasn't the leaves. It was between us. The leaves were only the witness.

The planning.

The going in one direction, then entering the water to float.

The looking up, and feeling what is below.

All transient, all in movement, one way or another.

The lying on water to feel the bottom underneath, to be carried away not knowing whether something will hold you up but having to find out.

I thought of this looking up, the sun blinding my face. I couldn't remember Johari anymore. I knew everything she had done in her life, all she was, the things she had said. I knew facts and instances. I knew what her moods were like.

What I didn't know is whether we would be doing either with each other, the letting go or the holding on to things we had outgrown.

My feelings for her were suspended. It was a joyous suspension. We were still connected, but the distance between us allowed us both to be free. I was no longer the younger sister, who at some point had to introduce people to the disturbing fact that in our family not everyone made it.

It wasn't like that. It was entirely different.

Like everyone, we had to learn about the cracking open. How to allow it, the falling apart, the catching each other.

To be caught you had to let go.

I didn't know whether we failed her. I didn't know.

I liked to think she was still swimming. Just like us. Just like we all were.

Acknowledgements

My deepest gratitude goes to Gabrielle Le Roux, for the friendship that traverses artistic and geographic boundaries. Many chapters of this novel were written while co-working via video chat. Having my work witnessed as it shapes up, in real time, is a special gift we don't often get as novelists. To share it with such depth, care and excitement is such an immense offering. Thank you!

Much gratitude to Ashai Nicholas for all the insightful conversations, the openness and perspectives, and being such a champion of my ideas.

I am grateful to be working with amazing people, who took the time to be invested in this novel, and by extension were invested in me as a writer: many thanks to Mary Armour and Layla Mohamed for such thorough and insightful editing. Many thanks to my agent Emma Shercliff for the support and openness to my ideas and plans. Deep gratitude and admiration to Bibi Bakare-Yusuf, as always, for the incredible and affirming belief in my work. This book, and its process, was met with the care it needed.

All of my thanks to Natalie Popoola for being all that you are, and all of what we are.

Many thanks to Pamela Lawino for introducing me to the Uganda scheme.

Much gratitude to Umut Erel for clarifying details on Gaza (and West Bank).

Some chapters of the novel have appeared as short stories, in slightly different form in: Riptide Issue 14 Collisions (*Inside Out*), *Timescapes-aller retour. Erzählungen aus afrikanischen Kontexten*, C.W. Leske Verlag 2022 (*The Swimmer, Sit Down*), and *New Daughters of Africa: An International Anthology by Women of African Descent*, Myriad Editions 2019 (*The Swimmer*).

I am immensely grateful to have received a grant from The Society of Authors and the Authors' Foundation, which enabled me to focus on the final editing of the novel.

To the little ones, Tamu and Elias, for being the joyous future, right here in the present.

And another big thank you to Tamu, for making the final decision on the cover design.

Support **Like Water Like Sea**

We hope you enjoyed reading this book. It was brought to you by Cassava Republic Press, an award-winning independent publisher based in Abuja and London. If you think more people should read this book, here's how you can support:

Recommend it. Don't keep the enjoyment of this book to yourself; tell everyone you know. Spread the word to your friends and family.

Review, review review. Your opinion is powerful and a positive review from you can generate new sales. Spare a minute to leave a short review on Amazon, GoodReads, our website and other book buying sites.

Join the conversation. Hearing somebody you trust talk about a book with passion and excitement is one of the most powerful ways to get people to engage with it. If you like this book, talk about it, Facebook it, Tweet it, Blog it, Instagram it, BookTok it. Take pictures of the book and quote or highlight from your favourite passage. You could even add a site link so others know where to purchase the book from.

Buy the book as gifts for others. Buying a gift is a regular activity for most of us – birthdays, anniversaries, holidays, special days or just a nice present for a loved one for no reason... If you love this book and you think it might resonate with others, then please buy extra copies!

Get your local bookshop or library to stock it. Sometimes bookshops and libraries only order books that they have heard about. If you loved this book, why not ask your librarian or bookshop to order it in. If enough people request a title, the bookshop or library will take note and will order a few copies for their shelves.

Recommend a book to your book club. Persuade your book club to read this book and discuss what you enjoy about the book in the company of others. This is a wonderful way to share what you like and help to boost the sales and popularity of this book.

Attend a book reading. There are lots of opportunities to hear writers talk about their work. Support them by attending their book events. Get your friends, colleagues and families to a reading and show an author your support.

Thank you!

Stay up to date with the latest books, special
offers and exclusive content with our
monthly newsletter.
Sign up on our website:
www.cassavarepublic.biz

Twitter: @cassavarepublic
Instagram: @cassavarepublicpress
Facebook: facebook.com/CassavaRepublic
Tiktok: @cassavarepublicpress
Hashtag: #LikeWaterLikeSea #ReadCassava

PRODUCTION CREDITS

Transforming a manuscript into the book you are now reading is a team effort. Cassava Republic Press would like to thank everyone who helped in the production of *Like Water Like Sea:*

Publishing Director: Bibi Bakare-Yusuf

Editorial
Editor: Mary Armour
Copy-editor: Layla Mohamed
Proofreader: Boluwatito Sanusi

Design and Production
Cover Design: Jamie Keenan
Layout: Abdulrahman Osamudiamen Suleiman

Marketing and Publicity
Marketing and Content Manager: Rhoda Nuhu

Sales and Admin
Sales Team: Kofo Okunola & The Ingram Sales Team
Accounts & Admin: Adeyinka Adewole

ALSO BY OLUMIDE POPOOLA

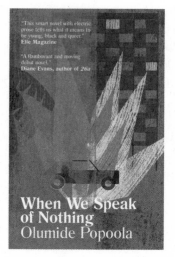

WHEN WE SPEAK OF NOTHING
Olumide Popoola
ISBN: 978-1911115458

It's 2011 and racial tensions are set to explode across London. Best mates Karl and Abu are both 17, dealing with infatuations with classmates and avoiding the local 'wannabe' thugs that target Karl for being different.

When Karl finds out his estranged father lives in Nigeria, he escapes the sound and fury of London for Port Harcourt to meet him. Rejected on arrival, he befriends a local activist who wants to expose the ecocide in the Niger Delta. Meanwhile, the murder of Mark Duggan triggers a full-scale riot in London. Abu finds himself caught up in its midst, leading to a tragedy that forces Karl to race back home.

When We Speak of Nothing launches a powerful new talent, with its stream of consciousness prose, peppered with contemporary slang. If grime music were a novel, it would be this.

"Refreshingly original, energetic and ambitious storytelling." – Bernardine Evaristo, author of *Girl, Woman, Other*

"Edgy, lyrical, and vivid, this is a novel for this very moment." – Laurie Frankel, author of *This Is How It Always Is*